WHEN

DARKNESS

FALLS

Cover design by Chiara Girardelli

FOR YOU MUM

INTRODUCTION

Time will wear wings indeed!
Charles Dickens: Martin Chuzzlewit (1844)

She lies in the narrow bed beside her sister, warmth from the stone bottle at her feet, the thick blankets and eiderdown across her body, and listens to the comforting sound of the clock coming through the thin prefab walls, its developing chime sounding every quarter hour. She loves the sound of her grandparent's clock, though time itself is of no importance to a small child, not yet four. She also loves the smells that emanate from the cupboard in the little back bedroom, for in it, are her grandfather's bookbinding tools; paper and glue, impressive and heady, seeming to creep from under the door. These will be the sounds and smells that remain with her all her life.

In later years, her middle age, she knows how time stands still. In death for example, but also in split-second decisions; words that come before they have even been properly formulated, as though it is not her voice she hears. Decisions and words that will change whole lives. She will come to be intimately entwined in those darkest of dark places, as time pushes her towards wanting it to cease altogether.

In her retirement, she lies in bed most nights, listens to the tick tock, tick tock of the small alarm clock by her side, reflects on what might have been, thinks of hurt inflicted, sometimes of her achievements, but not so often, of how time projects her towards her end years. She is aging. The face in the mirror is lined, the body sags, and she covers it up as best she can. The days pass more quickly now. One flies into another. She thinks, if only we could turn back time…

1

Brighton December 11th 1891

In the evening my boss, Mr. Morley comes to find me again, but now his face is grim and I think he must have changed his mind about firing me. What will father say? How will I face mother when all she's ever done is believe in me?

'Come with me,' he says as he takes my arm and leads me towards the entrance of the yard. A policeman stands there, comes towards us and Mr. Morley almost pushes me forward.

'My name's Detective Inspector Charles Potter. Where were you last night?'

'At the circus,' I hear myself say, without any notion of why, except the noise and lights in my head remind me of it.

'I need you to come with me to the police station,' and he takes my arm at the elbow, his grip tight so that I'm forced to move. It's dark now as I walk with him. I don't know why he takes me, but think perhaps I was in a fight last night. Perhaps I hurt somebody. When we get to the police station, I see a line of men against the back wall of the town hall. He tells me to stand at the end of it and when I'm there, he shouts for me to stand up straight and look in front. Several policemen wait around, watch us all and three have drawn their truncheons, so I think they might expect us to run. But how can we. There are more of them than there are of us, and it makes me want to smile, but my legs begin to shake and really, I'm so scared now, they might not hold me up.

Several people are brought in to look at us. The policeman who came for me, talks to them one at a time and then they come towards me... point at me and go away. I don't understand what it's all about. I look along the line of men, but am shouted at again to look in front.

It seems to be taking such a long time. They are mostly women who come, with one or two men, but children come too. Little ones who should be in bed. The look on all their faces as they point to me tells of hatred. My whole body shivers, my heart beats fast, my mouth dries… Sweat trickles down the back of my neck… my face is wet with it. When all the pointing is done, Detective Inspector Charles Potter comes towards me… tells all the others they can go… then says,

'I'm arresting you on the charge of murder.'

I hear the words but they don't make any sense. I feel my body sway, look at him and try to make words come from my mouth, but I can't speak them. I'm taken downstairs by another policeman. As I go further down, below the Town Hall, it gets darker… there are no windows… I'm stopped in front of a heavy door to a cell. I'm confused… wonder if I really heard what he said. Was it murder? Have I really killed someone? Who?

'Do you understand the charge against you?'

'Yes, but I don't remember anything about it.'

'Please take off all your clothes. We'll need them for examination and I'll have an officer come and examine your body.'

The cell door slams shut. I'm alone in a small space… silent and damp. The walls are brick and there's a window covered with iron bars, high up in the end. On one long wall there's a bench set into a stone floor… the cold of it creeps up my body. There's only a little light from the small window… and a bit that shines under the door, so it feels black, like my spirit. I hear the thick door unlock and a policeman comes in with another man. The man looks all over my body… I don't know what for… but he holds my arms up… looks underneath… I have to spread my legs and he looks all round… says things to the policeman who writes notes in a book. I don't hear what he says… my mind's too full… makes pictures of what it thinks I might have done… all of them terrible. Then I think of Elly, mother, father… William. When they leave, I still have no clothes on… my nudity shames me. I sit on the bench… stare for a while… hold my head in my hands and weep. 'What have I done?' 'What have I done?' They fill my mind these four words... over and again I hear them… I cross my arms over my chest to ease the pain that sits there… lay my head on my knees… then I don't seem to feel the cold and pain… just strange sensations in my head and limbs…

December 12th 1891

His father leaves the house early on Saturday, places a notice on the door two houses away, to let his customers know the business will be closed for the forthcoming week, then makes his way towards the Town Hall in the centre of Brighton. As he approaches, heart beating, head held low, he is aware of groups gathered for the spectacle. Mostly they ignore him, though one or two recognise him and point him out to their friends. He makes his way up the steps and into the courtroom, taking a seat at the back. It is not long before the entire gallery is full, the main entrance closed, and from a door in the opposite corner, his son, flanked by two constables, is led into the dock.

His son still wears his railway uniform, and as he stands there, his hands in front of his body, he looks about the room. He is no longer a boy, but a young slightly built man, not very tall. The fair hair he always had, is the same but is now more wavey than straight. His eyes are bright, his face thinner than his father remembers. Above his top lip he has grown a light moustache, and his chin is deep, protruding somewhat, but despite this, he thinks his son is of very passable appearance. Looking quite relaxed, almost unconcerned his father cannot imagine what must be going through his mind, hoping his son will see him there and take heart from his presence.

His father wonders if he realises the gravity of his situation, whether he has had any counsel, but his thoughts are interrupted by the entrance of eight men, who make their way to the raised platform behind the bench, opposite the dock. Mr. Steers is the Stipendiary. The Mayor is there also and of the rest, five are Alderman… he recognises some of them… thinks such high powered men indicate the seriousness of the investigation. He forces himself to sit tall… after all, his son has not yet been found guilty of this crime, but inside he shivers and is close to feeling overwhelmed.

They ready themselves, murmurs among the gallery reduce to nothing, the resulting silence palpable. His father's hands sweat… he rubs them along his thighs… looks back at his son, who remains unmoved. Mr. Wilkins appears for the prosecution, Mr. Samuels for the defence. He does not know Mr. Samuels but prays he will be robust in his role and defend with vigour. His son is formally charged with wilful murder. He struggles to hear it, to understand how it has come to be. Mr. Wilkins stands, beginning the proceedings by outlining events of the last two days and then calls witnesses.

As he listens to the grim details his heart sinks... he cannot believe his son capable of such barbarity. Descriptions so intimate... so graphically told. He feels sick. The clothes his son was wearing underneath are produced... the court told of blood stains, not only on the outer garments, but on those beneath as well. It is unreal. Surely, he will wake any minute and tell his wife of his bizarre nightmare. He watches his son who averts his eyes towards the floor of the dock or up towards the ceiling. He is serious, sometimes looks dejected, takes deep breaths now and then. When the child's body is spoken of, his son turns away but does not appear to be agitated or emotional.

His father does not know what to make of it, cannot understand the lack of mortification in his son. When the child's father is called to give evidence, he sees the agony on his face, the way he crumples as he speaks of it and has to compel his own body to remain seated, truly feeling the pain he suffers. All he wants now is to fly from this place. At the end of the statements, his son is remanded in custody, taken back to the cell, leaving his father to exit the court as quickly as he can.

He needs air, not realising how hot and stuffy the courtroom has been. It is cold when he steps outside, but dry, so he walks home along the seafront, breathes deeply as he tries to order his mind. What he has heard leaves him in turmoil, not knowing what to think. He is devastated they would not let him see his son, and from somewhere deep in his thoughts, he remembers the constable giving evidence that his son was drunk on Thursday evening. It hits him like a blow to the head, makes him double over, lean on the nearest solid thing, watch as the contents of his stomach are forcibly ejected onto the promenade. His emotions somersault wildly. He weeps openly for his son, but as he moves on an anger builds. He wants to yell out, shout loudly, scourge his mind for tormenting him so. He wants to take his son by the shoulders and shake him. He wants to rewind time, go back to Thursday night, so he looks for him when he does not return home. If only.

He goes straight to the scullery when he arrives home, asks for hot water, otherwise ignores the expectant faces turned towards him. With the door shut, he strips, feels and smells the violence of his intestines, scrubs himself, wonders if he will ever be clean again. He

6

sits on the stool, lets his body sink into its own shape. Did his son break the pledge on Thursday, or long before then? What else but drink would have made him behave so cruelly. He puts his clothes on and makes his way upstairs. Inside he weeps.

2

Pride is one of the seven deadly sins; but it cannot be the pride of a mother in her children, for that is a compound of two cardinal virtues – faith and hope.
Charles Dickens: Nicholas Nickleby (1839)

Brighton 1862

Alice Mary Tyler wakes early as is often the case these days, but at least today there is some vestige of light. The moon shines through the tightly drawn drapes, which do not quite meet at the centre of the small window in their bedroom. She slips silently from the bed, not wishing to disturb her husband, and reaches for the warm winter shawl ready waiting by her bedside. In her condition she is unable to use the chamber pot, so slipping her shawl over her shoulders and knotting it tightly at her breast, she creeps to the door and eases it open. Her husband turns but does not wake. She pauses at her daughter's bedroom and sees that she is still sound asleep, so negotiates the narrow, twisting stairs, while concentrating on missing those treads that creak. She makes her way to the ground floor, through the narrow door at the bottom. In the quiet of the morning every sound seems to be enough to wake the whole street and she wonders how she manages to close the latch on the staircase door without waking Maud. She goes carefully into the kitchen and the scullery and then beyond into the early morning air. The privy, though not far from the scullery door, is at the back of the house, adjacent to the garden wall. She only just makes it this time.

The November morning is cold, but she stands by the privy door afterwards and looks to the sky. Only a few thin clouds scuttle across on the wind, which catches her shawl and the hem of her nightdress. Recent weather has been wet and she hopes today there will be no rain. Her back aches. It has ached throughout the last few months and she places her hand at its centre; gives it a gentle rub. She cups her other hand under her abdomen as though it might lessen the burden of her body's condition.

'Are you there, little one? You haven't moved much lately. Your sister kicked for all she was worth. Her tiny foot would bulge out so much I could almost hold it. She was telling me how fine and healthy she was, so will you give mummy a kick, then I'll know you're alright?' The wind begins to increase as she stands there. It is coming off the sea from the south and seems to slither round the corner of the privy to find her ankles and nip them with the cold. She is used to the wind though and thinks of her father. The mill paddles will be turning, and even on a Sunday he will be making good use of the wind. It takes her back to her childhood and those long days when she would accompany him to the mill on the South Downs, watch the huge stones turn and the grain fall like sun soaked rain, marvel at the transformation it goes through. She allows herself a memory of her mother, whom she had loved dearly, but who had died before her only daughter married and her first grandchild born. *I need you now mother*, she thinks, though she has learned not to give in to the grief that had beset her two years ago, needing to be strong for her own children now. And it is Sunday. Her yellow day; always her yellow day. Full of brightness and her mission to God for thanksgiving. Usually, all the family come for dinner and there are games and reading, laughter and rooms filled with brightness. Today though, dinner will be with Alfred's parents, William, and Lily, who live just two houses away.

Feeling the cold acutely now, she returns to the house. The stove needs lighting, so as gently as she can she lowers herself to her knees and begins clearing away the ashes left from the previous evening, which Alfred will take to the ash store in the garden and mix with the contents of the privy. She crumples old newspaper, lays it on the bottom of the firebox and adds some kindling, on top of which she carefully places coal from the bucket. It takes three matches before the flames are steady enough for the kindling to catch. Just as she is beginning to feel the warmth and about to get herself up, she hears creaking on the stairs and too late, the familiar voice of her husband.

'Alice my dear. What are you doing? You know how I worry when you do these difficult chores. Why didn't you wake me?' She turns to see that he has carried Maud down from her cot setting her on the ground so she can waddle over to her mother.

'I wanted you to have some extra sleep Alfred. I woke up early. The baby rests heavily and I needed to relieve myself... and I've always done it. Why should it be any different now?'

'Because I'm as worried as you are that this baby isn't moving and I think I should try to be a bit more helpful now. You need to be careful,' he says, with a smile that she knows means all too well, he is to be listened to.

'Hello Maud. Did you sleep well?'

'Yes Mama. All night with Dolly.'

'Hm... you're lovely and warm,' Alice says putting her arms around her daughter and kissing her softly on the cheek. Alfred comes across to help her and with a good heave, she manages to get to her feet. He kisses her on the forehead and touches the perfect little birthmark just under her left eye.

'I love this little place,' he says, touching the petal shaped mark she was born with.

'You tell me that everyday Alfred, but don't stop. It makes me feel special.'

Once the fire is established, water, collected the previous evening from the pump and stored in the kettle and pots, is placed on the hot plate. When there is sufficient for both of them, Alfred takes it to the scullery and pours it into the large sink. Alice follows him, shuts the door when he leaves, takes off her night clothes and shivers. It is really icy in the room with its bare brick walls and because it is Sunday there is no copper on to warm it through. After her wash she leaves the water for Alfred and returns to the kitchen, where the aroma of breakfast instantly makes her feel hungry. Alfred likes to cook simple things and has made Sunday breakfast ever since they had been married. He says it is his gift to her that on one day of the week she does not have to do it. Maud is waiting at the table talking to herself in the way she does, with little words and short sentences she is beginning to know, 'Mama' and 'Papa' sometimes audible. Alice stirs the porridge quickly before it catches in the pan, Alfred having already cut slices of bread, taken the butter from the cold store in the larder and found the cutlery. She is dishing up when he comes through and they sit down for their first meal of the day.

'Be careful Maud! Hold your spoon tightly and the porridge won't slip off and down your front,' Alfred says.

'We're so lucky to have this house,' Alice says, not for the first time. Do you remember that tiny kitchen and just one bedroom? And that small room we all had to live in!'

'What was worse was the pump, so far from the house, and the privy we had to share with all those other families. It was quite disgusting really'.

'Getting this house came just at the right time, didn't it? I'll always be grateful for it. So many families have no choice but to live in the slum parts of town.'

Mr. Hargreaves is a good landlord, installing a stove in the kitchen which is so much cleaner than the open fire she had been used to. It is not the latest, as those heat water for all the home but their street has not yet been connected to a water supply. Although they are not wealthy, they are beginning to purchase furniture and the necessary daily utensils which make life more comfortable.

They both like this Sunday morning breakfast, taking their time, this being the only day Alfred is not at work. It is his best time with Maud. He loves to sit on the floor with her and play, to cuddle her and feel her warmth, to smell the babiness of her. He always makes the best use of it. Once Maud has eaten as much as she wants, he takes her on his lap while he finishes his bread and butter. With another kettle boiled they are able to make a hot drink of tea, and there is always enough left for Maud to have a little. Tea is still quite expensive even though the government has rescinded the tax, but Alfred and Alice always have some in their pantry.

Breakfast completed Alfred goes upstairs while Alice sets the used things in the scullery sink. She puts warm water in a large bowl on the table, washes Maud, combs her hair and wraps her in the winter shawl she has worn to the privy, setting her on the floor to amuse herself. Before going upstairs, Alice uses what is left of the water to wash the dishes. She tidies the scullery and the kitchen table, and puts the last of the water on the hot plate. Maud feels lovely and warm when Alice takes her hand to climb the stairs. In their bedroom, Alfred is already dressed in his Sunday suit.

'Thank you for getting my favourite dress out.'

'It's the only one you can wear at the moment, so I didn't have to look hard.'

He kisses Maud before leaving them to prepare and goes to the parlour to read the 'Brighton Herald'. Maud is on the bed, rolling around in the blankets, pretending to hide.

'Now Maud, will you sit still for Mama today? Let's get these warm undergarments on first.'

Next, come the pantaloons over which is worn a white dress that Alice made. Then, by now being used to the routine, Maud plays with her rag doll while her mother coils her own long dark hair, pinning it at the back of her head, before beginning to dress. Over her woollen undergarments, she fits a half corset, now fashionably worn while expecting, and then steps into her dress. She made this dress too, when she was carrying Maud, but now it seems as though it will not even go round her, so much larger has she become in this last week.

'Alfred,' she calls, 'I need some help.' She tidies the bed while she waits. 'Would you please help me do up this dress?'

He begins with the lowest button working his way upwards until he reaches the largest part of her abdomen.

'Oh Alice. You won't be able to wear this dress for many more Sundays. I hope the baby arrives soon.'

'I think it will.'

As he continues, with some struggle, she pulls herself in until the dress is taut around her and though he does not need to, he fastens all the buttons to her neck.

'Thank you.' she says, enjoying the feel of his hands at her throat. She takes them in hers, holds them for a brief moment before reaching for her warm coat and presenting it to him to help her again. Alfred collects Maud in his arms and descends the stairs, Alice following on behind rather more slowly. The baby carriage is taken outside and Maud comfortably settled with Dolly, both wrapped in blankets.

3

St. Nicholas Church is a reasonable walk even without being in the later stages of pregnancy, so I hold onto Alfred's arm while he pushes Maud. I've always liked this route to church and today we leave home in plenty of time so I don't feel hurried. We walk along Rock Street towards Easton Road, the main road from Kemptown to Brighton. The day is dry, and the trees are splendid in their late autumn colours; yellows and golds; reds and browns; all vying for a space to drink in the day's unexpected sun. The road is covered in their glory too. Sometimes patches of dry leaves crunch under my feet, a sound Alfred particularly likes.

'Mind those wet patches Alice. They'll be very slippery.'

'Can you not feel how tightly I hold on to you?'

'And keep doing so, please.'

We catch the bus into town, for the walk is too much in my current state, and look out at all the new building along Easton Road. Alfred is interested to see some of them now occupied. Not many are private homes, although one or two large three storey houses are dotted along the way. We pass the Female Orphan Asylum where girls are already lining up in the front garden to make their walk to church, their merry sounds drifting towards the road. It's an impressive building, double fronted with three storeys and is surrounded by a low wall with iron railings on top. Some of the girls are fooling about, thinking they're out of sight of their mistresses, but I could have told them that mistresses have eyes everywhere!

Further along the road we pass the terrace of white houses which are a little older, and which I particularly love for their bright, and cheery aspect. One of them has a grand portico with steps leading to it, and again, outside the whole terrace there are iron railings. Part of this terrace has been taken by the Institute for the Deaf. Then there's what many people say is the grandest of all the buildings, opened just a year ago, and is the School for the Blind. It's been built in the Gothic style with very fancy windows but I think it too heavy and out of place with the beautiful terraces close by.

'The land for this building was donated by the Rev Steven Watson who founded St Mary's Hall, close to us,' Alfred says. 'I'm pleased to see that it's now thriving.'

'Well, I think it borders on the ugly. I can't imagine what you like about it.'

'But it's a wonderful piece of architecture, Alice. Can you not admire it for that alone?'

'I can't. It's far too dark and heavy with all that decoration.'

I turn my attention to Maud so I don't have to engage in the splendour Alfred so clearly admires.

When we arrive at Brighton, we still have a little walk. I push the blankets more tightly around Maud before moving on, and we meet several people we know along the way. Some are just acquaintances but others are friends from Kemptown. We acknowledge them either with a nod or a simple greeting, before eventually reaching the church. I love this church with its squat square tower and rooves, showing how it's been added to over the years. It stands on a small rise, gravestones spilling out down the hill, mostly facing towards the east, and today they look rather sad and overgrown. We were married here, both of us having been brought up in the Anglican faith. I have to stop awhile to get my breath, before tackling the rise, by then feeling quite exhausted, my heart beating a little too quickly from the walk.

'Perhaps I shouldn't have come today. It has fair worn me out Alfred.'

'I think this'll be the last time I'll allow you to, until after the baby's born.'

Inside the church we find Alfred's parents and his brothers David, Henry, Harry, and Jonathan, and after greeting them, take our seats in the pew behind. Alfred's father, William, has his own boot making business. He is a fine looking man, tall and slim, with dark brown hair and eyes the colour of the dark tan leather he works with. All the Tyler men take after him, there being no real resemblance to Lily at all; almost as though she'd not taken part in their making. David, Alfred's older brother by two years, is also a boot and shoemaker, working with them in the basement of number eleven Rock Street. Henry at eighteen is learning a trade as a blacksmith while Harry, four years younger, works as an errand boy for his father as well as for other local businesspeople. The youngest of the five brothers is Jonathan, aged twelve, who has finished his schooling but not yet taken on any gainful employment, much to his father's disappointment, so he does whatever is asked of him, and helps his mother in the home.

Sitting between us, Maud swings Dolly around in front of her as though she's about to launch her through the air towards her grandparents.

'Stop that Maud!' Alfred whispers. 'People in church want to hear what the priest has to say. We must be quiet now.'

I listen attentively to the sermon, even though the pew is hard and there is no respite for my aching back. It's a sermon that challenges the congregation to live by the Lord and continue to read the Bible as our guide to an honourable and healthy life.

'Those of us in His flock are safeguarded… but if we stray from his Word… if we think we can manage by ourselves… then beware, I say to you. Beware of those who would tempt you from the paths of righteousness. They're everywhere you least expect them to be. Your closest friends… your work mates… your employers… Don't be fooled into believing that anyone can look after you like our God, the true father. He, and only He, can guide you in a life of purity. So, I say unto you, follow Him… take the straight path he offers you… keep your eyes on Him and Him alone. And you will be rewarded in Heaven.'

When I pray, it's for all my family, but my most fervent prayers today are for this unborn child and for a safe delivery. At the end of the service the congregation begin to gather outside on the gravel path, where many lively conversations are under way. People are relaxed. There is little talk of the sermon we've just listened to though.

We meet Mr. Hargreaves as he walks to his carriage, his wife having gone ahead. He's a handsome man, perhaps a little older than William, with a good head of fair hair which he keeps cut truly short. His blue eyes are rich and a little mesmerising, although I wouldn't dare to say so. He keeps a slim profile and his clothes, which are extremely modern, hint at his broad shoulders beneath. He carries himself well, given that he is rather on the tall side, and nobody would be in any doubt as to the standing of such a gentleman.

'Good morning Alice; Alfred,' he says with a slight nod of his head. 'This must be little Maud. You've grown since I last saw you. Alice, you appear to be worn out with the exertions of attending the service today. May I offer you a ride home in the carriage? Maybe Mrs. Tyler would like to accompany us also. There's plenty of room.'

I look to Alfred who says, 'Thank you Mr. Hargreaves. I'm sure both Alice and my mother would appreciate it.'

'I would. Will you take Maud with you and try to tire her out a little? She's been sitting for so long, a run about will do her good.'

'Of course. We don't mind do we father? Alfred asks, and looks to his brothers for their agreement also.

4

It's quite a unique experience for us to be travelling in such a grand carriage, with its two fine horses, trotting through Brighton, heads held high. I feel as though I'm taller than the tallest man as we pass the crowds in town. I sit straighter. My shoulders are loose and not hunched as they often are and it's so grand it makes me believe I'm grander than I am. It's nonsense, of course, but such a privilege I must make the most of it.

'It's exceedingly kind of you to take us home today. I think Alice won't be able to go far for a while,' Lily says.

'It's our pleasure,' Mrs Hargreaves replies. 'What kind of people would we be, to take off on our own knowing that you'd have to walk home, and with us living so close to each other?'

I'm taken out of my reverie as I hear the words and notice for the first time, how similar Mrs. Hargreaves is, in stature, to her husband, being also quite tall, and slim in the hips, and, I consider, equally well attired. Her wool dress is a mixture of pinks and greens, with beautiful, embroidered patterns. The skirt is so full I think I would find it difficult to handle its making. As she sits there, it spreads out such a way, it almost covers her husband's legs! The tightly fitted bodice, which I manage to see when her shawl slips, has many small pleats from the shoulder to the centre point, and the sleeves are magnificently bell shaped with matching pleats. How I do envy the workmanship of it and wonder who her dressmaker is, for although Mr. Hargreaves has his boots made at 'Tylers', I've never been asked to make anything for his wife.

'Did you enjoy the sermon? I do believe that sometimes our Priest thinks we spend our time between Sundays in sinful engagements,' says Mr. Hargreaves, laughing gently, but his wife gives him a brief look to suggest he is not being quite proper.

'I did enjoy the sermon sir. I thought it very suitable for the younger members of the congregation to be reminded of the fates that will befall them, should they stray from the Lord's path,' I say, thinking that maybe my ride in such a fine fashion has emboldened me rather too much.

'You are awfully close to the end, Alice. I expect you're anxious now to have it over with,' says Mrs Hargreaves.

'In truth, I can't wait for this year to be finished. 1863 will be a relief. Oh. it's fine for you to let us down here. It means you won't need to go out of your way, and it's only a short walk to the house.'

'We wouldn't hear of it, dear girl. You in your condition! Whatever will people think?' she says with a broad smile.

'It's been so kind of you,' Lily says as we arrive at the house, and after I rather awkwardly clamber down, my belly not allowing me to see the steps, so that I almost fall into the road, we wave our thanks and watch as they disappear round the corner.

'Sit yourself down in the parlour Alice. I'm going to find Emily to see how she's getting on with dinner.'

A fire has been set and I'm thankful for the warmth emitted. I hold my cold hands to the flames, try not to breath in the smoke infiltrating the space, and when they are warm, hold them against my face. Sitting back in the chair, I look around the room, which I've been in so many times before, but somehow have never really noticed. It's funny how one can be in a place many times and yet not see what is there. I suppose I've usually been busy and not on my own. A large number of photographs, heavily framed in black, hang on the wall opposite the fireplace. I recognise those of Alfred and his brothers but not others which I think must be of their grandparents or aunts and uncles. There's certainly a likeness in most of the faces. The same oval shape and thick dark hair. Their eyes are darker than dark brown and being deep set, look almost black. They all have narrow lips which turn up at the corners in a smile for the camera. Both the men and the women are fine looking. A handsome family indeed.

On the wall facing me, hangs a rather large embroidery featuring peonies and lilies in a bouquet, with fern leaves and little daisy flowers. I think this a new addition, for surely, I would've noticed it before. It must be Lily's work. I'll ask her about it, since I'd like to be able to embroider as well. My mother was a dressmaker and taught me all her skills, so I've become quite adept, though not as good as she. But I can design and make well enough to have a reputation among many of the upper middle class ladies about here. The transformation of a flat piece of fabric into something shapely and well-fitting fascinates me. It's like a puzzle, and the sight of something finished gives me such joy. Alfred wanted me to give it up after we married, and I must say that Lily said as much too, but I was rather petulant and persuaded him of the satisfaction it gives me. Of course, it provides a small extra income now that we've moved, and I've the space to work. Lily still thinks it's quite wrong for a woman to continue working after marriage, but it doesn't stop her from loving the dresses I make her. My father wanted us to live with him at the mill, to start with, but Alfred was determined that we should not rely on our parents. I think he wishes we had when the cold and damp, in our first house, got to his fingers. We're in a much better area now though. We have our own privy, three bedrooms, a parlour, a cellar, a good sized garden. So much space we didn't know what to do with it at first. More than all that, we have a kind landlord. The business is providing well for both families, so Alfred says, and I look forward to better times ahead.

While I muse, Lily and Emily have been busy in the kitchen and Emily brings me a cup of tea in a splendid china cup and saucer.

'You must be thirsty Mrs Tyler', she says. 'Mrs Tyler will be through in a while. She won't be a minute.'

'Thank you, Emily. This's just what I need. And we've the best china today!'

After a while, Lily brings two dishes through with her, places them carefully on the table, and sits in the chair facing me.

'How are you feeling now Alice?'

'Much better thank you Mother. The rest has done me good. It was kind of Mr. and Mrs. Hargreaves to bring us home. What do you know of him?'

'What do you want to know?'

'I suppose I find it out of character for such a gentleman. I'm rather interested now.'

'Well. I know him well Alice. He was friendly with Alfred when they were young.'

'I didn't know that! I've never heard Alfred speak of him other than as our landlord. How were they friends?'

'I'm not sure I should say, Alice.'

'Please mother. Do tell me. There surely can't be a reason for me not to know.'

'Well. Old Mr. Hargreaves ran the grocer's shop round the corner. He was friendly with Alfred's father. They were both tradesmen you see, about the same age and both with young families... yes, they got on well. Shared an interest in architecture and nature. So, Alfred and Edward, that's Mr. Hargreaves given name, played together... I suppose they grew up together.

'I'm a little confused. How did Mr. Hargreaves become such a gentleman from a tradesman's son?'

'There's rather a long story behind it Alice, and I'm not sure I even remember half of it. There was some distant uncle somewhere... I can't remember which side of the family he was... anyway he was wealthy... he owned a large mansion in the north, with a lot of land and several cottages. At some point he died without leaving any direct heir, and after a few years, it was discovered that old Mr. Hargreaves was the beneficiary. Of course, it changed everything. It wasn't long before the family moved away... out towards Rottingdean I believe. It quite upset the boys and father too. Alfred missed his friend terribly... I hadn't realised they were so close.'

'Where you friendly with old Mrs. Hargreaves?'

'Oh. No, my dear. We had nothing in common. I rarely saw her, only when I needed to frequent the shop.'

'What happened after that?'

'We heard that old Mr. Hargreaves and his wife died in some sort of accident... not sure now what it was...think it might have involved a train. Anyway Mr. Hargreaves, Edward that is, inherited the estate and all the money, as the eldest son.'

'Oh, my goodness. What a story Mother. How did you meet again?'

'Well, my dear. Alfred's father and I have lived in this house since we married. The landlord was already getting on in years and died suddenly. The next we know our Mr. Hargreaves buys the house, along with all the others in the road. So, you see, he became our landlord.'

'What amazing twists and turns. But why does Alfred not call him Edward?'

'It wouldn't be seemly Alice! Mr. Hargreaves is a gentleman of some wealth, wherever he started out, and he's our landlord. How can any of us call him anything but Mr. Hargreaves? Mind you, for all he's become, he's never forgotten where he came from. He looks after his tenants, and you've seen how generous he can be. He does a lot of good work about the town.'

Mother leaves me then to check on Emily and I turn to thinking about what she's told me, which runs into thoughts about how I'd like to furnish our house. When she returns, I say, 'I do so want to make our home comfortable for Alfred and the children. I have some large pieces of fabric my mother left me and I think I'll make some new curtains for our bedroom. The windows there are quite small so it won't take much.'

'Now my dear, don't let your thoughts get ahead of you. Once this child arrives there'll be little time to even think about your sewing. Now, where are those men folk of ours? The light's already fading fast and I for one am ready to eat something.'

5

Alfred, his father, and brothers remain in the church grounds for a while, catching up with the local news.

'Father, did you see the piece in the 'Brighton Herald' about the application for a water company to be put to Parliament in the next session?' Alfred asks.

'Not yet. I haven't had time to read much of the paper.'

'Well. It says that by November 30th there'll be notifications of the plans in the Town Hall for public inspection, and of the properties to be taken for the site of the reservoir. We should try to go and see if there are any plans for Kemptown.'

'We should my dear boy.'

'I've also given some thought to our water situation. I think it'd be sensible, with the birth due soon, for us to have as much water as we can store at both homes. There's room in the sculleries and if I collect together as many buckets as possible for storage, there're six of us who could collect from the pump. I know Alice will try to collect it herself and she's so near her time, I think it unwise.'

'A very sensible idea Alfred. We can start tomorrow after the close of work and then your brothers can keep everything topped up each day.'

Deciding to take a more leisurely walk home, the day having stayed dry, they take turns to push Maud in the carriage. Heading towards the promenade, to show Maud the sea, they watch as waves break on the beach and delight in Maud's high pitched laughter. She waves her arms about, with Dolly flapping in the wind, enjoying the splashing sound of the waves and the slurp as they recede over the stones.

'When the weather's hot again after this cold winter, Grandpa will take you paddling in the sea. Maybe Papa, Mama and the new baby will come with us Maud.'

'We'd love that. Perhaps we can arrange a whole family picnic on the beach,' says Alfred, who then asks his brothers to push their niece for a while so that he can talk to his father. Once they are alone, he confides,

'I'm worried about Alice, Father. She isn't having a good time with this baby, and I can't stop her doing some of the heavy household chores because she's too stubborn to wait for me. There's too little movement from the baby and we think it bodes ill. At least we can afford a doctor this time but I think she shouldn't be left on her own now. I wondered if Mother would be able to stay with her during the day while I work at the shop. Maybe Mother might manage some of the small daily chores so that Alice is able to rest more.'

'I know what you mean. She's always had her father's stubbornness. We'll talk to Mother when we get back. I feel sure she'll be only too pleased to help.'

'Thank you, father. I'd feel better for it.'

By the time they catch up with the others, Henry is carrying Maud in his arms and showing her the Chain Pier, telling her that this is the first pier to be built in the country and that it is a great feat of engineering.

'I don't think Maud's too bothered about the pier Henry,' Alfred says as they approach.

They all laugh but Henry knows enough about working with metal to be in awe of this magnificent construction. He turns his back to them, shuts them out in mock hurt.

'When the summer comes, I'll take you out on the pier, Maud, and you'll be able to see all the fancily dressed people who come down from London to visit,' he says.

They continue along the promenade until they reach Chichester Place, which they take until the roads cross. Turning right into Chesham Road they soon reach Rock Street and home. The sound of the front door opening and a mixture of voices brings Alice and Lily out to greet them.

'Here you are Alice, one very tired little girl.'

Alice takes Maud upstairs and lays her on a bed, where she closes her eyes and falls asleep almost immediately while Alice watches, feeling an immense love for her child.

'Boys,' says William, 'I need to talk with your mother and Alfred, so will you leave us for a while? We'll be in the front parlour.'

William explains his conversation with Alfred and Lily says,

'I've noticed she's struggling, though I've said nothing, but I'd love to be able to help. How will you manage though?'

'We've Emily and we're all out at work each day. Emily's a good lass. She'll do as much as she can to help us.'

'Then it's settled. I'll go before Alfred needs to leave for work and return when he's home again!'

'Lily, there'll be no rush in the mornings. Alfred has only one house to pass and he works with his father, who's not going to worry if he's a minute or two late! We're well on with the work and have only a few more orders in hand.'

Being careful on the stairs, Alice arrives back in the parlour to find that Lily and Emily have furnished the table with sumptuous looking dishes, the younger men clearly anxious to devour them. It looks wonderful and she realises she is hungry. Emily brings a shoulder of mutton with onion gravy and there are dishes of potato, cabbage, and turnip. Pitchers of lemon are skilfully settled between them. With the lamps lit, the drapes pulled, the fire banked up with more coal, the room feels like a warm blanket which pulls her in and makes her smile.

William allows the younger boys to leave the room at the end of the meal, and they disappear into various parts of the home.

'That was such a welcome meal Mother. I feel as though I've eaten for three, never mind two!' Alice says, selecting a piece of fruit.

'How've you been feeling this last week?' Lily asks.

'Well Mother, I admit to having been particularly tired. Some mornings it's all I can do to get out of bed.'

'How much longer do you think it'll be before it decides to grace us with its presence?'

'Oh. I don't know... I hope it isn't long though. This dress is about as tight as it can be.'

'While you were upstairs, we talked about how we can help. We've agreed, if you want it that is, that as of tomorrow, I'll spend the days with you while Alfred works. It means you can rest and I can busy myself with some of the daily chores and look after Maud. What do you think?'

'Have you really thought what it would mean for all of you?'

'Yes, dear girl. But you're the one who needs help now. Isn't that what families are for?'

'Then I'd be pleased Mother, not just to be able to relax a little more, but to have another woman to talk with.'

'Well,' Alfred says, 'I'm much relieved, but you make sure Alice, you don't use it as an excuse to do even more in the house!'

Back at home with Maud settled in bed, they sit in front of the stove in the kitchen to warm their hands.

'I look forward to spending some time with Mother. I'll ask her to teach me some embroidery! She's incredibly good with her needle and that hanging in the parlour is so beautiful, I can't believe I've never noticed it before.'

Well… perhaps after this baby's arrived you and Mother might spend an afternoon or two together. I think Mother would enjoy that as well. After all, she has to contend with six men and only Emily to talk to. I think she might have been wanting to offer herself, but thought you might see it as an intrusion.'

'Oh! I do hope not. Why would she think that? I know we don't always share the same opinions, but she's your mother, and being the only women among so many of you, we really should be closer than we are. Don't you think so?'

'I do. Perhaps it will begin to happen now, and I'll be glad of it for both of you. Shall I get our nightgowns to warm by the fire?'

'Yes please, and will you bring me down my winter shawl as well Alfred? It'll be very cold upstairs. Perhaps you'd put the stone in its cover and place it in the bed.'

While Alfred is upstairs, Alice checks on the parlour fire. She knows it will not be long before she needs to sleep and Alfred will want to sit comfortably to finish reading his paper. When he returns, he warms their clothes by the stove and Alice dresses. Alfred kisses her lightly on the forehead holding her as closely as he can.

'I love you Mrs. Alice Tyler.'

'And I love you too Mr. Tyler.'

'I won't be long reading and I'll try not to disturb you when I come up. Sleep well my dear.'

Alice treads wearily up the stairs, feeling that the day has slipped past all too quickly. She looks in on Maud, sleeping soundly as ever and listens for a moment to the gentlest of breath emanating from her, says a silent prayer for her daughter and her unborn baby. She slips between the cold covers, eager to find the warmth of the stone on her feet. With a deep intake of breath, she closes her eyes and sleeps.

6

I wake early not remembering having gone to sleep and as I rise to collect my shawl, feel much better than I have for a while. Perhaps yesterday tired me more than I thought. On reaching the bottom of the stairs, I meet Alfred as he leaves the parlour with a bucket of ashes from the fire.

'Good morning my dear. I think you slept well last night.'

'Good morning Alfred. I did, thank you. I must hurry now as I've slept longer than usual.'

He stands back to let me go and then follows through the kitchen to the garden. While I'm in the privy, I can hear him emptying the remains of the fire into the ash store. I know this is quite full and hope it'll be collected tonight, or he'll have to do something about it himself. I don't linger outside this morning, for the wind has changed, coming now from the north. Even though we live close to the sea, and our street's sheltered from these northerly winds by the rise of the town and the South Downs, it still feels bitter. Back in the kitchen I hear Alfred on his way downstairs with Maud, hear him say, 'We must practise this because Mama can't keep carrying you now her tummy's so big!... Slowly now... that's it. Clever girl Maud.' I think about how much I love him. The kettle's hot enough for his wash so I fill the sink in the scullery and he disappears, leaving us to cuddle and warm ourselves by the fire. I prepare breakfast, which is porridge, bread and butter again today, and make a note to walk to the shop for some eggs later. Perhaps if I can find some spinach, we'll have it with egg for our evening meal.

Alfred's mother arrives just before eight o'clock to allow him to go to work, but before leaving he searches the basement and the scullery for as many buckets as he can find. Altogether he has six. He stacks them up in the corner of the scullery, away from where we'll want to work, says his goodbyes, and disappears through the front door. It's just mother, me and Maud now. I'd usually hurry round to clear things away so the washing is started, but suddenly I feel a bit lost. I think mother needs entertaining, as is normal when she's here, and realise that my normal is changed. Maybe forever. Mother's not here to visit. She's here for me, to help me. I wonder if we'll grow closer in our dual efforts, or whether our natures are so different, working together will prove too difficult. I tell myself; it's me who must be accommodating. She's older and set in her ways. I'm young, better able to adapt, to learn from her.

Alfred has a spring in his step as he enters his parents' home and goes downstairs to the workshop.

'Good morning Alfred. You look lively this morning,' his father says.

'Morning father. Well yes. I feel much better knowing Alice is taken care of. We both had a good night's sleep and little Maud… well thank goodness she's such a good child and healthy sleeper. We rarely have disturbed nights on her account.'

The workshop is, as always, an array of completed and almost finished boots and shoes, lying on tables and benches set against the outside walls of the cellar. On the wall at the bottom of the stairs hangs a large frame of pigeonholes in which the lasts are stored, and above other benches, tools hang from nails and old brackets. Shelves house the larger pieces of leather, rolled up to prevent creasing; pots and jars of nails and other paraphernalia have their own spaces. Under one bench, wooden tubs contain smaller pieces of leather and offcuts. Alfred loves the workshop; has never had any qualms about learning the trade, and for some reason today, he realises how much it means to him to be able to work within a family business. They know how each other operates and can all work on the same pair of footwear without any loss of quality. They have the same temperaments and attitudes towards their patrons and this allows any one of them to undertake every aspect of the business.

As he moves through the space, the pungent smell of leather and glue fills his nostrils; the sound of David knocking nails into the sole of a shoe rings melodically; the sight of his father bending over a last, his shoulders beginning to hunch permanently from the daily stance; each of these, small in themselves, add to the intense joy of life, which has increased tenfold since he found Alice. Watching his father now, he sees himself and David in maybe ten or twenty years, with calloused hands, bowed shoulders, bruises from knocks on benches, and thinks it will all be worthwhile just to be like him, for he loves and admires his father intensely and wants to be the man William is.

William built on the business having taken it over when his father died. At that time, they only made bespoke boots and built a reputation for fine quality work, increasing their customers, mainly on the basis of word of mouth. Many of William's patrons are wealthy gentlemen, requiring bespoke shoes and boots, but they now also provide a local shoe shop for general sale. 'Tyler's Boots and Shoes' became 'Tyler and Sons' in recent years. The first task for Alfred, as his father and brother David are already working on orders, is to tidy the space. He gathers all the lasts lying about and places them in pairs in their designated pigeonholes.

'It's good that we have shaped lasts now Father, but when they weren't, they were so much easier to store. These take up a lot more space.'

'Ah yes. And it was easy to match them if anything happened to one! I wouldn't go back now though. They're so much more comfortable.'

'I wish I'd stayed later on Saturday to clear some of these tools away. Perhaps we should all have a good clear up at the end of the day.'

'We used to didn't we. I think the volume of work has made us a bit lackadaisical. We must get back to that routine. It's good to have a tidy workspace,' says David.

'You talk some good sense sometimes, son,' William says laughing.

Emily brings them down a hot drink of chocolate during the morning, there being no heat in the basement. While they drink, they discuss various issues from the news, yet another aspect of working together they all enjoy, the time to share ideas and views, not necessarily about shoemaking, but more often than not they discuss the latest developments in tools and how other tradesmen work. None of them are against learning as much as possible to improve their product.

7

'Alice!'

I hear my name as in a dream, before I realise mother's standing in front of me, peering at me as though I'm some strange being. I look down at her, she being quite a bit shorter, and she's smiling up at me, her face softer than I've ever seen it before.

'You were a long way from home Alice.'

'I'm sorry Mother. I didn't know I was in such deep thought.'

'Are you well?'

'Yes. Don't worry about me… I'm just finding it a bit strange. Do you not find it so?'

'Us, about to do battle, wearing our old clothes and putting off all the good behaviour we're used to when we're together? I suppose I do. But you know Alice, I've been a lonely old woman for many years, and I confess that while you lived in that dreadful house, in the centre of Brighton, I couldn't bring myself to visit. I do believe that in some way I've failed you and Alfred because of it. Now I want to change that. I want to get to know you properly.'

I wonder who this person is before me. She doesn't look like Alfred's mother, well dressed as I've always seen her. She doesn't sound like her either. It's a transformation, but I'm pleased. I think we may be friends after all. I watch her fill the copper with water, light the fire underneath, her sleeves rolled up showing how her elbows are dry and flaky and the skin on her lower arms, loose. We go to the bedrooms, taking Maud with us and today, I don't worry about her on the stairs. I wonder if I've become redundant.

Lily takes the pillow cases and bottom sheets for the wash, leaving the top sheets to use on the bottom for the next two weeks.

Everything's taken from the beds. Lily shakes the blankets to remove as much dust and dirt as possible, and as I watch the guilt weighs strongly.

'These blankets get heavier every year, I swear, and they're nothing compared to the eiderdowns,' she says, somewhat out of breath. 'I really don't know how you've managed.'

When she's done, linen lies in a bundle on the floor at the top of the stairs; she bends down to collect it and I see the grimace on her face as her back twinges, so large is the pile she can hardly see to put one foot in front of the other.

'Mother! Stop. Put it all down and watch!'

I give one hefty kick of my foot, and we look on as the pile rolls down the stairs, collecting itself into a ball and coming to rest against the door at the bottom.

'Oh! Alice. In all my years I've never thought to do that,' and we laugh loudly like young school girls.

'The sooner we start, the sooner we finish,' Lily says brightly, after we've kicked the dirty linen all the way to the scullery. She's still giggling and I smile to see her having so much fun on wash day.

I lay a blanket on the kitchen floor, as close to the warmth of the fire as I dare, and Maud and Dolly begin building towers with her wooden blocks. I know she'll amuse herself for most of the day if necessary. Lily puts a bar of soap in the copper and works it for a few minutes to dissolve before the linen goes in, takes the long wooden pole, swishes everything around, all the while checking the fire to make sure the heat is up. I see the pains in her back catch her, further guilt tormenting my head.

While the washing heats, she rests a bit, watches me now, as I clean the breakfast dishes, but she's up and ready to start again almost before the last plate is stowed away.

'Let me help mother. I can do some of the pounding. It's the lifting and bending I find so difficult.'

'You can perch on that stool and watch your old mother-in-law do something for a change.'

She works tirelessly, pummelling and scrubbing the linen before transferring it to the sink.

'It's a good thing we've had so much rain lately; there's enough soft water for everything today,' she says as she refills the copper, and while the fresh water heats up, she attaches the mangle to the sink.

'Alice dear, would you give me a hand with this wringing? The sheets are so heavy and slippery, I can't get a proper grip and turn the handle at the same time.'

'Shall I hold the sheets or turn the mangle?'

'Turn the mangle dear. With your stomach you won't get anywhere near the sink to do the sheets!'

I can't help but laugh. I've never seen Alfred's mother so jovial. I didn't know she could be like this. I feel as though I'm peering into her; to where she keeps herself hidden, and feel privileged to be witnessing her doing these mundane tasks. I wonder about their situation, something I never considered until now. I know Emily's been with them a few years and before her, there'd been an older woman. Alfred spoke of her once, now I think about it. Even though the business is doing well, it had been a struggle for William to build it up and gain the good reputation they enjoy, so how could they have afforded a maid? Perhaps I'll ask Alfred about it, or maybe that's beyond my knowing until he chooses to tell me.

Once everything is back in the copper for another rinse, we stop for a drink. Maud still makes tall towers and then knocks them all down with a swipe of her hand, or throws Dolly at them, only to start over. A sigh of relief comes from mother as she flops onto a chair by the stove, and I feel quite conflicted. I take her hand as I put her drink on the table and see the redness brought on by soapy water.

'Would you like some cream Mother?'

'Do you have some. My hands are not used to this work anymore.'

I rub it in for her. It seems the least I can do. Dampness spreads through the kitchen, even though I make sure the door is shut so it does not permeate the rest of the house, and the perfume of soap mingles with our hot chocolate, souring its flavour. But on wash days we are all well used to that.

'Mother, did you make the embroidery hanging in your parlour?'

'Yes dear. Quite a long time ago now, but it's been in store and father's only just found time to hang it for me.'

'It's beautiful. Such fine work. Where did you learn to embroider?'

'I was taught at home. It was the thing to do when I was a young girl, and I've loved it ever since.'

'Will you teach me?'

'I can show you the stitches dear if that's what you want. Perhaps when the little one comes along and life is back to normal, we can spend some time with it.'

'I'd like that.'

I muse for a while, take Maud on my lap, and dream of a time when normal life will allow such a thing.

'I'll need to go and buy some eggs and milk this afternoon. Will you come with me?'

'Well, I think we should have this done soon enough, so yes a trip in the fresh air will do us both good. I confess that since Emily's been with us, she's done all our laundry and I'd quite forgotten just how much it made my body ache!'

After several rinses, and quite a bit of spilt water, everything's ready to hang out on the line in the small back garden. There's no rain today, but at this time of year it'll take several days to dry without the wind, and even then, it might have to be placed over the ceiling airer. Alfred put two of these up for me, one in the scullery for wet washing and one in the kitchen for finishing off. At about midday, Harry comes to the house.

'Hello Mother; Alice. Hello Maud. Are you building?' He picks her up and gives her a huge squeeze, making her giggle and flail her arms about.

'Father sent me to see if there's anything you need.'

'Well now. You've come at just the right time, son. All those buckets and things need filling from the pump, but before you start on that, will you ask Emily to come round if your father can spare her?'

Emily is a godsend, and because Lily is weary now, she asks her to clean up the scullery and make the beds with clean linen. I still have Maud on my lap and we play some clapping games, while Harry comes in every now and then, laden with buckets. I prepare lunch and we sit in the dining room, Emily eating with Maud in the kitchen, after lunch Lily says she must go and change if we're to go shopping.

'You don't need to Mother. It's winter. Nobody will know what's under your coat.'

'I will know Alice, and I can't allow people to gossip about Mrs. Tyler out and about in her work-a-day clothes. I won't be long,' she says, heading for the door and disappearing before I can say another word.

I have a sense of relief then. It's as though I've been playing host, even while we worked well together and laughed at ourselves, but even so it's alien to me and will take a deal of getting used to. I take Maud upstairs to find her coat and check that Emily has everything she needs.

8

I don't realise at first what has woken me, but know I have to get downstairs.

'Alfred! I've so much pain in my back. Please can you help me up?'

'Wait a minute, take my arm.'

'Ah!… gently… perhaps if I slide to the edge of the bed…'

'I think once you've been to the privy, you should come back to bed. I'll bring you a hot drink.'

My back feels better with an empty bladder and I'm dozing in the cool sheets and soft pillows when the first pain strikes. It's harsh across my abdomen and lasts for some minutes. When it subsides, I think back to having Maud, try to remember the pains and how long they lasted before she appeared, but that's the funny thing about having babies. The excruciating pain of it is forgotten almost immediately, and I think then, that were it not the case, no woman would have more than one child if she could help it!

Lily arrives, at the bedroom door just as another creases my face.

'It seems I've come just in time dear.'

She's all calmness, quite my opposite and I'm so glad of her, I take her hand and squeeze it tight.

'Let's keep a tally of the pains. Is there anything I can get you?'

'No thank you Mother. But would you take Maud, please? She must need a drink. She's been so good, on the bed with me and Dolly.'

I give Maud a hug and kiss the smooth skin of her cheek, knowing I'll not be seeing her for much of the day.

Lily talks to Maud in such a kindly way, as they descend the stairs, and I can't help but admire her serenity, thinking my mother would be so full of excitement she'd be all a fluster. Lily brings me some broth at lunch time and I can feel the heat of it travelling down to my belly, the taste of it good in my mouth. The pains are worse now though and closer together, so I spill some broth over the bedclothes, cross with myself for being clumsy, for not putting it aside before the worst of it hit me, but in the end, it doesn't matter, for just as it calms, the waters break, soaking everything.

'Mother!' I shout, and she rushes into the room so fast, I think she must have been coming anyway. I throw back the covers, the damage to the bed all too plain, and struggle to my feet. She helps me to a chair before she pulls all the bed clothes off and dumps them on the landing. I giggle.

'What's so funny?'

'I've a vision of you kicking them downstairs. Do you remember mother?'

'I do my girl. I'll not forget that in a hurry,' and she laughs with me.

This is the Lily I crave for. I understand her a little better each time we work together, and I suppose I accept that she has two conflicting sides to her personality.

'I think you'll have to use the spare bed now. This mattress'll have to be scrubbed and dried out. Here, let me give you a hand,' she says as another pain racks my body.

'I'm taking Maud to Alfred but I'll only be a few minutes. He'll fetch the doctor. Will you be alright my dear?'

Without waiting for a reply, she runs from the room and I hear the front door slam. I'm alone in the house now, feel so wretched, I cry. It's only me and my baby, and it's not moved for so long. 'Please be alive little one. Please don't be dead inside me.' I can't bear the thoughts that race through my head, as another more painful spasm comes, and I feel the need to push. 'Don't push,' I say out loud. 'Don't push. Wait for the doctor,' and mother is by my side. I grab her hands in mine. Pain shakes my body.

'Try to relax Alice. The doctor won't be long.'

'Mother, I'm so afraid for this baby. There hasn't been movement this week and I'm sure it'll be born dead.'

'Come now my dear. The doctor will do his absolute best to make sure you have a safe delivery and I'm anxious to meet my new grandchild.'

'If only I could believe that. I've been praying for the child… asking God to keep it safe… but Mother, this is so different to Maud.'

'Every birth is different. You shouldn't be dwelling on such dark things.'

Another spasm takes hold of me and I can't stifle the noise that comes from my throat, a sound that frightens me. I look at Lily, and see her face troubled, the cause of my pain reflected in her. My body tells me to push but there's no doctor.

'What if the baby comes before he gets here? Will you be able to deliver it?'

My head buzzes with images of death, coffins and burials and the pain is almost beyond bearable when Dr. Sayer shows his head round the door. I don't know why, but I instantly feel safe. When Maud was born, we had no money for a doctor, and I think of the grumpy old midwife shouting at me as though I was somehow being awkward, as she brought her into the world.

'Now Mrs Tyler, you will leave please and make sure everything's ready with the necessary towels and water. I've no need of you in the room until I ask for you. I can give you some chloroform, Alice, to help with the pain.'

'No doctor, but thank you.'

'Well, it's here if you need it. Try to relax. Ah… I can feel baby's head. That's good. On the next contraction I want you to push hard.'

When it comes, I think my body might be torn in two, but feel the relief of it as well, until there is a sharpness in my abdomen, making me cry out.

'That's probably a shoulder, Alice. Nothing to worry about. Well done. The worst is over. Now please just relax until the next contraction comes and then another big push.'

With the next bout of pain, my baby is born. I slump back in a pool of sweat, to listen for the cry I expect. I hold my breath. There's no sound. I watch as Dr. Sayer takes my baby aside, wraps it in a towel. I see him rub it and look in its mouth, still holding my breath until it bursts from me.

'It's dead? Doctor is my baby dead?'

'Mrs Tyler,' he calls, 'will you please come back in the room and sit with Alice? I've work to do here.'

He struggles. I can see from where I am, there's a blueness about the face and I know that if my baby doesn't cry soon, he'll pronounce it dead. Lily is by my side in seconds. She holds my hand; smooths my brow and we wait anxiously.

It seems hours pass as I lie there, convincing myself I will never hear it; that my baby is dead; and I think I already grieve. Lily makes me comfortable, turns frequently to see what Dr. Sayer is doing, and all the time assures me that only seconds have passed. We pray to God for its life. I see Dr. Sayer rub my child's chest gently and there's a weak intake of breath. He continues until there's an unexpected cry, an explosion in my head. I sit up stretch out my arms towards him, tears of joy on my cheeks. Lily puts her hands to her own face and weeps for the miracle.

'You have a baby boy Alice. He hasn't had the best start to life but he's alive,' says Dr. Sayer as he brings him and lays him in my arms. Almost immediately he drops into a chair exhausted. I look at him and see worry there, above the fatigue but he smiles, writes something in his notebook and looks up. It's as though he's about to say something, but instead he leaves us and I hear him shout down to Alfred.

'Alfred! Come up… come on,' he yells and in a second Alfred is beside me.

'This's your son. I want to call him after you. Alfred, I say, as I hold out our baby to his father, 'this's your father.'

Alfred takes the child in his arms and it seems the sun shines for the first time today, on our first boy.

'He's a fine baby Alice. All his limbs are here and his tiny fingers and toes. And look at his beautiful little face! He has my nose already!'

'He's beautiful Alfred, but it was a long time before he took any breath and cried.'

'You're not to worry Alice. Look at him. He's perfect.'

Emily and Lily take a quick peek at the new arrival, before going down to the kitchen to organise hot drinks and the cleaning of the bedroom. Dr. Sayer stays for a while and I see in his face some reluctance to go.

'It hasn't been the easiest of births,' he says, and his voice trails off as he gets up to leave, but I stop him and say,

'You look rather anxious. Is there a reason?'

'Err… no,' he says.

All the worry of this pregnancy and the doubts I had as to my baby's lack of movement, disappeared the moment I took him in my arms.

'Mother has been magnificent. I wouldn't have managed without her and I wish to repay her somehow,' I say.

'Tell her that, Alice. It'll be enough for her.'

We pray together for our son and family and thank God for his blessing in giving us another life. Alfred goes downstairs to see if there is any food left. I'm alone with you for the first time. I hold you to my breast and you suckle.

'Hello, my little boy. What a miracle God has wrought. My head knows you shouldn't be here but my heart praises him for his kindness. Has he saved you for something special? Will you be a great man? You, and your sister Maud, are the most precious things in Mama's life. I'll always protect you from harm, and I'll never abandon you. You'll grow up to be a fine man so Mama and Papa will be proud of you. You'll know every day of your life that you are loved because Mama will tell you so.'

9

Freddie's a good baby. He takes to the breast easily, feeds well, and I enjoy these times. While I hold him in my arms, I scrutinise him, the better to remember his physical features when he's out of sight.

'You've got your Papa's nose, little one, so tiny… and look at those beautiful ears…. not too large and not too small… that tiny turned down mouth will soon be smiling.' His eyes are a perfect blue, his hair pale brown, and there's lots of it, quite a mop in fact. When I put him down, he sleeps soundly and I'm amazed that he hardly ever cries. He lies on the blanket in the kitchen or in the baby carriage, while I work and often there's no movement of limbs, to the extent that sometimes I hardly know he's there and need to check his breathing. Maud loves him. She peeps at him while he sleeps, and offers him her toys when he wakes.

'Mama. When he as big as me?'

'Well now. You're nearly two years old, aren't you? So… I think it will be about two years.'

'Then he be like me?'

'Not quite Maud. You'll always be nearly two years older than him.'

'When I play him Mama?'

'When he's a little bigger and can sit up. Then you can help him to start walking.'

'I carry him and give him hug?'

'I tell you what. When I've finished this chore, we'll go and sit down. If you're very careful you can have him on your lap. How would that be?'

Dolly flaps about in excitement, and it becomes a regular afternoon treat for her to hold her brother. If she doesn't, she badgers me until I give in.

'Come in Father. It's such a dreadful day, come out of the cold. The fire's on in the parlour, and I've got some tea ready.'

'Hello, my girl. My… let me look at you. Motherhood suits you, just like it did Mary.'

'Where are the boys? I thought they were coming too?'

'They won't be long. Popped in to see Alfred and the crew next door!'

'Perhaps Alfred will come back with them for a while. Father, it's so lovely to see you. I've missed you these last months.'

I hug him tightly and he responds. I know he still mourns mother and misses the physical closeness they enjoyed, so I always try to comfort him as best I can.

'The mill's been so busy, I've hardly had time to sit down, never mind walk across the Downs. Doesn't mean I don't think about you though.'

'Are the boys helping you out?'

'They do their bit, but they've got their own jobs, so most falls to me now. I'm just not getting any younger! Here, look… I've brought you some more flour and you must let me know when you're getting low… one of your brothers will bring some down.'

'Thank you, Father. As long as we've bread, we won't go hungry. Now, warm yourself. I'll bring in the tea. Lily's in the kitchen and can't wait to see you.'

'I can't wait to see my new grandson,' he calls after her.

My brothers, Charles, Matthew and Thomas, come in shortly after with Alfred, who's been able to take the rest of the day off. After all the greetings, tea and cake, I carry Freddie in.

'My, my. What a handsome fellow he is,' Charles says. 'He looks like his father already!' and he punches Alfred lightly on the arm, whereupon a mock battle ensues between the two men.

'Ah, but he's got our colouring,' chimes in father, as though this is the most important trait in him.

'I don't care who he takes after. He's alive and in one piece, and thank God for that,' I say.

During the evening, I watch father. Life always seems to get in the way of us seeing each other, and when he brings flour for me, he stays only for a quick cup of tea, the climb over the Downs beckoning him before he tires too much. Now, I can see he is indeed aging. His hair's thinning and his back, which had once been so straight, is rounding at the shoulders. I suppose it's the years of carrying sacks of grain up and down ladders. It occurs to me that when the time comes, he'll move in with us and I'll look after him, as the only daughter, and none of my brothers yet married. I'll not mind it. He's a happy man and I think he'll enjoy being with the children. He's never wanted for much and I know we can make him comfortable. Lily enjoys seeing father again and if William had been able to leave the workshop, he and father, would've hidden themselves away somewhere to chew the fat.

10

What Lily does not enjoy, or intend to continue, are the labours of home chores that she undertook during that final week of Alice's confinement. She and William relax in the parlour one evening. William reading his newspaper, Lily musing on recent events, while at the same time attempting to concentrate on her latest embroidery.

'It was lovely to be with Alice that last week... but William, I'm no longer used to all that bending and lifting. I think this cough and cold I have is due to the exertions. My body feels as though it's been through that mangle!'

'I don't see you having to do any of that now, so you must relax and let Emily do the heavy work.'

Without realising it, a slight smile plays on her lips and when William looks up, he is pleased to see his wife content, in spite of her coughing.

'I wonder what's causing that smile, Lily.'

'Oh... I was thinking about our beautiful grandson... but also, about how I might be able to help Alice. She'll find things hard now with two children to look after, as well as all the household chores... I know she wants to return to her dress making, although of course I don't agree with it. But I suppose I'll not be able to stop her and if it gives her so much pleasure, she'll be happier for it, don't you think? And I confess William that I'd very much like a new day dress.'

'I'm sure you do Lily! So, what're you really thinking?'

'I'm thinking William, that we're comfortable and don't have need for much... So... maybe... we can afford to help them financially?'

'Ah, I see. Let me think about it over dinner.'

'The boys are all still at home... they've everything they need'...

'Yes, my dear. Give me a little time to see what can be done.'

At the end of their meal when they sit once more by the fire, William says,

'I've had an idea. We could give Alfred and Alice an amount from your money'. Lily is pensive for a moment, her face clouds over slightly. William can see her thoughts tumble and thinks she is disapproving of the notion, so says,

'I know I said we were not to touch it… that it's there for the children, but isn't it at times like these that they should benefit from it?'

'In fact, dear, I think it a good thing. I was just wondering how we'd… well… you know, how we'd explain it.'

'We should be honest… tell them the truth. After all they're grown men now and will understand.'

'I don't want all the children to know now.'

'Why not?'

'Because the youngest are not men enough and may take advantage of such good fortune. We've managed well and they should too. At least until, like Alfred, there's a need.'

'And you don't think that only Alfred knowing would compromise him in some way?'

'David too then, as the oldest. Alfred won't be alone with the knowledge and David is sensible enough to manage it. It would mean that Alice could have a maid.'

Lily perks up then, a broad smile on her face, a twinkle in her eyes and continues, 'And I think I know just the person who might help us find someone… Reverend Williamson's bound to know of a lass who needs work, and it's always best to employ on a recommendation. Will I talk to Alice about it?'

'Lily, it always amazes me how swiftly you switch from serious to joyful. Let me talk to Alfred first please.'

Next morning, unable to wait, Lily goes to the hall, takes her coat and hat, and makes herself ready for the walk to the Rectory. However, William comes through on his way to the basement and asks where she is going at such an early hour. When she tells him, he reminds her he has not spoken to their son yet, and of course Lily knows he is right. He does not want to dampen her spirits, though it will take a lot to do so, but he has always been a fair man and one who wants to manage things in the right order; Alfred first, then Alice and then Reverend Williamson.

'I'm quite sure you'll be able to take that walk later today and perhaps Alice will accompany you.'

'You know William, you're always right. It's good that I have you to tether me sometimes.'

'Tether you like a goat my dear?' he laughs.

'You know what I mean. Sometimes I can be led by excitement when I should stop and think about what I'm doing!'

When Alfred arrives for work his father takes him into the parlour. Lily is baking a cake, with Emily, in the kitchen. He sits him down with a cup of tea which is quite unusual.

'What is it Father? Is there bad news?'

'No dear boy. I want to speak with you away from your brothers regarding a decision mother and I have made. We're going to give you a sum of money to help so you can have a maid and be more comfortable. We won't hear of any reasons why it shouldn't be so.'

Lily has crept through the hall to listen outside the door and smiles at her husband's forcefulness, knowing how Alfred will argue against it. Alfred is astounded and thinks perhaps he hears incorrectly, so asks his father to repeat himself.

'Father. I don't really know what to say. Can the business sustain such a large sum?'

'Well now, my boy. I need to tell you something mother and I have kept secret all these years'… William hesitates as though what is to come is some awful news. 'There's no other way of saying it… your mother married below her. She was born into a rather wealthy family, and when we wanted to marry, her parents were set against it.'

The shock strikes Alfred into silence. He wonders how he had never known such a thing about his own mother, and why it should have been hidden from the family. It is not something to be ashamed of after all.

'I don't know what to say! How did you meet her?'

'That doesn't matter now, son. The fact is we did. I won't go into too much detail, just enough for you know how things were. Mother's father offered her a substantial amount of money, when he realised she wouldn't give me up, but if she took it, it would be on the understanding that he wanted no more to do with her and she would be disinherited. I've never said this to anyone before Alfred. That she loved me so much she could take such an offer, was the best moment of my life. But I was a proud man. Mother wanted us to use some of it to buy ourselves a house. I couldn't accept that. As her husband it was my duty to provide for her.'

'So, this is why we've never known our grandparents?'

'It is son. We thought it better to say they had died. Mother found it difficult at first… we had our moments… I often felt in those early years that I should have let her go, but… well,

we've come through. We decided to place her money in a bank and only use it if we really had to. Otherwise, it was to be kept for our children.'

Alfred simply cannot believe it… that his parents had been so selfless to have given up what would have been an entirely different life… and for children not then born.

'Father… I don't know what to say, I really don't. It's come as such a shock. In truth, I should be like you and say no… that I'll provide for my family now.'

'No son. This is what we want and we're going to tell David about it, so you don't have to carry our secret on your own.'

'What about the others?'

'Not yet. Mother thinks them still too young.'

Alfred sits back in the chair, relieves the tension in his body, and looks at his father. Could I ever be as magnanimous as he?' he wonders.

'Now. Go and talk to Alice. Your mother is chafing at the bit to see her and find her a maid.'

Lily scuffles back to the kitchen before she is seen eavesdropping and picks up her mixture quickly. She is, however, rather out of breath and William is not fooled.

'Have you been listening Lily?'

'I confess to it,' she says, smiling broadly.

'I don't know how to thank you mother. It will make life so much better for us. I'm actually a little embarrassed about your generosity… lost for words, but thank you both.'

It is still early in the morning, the breakfast dishes unwashed, and I'm taking things through to the scullery. Freddie lies on his blanket with Maud and Dolly beside him. The stove's lovely and hot so I can feel the warm air being drawn through into the scullery. I look frequently at the children, and I'm so happy it feels almost sinful. I'm thinking of asking Alfred to fetch my sewing trunk up from the cellar, when there he is, all a dither.

'What is it Alfred?'

'Dry your hands Alice and sit with me. Is there water enough for tea?'

I make a pot and sit at the table not at all sure of what's coming, and listen with incredulity as I hear more and more of Alfred's tale. Surely, it's beyond belief, and when he stops, I think I've missed most of it.

'Alfred. What is all this. Have you fallen and hit your head?'

'No,' he says, laughing so much he can't speak again for a moment. 'It's true Alice. I know it's hard to believe but it's true. Imagine mother's family being wealthy and us children never knowing of it.'

'It explains quite a lot about her though. Her haughtiness when she's in company; her views about me not working. You know Alfred... I can actually see her in a grand place with servants and nothing much to do but needlework. No wonder her embroideries are so fine!'

We're silent for a bit, not knowing what to say and I watch my husband stare into the room. Freddie cries. It's his feed time so I pick him up from the blanket and hold him to me, breathing in his wonderful baby smell. Maud's been so engrossed she's not made a sound, or perhaps I've just not heard her, the news blotting out all around me. I give Freddie to Alfred and prepare some bread and cheese for our lunch, remembering now that the breakfast things have still not been washed.

'To think my dear that mother almost delivered Freddie; that she worked so hard for us during that week, as though she were the servant and not the one to be served. How much Alfred?'

'How much what?'

'How much are you to be given?'

'Oh. Five hundred pounds.'

'What! But that's a fortune. I can't believe it.'

I feel giddy with excitement, but also because it feels like a confirmation of my worth as her daughter-in-law, when for so long now I've thought mother didn't really approve of me. Perhaps I've misjudged her all this time. Alfred goes back to work and I prepare some hot water for the dishes, only just finishing as mother comes down the hall, almost running to the scullery. Her face is a picture of joy and most unusually, I hold out my arms to embrace her. I think it's the first time she really holds me, her arms tight round my body.

'Mother! How can we thank you for your generosity?'

46

She draws back from me to say hello to Maud who has been calling Nana.

'It's the right thing to do.'

'It must have been so hard for you… you must have loved father enormously to leave your family and the life you were entitled to.'

'It was Alice. One of the hardest decisions I've ever made… my father was adamant though.'

'Have you ever had any regrets?'

'Never. Not for a single moment. I trusted William with my life and he's never given me cause to wish I'd made a different decision.'

'But you might have been a great lady…'

'Instead of the humble wife of a shoemaker, you mean,' she interrupts, and I think not so humble, while she continues. 'You, on the other hand, might have been a maid, yet you too are the wife of a shoemaker. What changes we have seen Alice.'

'Indeed Mother. I don't believe I'd have been a maid though,' I say, with just a little indignation, 'my mother taught me a skill, for which I'll always be truly grateful.'

'Ah. Yes. Your dress making. Now, my dear, let's get ready. I want us to see the Reverend Williamson. I've already sent word of our visit. I believe he's bound to know of some young lass who's in need of work.'

We walk in silence along the Easton Road, mother's head bowed against the cold wind blowing straight towards us from the west. She's never liked the wind and yet it blows strong and often through Brighton, you'd think she might be used to it. I think of the sacrifice she's making for me and wonder at this woman whose life changed so drastically for the love of a man.

'Mother. Do you believe Alfred married below himself?' I venture to say, hardly wanting to hear the answer but needing to know how she feels.

'Did you say something my dear? I can't hear with this wretched wind rattling in my ears.'

'It's nothing. We can talk later when we're home.'

The visit's a profitable one, Reverend Williamson fortuitously knowing of someone.

'She's a good girl… works hard… but really needs to earn a wage now to help the family. It would also do her a deal of good to be out of the crowded home,' he says.

'What can you tell us about her,' I ask.

'Her name's Rebecca Smith and she's seventeen… well almost eighteen now. She hasn't had work because her mother's an invalid, so she's been looking after her and running the house. There's another daughter who can do that now though.'

'She's able to cook then?' Lily asks.

'Oh yes. She's taken care of the little ones too, so will be good with Maud and Freddie,' he says.

'She sounds ideal,' says Lily, looking my way, and I nod in agreement.

I'll ask her to come and see you then.'

Back in Rock Street I settle the children to sleep and we warm ourselves by the stove, with tea and cake. It feels almost like a celebration.

'Mother. Do you believe Alfred married below himself?' I ask again, and she looks at me, her face quizzical but kindly. She's clearly thinking about her response.

'Alice. We're at a sort of junction here… from now on father and I do not wish to hide things… to pretend… the answer to your question is yes. I did think that, though I don't know why. Now you know the truth, I can imagine what's going through your head, but you must know that whatever I thought then, changed a long time ago. After all, who am I to judge you, when the gulf between our pasts are so great? What matters is that we love those we marry and work hard to make them happy. Alfred loves you. I can see clearly that you love him too.'

'Thank you, Mother. You've no notion of what it means to me to hear you say that.'

'Well. I do believe that's quite enough heart searching for one day, don't you?'

11

I'm nervous waiting for Rebecca's arrival to live in our house, so when I hear the knock, it startles me. Reverend Williamson stands at the door with her, a small luggage bag in his hand.

'Come in. Welcome Rebecca and good morning Reverend,' I say feeling the smile on my face.

'Thank you, Mrs. Tyler,' she says rather meekly, and it occurs to me that she's probably more anxious than I am. I take her coat, hang it on the stand and we go through to the kitchen, where I make tea. I want her to know that I'm really happy to have her here, and we sit talking of little unimportant things, until the Reverend bids us farewell. I take her down to her room, which she didn't see when she visited us, since the men only finished it two days ago.

'Mind the steps,' I say as we negotiate the cellar stairs. 'I hope you like it. There's everything I think you need, but should you want anything else, just ask.'

'Mrs. Tyler! It's lovely. I don't know what to say. It's more than I could ever hope for.'

'I hope you'll be comfortable. Take a moment to sort your things, and then meet me in the kitchen so I can show you the house and where things are kept.'

'Thank you.'

Alfred and I go downstairs, with Maud and Freddie, and the moment he opens the door to the hall I'm instantly enveloped by warmth and the wonderful aroma of breakfast. It's such luxury, I think staying in a hotel must be like this. Rebecca's done all the early morning chores I usually do. Will I never have to do them again? Will I become a lady now? Will it change me? I vow not to let it. I don't want to become

Alfred's mother, but I'm so happy this morning, I feel sure I'm grinning like a Cheshire cat, and I see Alfred's face beaming too.

'Good morning Mr. and Mrs. Tyler. Shall I take the children?'

'Good morning,' we both say together.

'If you would, please,' I say, handing over Freddie. 'Did you sleep well?'

'Yes. Thank you. I've never had a room of my own, and such a peaceful night's sleep… the first in a long time. I'm normally woken by one or more of the children crying or coughing. Sometimes they wake me up just to climb into my bed. I've never known such comfort, so thank you both for your thoughtfulness. Now… listen to me. I'm talking far too much.'

'I'm pleased,' Alfred says, 'and you must tell us if there's anything you need or want changed. This is a new experience for all of us. We'll make it work together.'

'Your breakfast is getting cold. I'll wash the children while you eat, she says.'

I'm astounded that she's taking on such a duty without being asked, but I suppose it's what she's done at home. It must be natural for her. It's not natural for me though and I feel a tiny pang of loss at seeing Maud and Freddie disappear into the scullery while we eat on our own. I must decide how much of them I give away; washing and getting them ready for the day is such an intimate time for me, I don't want to lose it.

Our mornings are considerably changed. Rebecca brings hot water to the bedroom for us and I wash and dress the children before we go down to breakfast. I feed Freddie too, so Alfred can have time with them before work. We eat in the dining room, which I still find rather strange, but it means Rebecca can have her meals in the kitchen and clear the dishes in peace. I can't believe the time I have now, to play with my babies. It's such a joyful time; I realise how much I missed with Maud.

Alfred has brought up my sewing trunk so I've been preparing the parlour to use as my workroom. I'm excited as I take the threads and order them in their colours, fold the fabric neatly according to its weight and use, sort through all my patterns and stack them in their sizes and styles, find a place for my scissors, thimbles, needles and other sundries. Rebecca helps me when the chores are done and I confess to delighting in sharing the work. This morning we stand by the door, admiring the order and readiness of it.

'It won't be like this for long,' I say. 'When my customers start returning, there'll be pieces of fabric and cottons all over the place. A dressmaker's workroom isn't easy to keep clean!... Do you think we need a more comfortable chair for my ladies? It never used to bother me, but now I think it would be good to offer a little more relaxation.'

'Perhaps you don't need to, but I suppose it would be nice to offer something soft for their nether regions,' she says and we both laugh.

'Would you answer the door to them and provide refreshments?'

'Yes, Mrs. Tyler, of course.'

'Will you be able to manage the children as well as the chores, if I work during the mornings? It's my intention, to begin with, to have the afternoons free, so that mother and I can spend some time together; or maybe we can all go out somewhere'.

'I'm pleased to do anything you ask of me. For the first time in my life, I'm happy to be away from my parents… they're lovely you understand… but father can be a bit overpowering and what with the small house… well, I used to feel I'd like to run and hide. And now I earn a wage for doing what I've always done for nothing, so I can send something home to help them.'

'I've written to my old customers to let them know I'll be working again by the beginning of March,' I say while we sit comfortably by the fire one evening.

'That's good. I'm pleased to know you're not thinking of starting before then, with all the events coming up,' says Alfred.

'Yes. It'll be a busy time till then. Mother's said she'll organise Christmas and the birthdays… yours and Maud's… so we can concentrate on the christening. Have you organised it yet?'

'I have… as instructed!'

'Oh Alfred. Sometimes you make me out to be a tyrant.'

'But you are my dear! Your wishes are for me to perform… and before you say anything, I perform them gladly. January the eighteenth is the day.'

'Who shall we ask to be godparents?'

'Who would you like to ask, my dear?'

'I've been thinking about it and would like to have Dr. Sayer as one godfather. After all he did save Freddie's life and perhaps it's a good way of thanking him.'

'We can ask him. Who else?'

'Mr. and Mrs. Hargreaves.' Alfred looks at me for a long moment and I know what he's thinking, but I'm quite determined whatever he says.

'I'm not sure Alice. We're their tenants. I'm his bootmaker. They're well above us socially and I'd be worried to put anything in the way of the good relationship we have. Is there no one else?'

'But you were good friends once.'

'Ah... I don't need to ask how you know of that. Mother's been telling you all my secrets?'

'I simply asked her about him since I thought it unusual that they should carry us home from church that day. And do we have secrets Alfred? I'm a little surprised you haven't spoken of it yourself.'

'I haven't deliberately kept it from you. I suppose there's never been a need to raise it. The truth is that over the years I've found it difficult to believe that the gentleman he is now, would still want to be the friend he was... Maybe I've created a distance between us to help me manage it.'

'He thinks well of you though... and he still uses your given name... mine too. So, I wonder if he wouldn't be delighted to have more of a connection.'

'Maybe. It won't hurt to ask them. They can always decline,'

It gets late and the fire dies down. Rebecca comes in to see if we want anything, before she goes to bed, but we're comfortable just to stay for the last of the warmth. Alfred returns to his paper, the house so quiet now I'm overcome with peacefulness. I think about the children. Maud is almost two and I can't believe so much time has passed since her birth. Freddie, just three weeks, is a puzzle to me. He hardly ever cries and Maud used to look at me while she fed, but Freddie's eyes never seem to focus on me. It's as though he's far away. I wonder if it's to do with his birth... not breathing for so long... that his brain might have been affected somehow. I know nothing of such things and yet it niggles away at me. Alfred says I worry too much. Mother says I fuss too much. There's no point in talking to them about it. But am I not the one closest to him? Am I not his mother? Surely mother's know instinctively when things are not quite right?

I try to put it out of my mind, but it's only when I'm occupied that I manage it. With this extra time, I spend more of it with him. Some days I watch him like a hawk watches its prey. I determine to make a start on the dress for mother. That'll give me much to think on.

52

12

It's Freddie's Christening today. Rebecca's lit the fires downstairs, including the one under the copper, to keep the heat from leaching out through the scullery.

'Have you remembered to put water in the copper Rebecca?' I call through the door.

'I have Mrs. Tyler. I learn quickly.'

She comes in to the kitchen smiling. It pleases me that we both see the humour of it now.

'I was so embarrassed… making such a stupid mistake. I can't remember what I was thinking about. Imagine what might have happened had you not noticed the empty copper. I've filled it up today so there'll be enough water for all the cleaning and dishes later on.'

'You'd never used a copper before, so don't worry about it. I'm sure you're not the first to have forgotten.'

I want everything to be exactly right today, so Rebecca and Emily enjoyed themselves preparing mush of it yesterday. I heard them laughing and chatting as they went about their work.

'Make sure the best crockery's used please, and don't forget to stop for a drink and a chat before we return. You'll not have much time afterwards!' I say before leaving them.

The day is exceptionally cold, although recent snow has thawed and thankfully drained away, but it's necessary to wrap both children in their warmest winter clothing and to swaddle Freddie in a blanket and the beautiful shawl Lily made him. I think how adorable he looks in the christening gown, a matching bonnet tied neatly at his chin. Maud has a new outfit for the day; a pink and white dress with a frill at the hem which shows her matching pantaloons, below which her woollen socks and shoes protrude.

'You look so pretty Maud. Give your Grandmother a twirl. Oh! Careful now. Don't get giddy and fall.'

'It's alright Mother. I've got her,' says Alfred.

'Aren't our children beautiful Mother? I'm so proud of them.'

'Now. Haven't I told you before that pride's a sin? If you carry on like this, there'll come a day when you'll be sorry my girl,' Lily says in her authoritative voice.

'Mother please. Of course, I know it is, but can't a mother be proud of her children? Look at your boys. Can you tell me you're not proud of them?'

'Well. Maybe in my heart, yes. But I don't say it. Remember Alice, God can hear everything.'

'And He can't tell what's in our hearts whether we speak it or not? I'm not ashamed of it,' and I hope she 'll mellow a little before we arrive at church.

Alfred wears his Sunday suit and I've lost enough weight to be able to wear my favourite dress again; the one I made after Maud was born and which is much like those I create for my customers. The fabric is dark brown, suitable for winter months and has a pleasing sheen that catches the light as I move. The fitted bodice closes with large buttons to my neck, and it has long sleeves, which are wide at the elbow for movement but tapered at the wrist for comfort and ease of wear.

'Alfred, will you fasten Mother's brooch for me?'

'Where do you want it?'

'At the collar please.'

'You look splendid in this dress. It accentuates your waist.'

'That's the corset too,' I say laughing.

The full skirt, flat at the front and gathered at the sides and back hangs beautifully over my half crinoline. I pin my hair at the back and tie the matching bonnet at the side, below my chin, the wide ribbon making a splendid bow. I turn to Alfred to seek his approval.

'You look magnificent my dear.'

Lily and William have gone to the expense of securing a carriage for our journey and as this arrives in the small street, we settle ourselves in, while the boys walk on ahead. Inside the church we meet our guests, greeting them as we walk to the front pews. My father and brothers are here, smiling and talking happily with those they know, and I kiss each one before they kiss Freddie. I'm happy and relaxed.

Freddie looks up at me, a rare pleasure, and I speak to him and stroke his forehead as I make my way to our pew.

I have known St. Nicholas Church all my life. Maud was christened here. It is my spiritual home; a place where I tell God about all that makes me happy, all that makes me sad and all that worries me. Not since I was a child, have I felt as safe here, as I do today among family and friends, bringing a new life to the Lord and thanking Him for it. I feel blessed that Freddie's god-parents are such important people who'll look after him whatever happens to me and Alfred. As the Reverend Williamson prepares to take the baptismal service, I hand Freddie to Mrs. Hargreaves whose face lights up with admiration. She cradles him as she walks to the font to meet her husband and Dr. Sayer, while we stand behind them. At the end of the service, everyone gathers outside and though it's cold and windy on this little rise, there's laughter and banter enough to keep us all warm. Reverend Williamson approaches and says,

'In all the years I've been baptising babies, I've never known one not to make a single sound. They usually yell out when they feel the water, if not when I take them in my arms!'

'Will you come back to the house, Reverend?' says Alfred.

'I'd like that. I'll finish here and see you a little later.'

Our little house brims with family and friends, gifts are received and love and warmth fill our home. Freddie is passed from one pair of arms to another, and Maud makes the most of all the attention she's receiving. I'm overjoyed at the success of the day, proud to share my daughter and son with our guests. Rebecca's a godsend and I'm humbled at our good fortune.

'I'd like to say a few words, if I may', Mr. Hargreaves announces. 'We're here to celebrate the christening of this little baby. Alice and Alfred have given him into our care as godparents, and we're very excited that they have… It's been a long time since I held such a small bundle, but the way time is moving, for those of us getting older anyway, it won't be long before Freddie's running about. My wife and I… and I'm sure I speak for Dr. Sayer too… assure you that it will be a joy to share his life… to watch him grow into a fine young man and achieve great things, just as his parents have. Thank you both for this wonderful spread and for trusting us with your son. We're honoured to have Freddie as our godchild from this day forward.'

'Thank you, Mr. Hargreaves, for such kind words, and to all three of you for taking on, what I hope will be a memorable task,' Alfred replies.

13

A month has already passed since Freddie was christened and mother arrives for a dress fitting. I'm taking in some fabric under the arm, my nose rather too close to her breast for comfort, and although this never bothers me with customers, it seems to unnerve me with her. I don't understand why and think it should be the other way round. Perhaps it's because I now know her to be from high society, when before she was just mother.

'Does that feel better?' I ask when all the tacks are in. 'You should move round in it to make sure it's comfortable.' She parades up and down the parlour, making her arms swing.

'It feels wonderful Alice.'

'Do you like it?'

'I do. And the colour is perfect for me.'

'There are so many to choose from now that chemical dyes are available. Society will be much prettier and more colourful. Do you remember our shopping trip to buy the fabric?' I ask.

'I do. All those yards of material I made the draper pull out so we could see the patterns better. Then watching while he rolled them up again only to ask for another. How we laughed at that on the way home.'

'At least we only needed eight yards for a day dress and didn't have to carry it with us. It was good of him to deliver it, wasn't it?'

She takes the bodice off carefully and we have tea in the kitchen with Rebecca before fitting the skirt.

'I'm quite excited today mother. Alfred's buying me a sewing machine.' I show her the advertisement.

'That's an expensive piece of equipment, Alice. Do you really need it?'

'It'll mean I can make dresses in half the time, so I can take on more ladies. Surely that will be worth it? Look how long it's taken me to make your dress; every stitch done by hand. With this machine you could've had it weeks ago.'

'You'll be telling me next you're employing a seamstress,' she says with a sideways glance.

'I'm working towards it Mother,' I say, and she turns away so I don't see the sourness on her face, but Rebecca does, and lifts her eyes.

We manage to fit the skirt before lunch is ready, and I know what needs doing now, so she helps me clear the parlour. I show her some of the fashion plates in my latest literature, 'The Englishwoman's Domestic Magazine' and she admires them, but as she flicks through it, she sees the large number of stories printed and asks,

'May I borrow one of these books?'

'Why of course, Mother. Does it interest you?'

'I've not seen one before. I tend not to look at such trivia, but I see it has some interesting articles and maybe a story or two I might enjoy.'

I find an old one for her to take home, ignoring her words. Sometimes I wonder if she realises how she sounds, and if she could hear herself whether it might shock her to know. I'm getting used to her ways gradually, trying not to let her upset me, for what's the point? We are who we are, and nothing I can do will change that.

It's the end of February already, the day being wet with a continuous drizzle and grey blanket clouds, and we spend the afternoon by the fire, which Rebecca keeps well stoked so it glows a comforting red and emits its heat right into our faces. Maud sits with her grandmother, the two of them playing hand claps and singing, while I cuddle Freddie and try to tickle him for a reaction. I try his belly first and then under his arms, his chin, back to his belly, but he hardly moves, his tiny limbs unresponsive. I put him over my shoulder and jiggle him about for a while, in the hope of hearing some small sound, but there's nothing. He's lifted his limbs before and gurgled but it's almost as though he's an empty shell today. I can't stop fretting over him. There's something not right. Eventually I lay him over my lap on his belly and stroke his back, whereupon he goes to sleep.

I think mother and I must have closed our eyes, because we both sit up together to the sound of a loud knock on the door, and Rebecca shows Dr. Sayer into the dining room.

'This is a pleasure doctor. It's very good to see you, but you must be extremely busy. What brings you hear today?'

'Do I need a reason to visit my godson?'

'Of course not. Would you like some tea?'

'That will be most welcome. How are you all? Well, I hope?'

'We're very well, thank you. Rebecca has made life so much easier. I'm even planning to take up my dressmaking again. And Freddie is so good! I put him on a blanket and he doesn't wriggle off, like Maud used to; he doesn't cry… in fact, there're times when he could be quite forgotten. Though he isn't of course,' I add quickly. 'He's always either with me or Rebecca, and Maud loves him.'

Dr. Sayer takes Freddie from me, once his cup is empty, and cradles him in his arms.

'I'm pleased to see that he's putting on some weight.'

'He's taking a little pap with his milk now and would have more if I let him!'

Dr. Sayer lifts Freddie over his head so that his face is towards the floor, and then moves him from side to side, quite roughly, I think. I look towards mother who is watching, her expression a picture of terror, and our eyes meet in recognition of concern. Freddie makes no sound though.

'Mrs. Tyler, have you noticed Freddie moving his head towards noises?'

'I have doctor… but not very much that I can recall.'

'I'd like you and the family to be specially observant over the coming weeks and to have Freddie on your laps or in your arms to watch for certain movements. There's nothing to worry about, but I feel that he isn't responding as I'd expect for his age. Do you remember when Maud began to move about more; to look at you when you spoke to her or make cooing noises?'

'I'm not sure I do, but I know there was no concern for her.'

'I want you to hold Freddie's arms and legs while he's on your lap and move them about playfully. Talk to him as much as you can, note whether he smiles at you or if he makes little noises. Hold a toy above his head, something like a rattle, and move it about to see if his eyes follow it. I'm sure that with some gentle persuasion he'll soon be doing all the things we expect of him.'

'Is there something wrong, Dr. Sayer? I'm rather unnerved by what you say.'

'I'd expect to see more movement in a child of three months… although it may be that Freddie's just a little slow in his development. If you can do the things I ask, I feel sure he'll respond well. There's nothing to worry about. Now. How's Maud doing?' he says as he collects her up and settles her on his lap.

She giggles and I can see that he's checking her over while pretending to play, and I think maybe a doctor as a godparent is an asset. It's not long after, that Dr. Sayer and mother leave and I check on how Rebecca is coping. I really don't need to though; she's confidently managing, and I think I could leave her alone and stop checking. But I'm also much against the notion of us being separate. I want to develop a relationship where we can work together or apart, so there's no barrier to what we can achieve. There's plenty of time though so I ask her if she'll make another pot of tea and go back to the dining room. As I pick my baby boy up, I can't help but wonder what lies behind the doctor's words.

'Hello Freddie,' I say as I cradle his head in the palms of my hands. 'What's all this about? Don't you want to grow up into a fine man for your mother?'

I look at his eyes but they seem to stare at me, so I lay him flat, talking to him all the while, and take his tiny little hands in mine, rub my thumbs into his palms in the same way I used to tickle Maud. His fingers twitch, making me smile, and the more I tickle the more he twitches. I try the same thing with his feet, holding his legs up and bending his knees. There're small movements apparent in his toes but otherwise I detect nothing. I don't know how I feel. I put Freddie over my shoulder, drink the tea and walk with him between the dining room and the kitchen, where Rebecca's minding Maud. Two or three times I walk the floor; desperately trying to remember what Maud had been like at three months old.

14

A loving heart is better and stronger than wisdom.
Charles Dickens: David Copperfield (1850)

Today is wash day. There is a mound of linen to get through. The copper's hot and steamy and there's little breeze to lighten the fug. Freddie loves wash day. He rolls in the dirty linen and while Maud tries to help, she only makes it worse by laughing at him as she pulls the sheets from underneath.

'Stop it please,' Rebecca says in mock anger. They know her too well though, know she cannot be cross with them. They are such darling children. She picks Freddie up and tumbles him about as if to put him in the copper. Maud bends double with laughter and Freddie shrieks in her neck as he holds on tight. She puts him down, tells them to go and play in the garden. Next time she looks round, he is standing quite tall behind her, his face turned upwards, eyes closed, as still as he's been all morning.

'What're you doing Freddie?'

'Drink,' he says.

'You want a drink?'

'No Becca! Drink smell.' His eyes are still shut but now there's such a huge grin on his face, she can't help but laugh.

'Drink smell? What smell?'

'Soap.'

She dries her hands, stoops down, puts her arms round him, hugs him tightly. 'Do you like it?'

'Yes.'

'And you drink it?'

'Yes.'

She loves this little boy with his funny ways. He makes all her days bright, no matter what happens. 'Do you drink other smells?'

'Yes.'

'Which ones?'

'Fire smell… and… Mama!'

Rebecca realises then why he's always about her ankles on wash day, and why he sits so patiently at the fire; hugs his face into his mother's neck, and wonders what can be so gratifying about smells, that he 'drinks' them. She thinks to mention it to Mrs. Tyler.

Rebecca takes the first wash to hang on the line and finds Maud lying on the ground like a proper lady sunning herself. She is a character. She has a clever mind, perhaps taking after her mother and there is a book by her side. Even though she is not yet at school, she can read many words and tells wonderful stories from pictures. Rebecca thinks when she starts at the end of this summer, she will do well. Freddie though, is sitting beside her, quite still and staring at something Rebecca cannot see. He does this sometimes, afterwards unable to say what he is looking at. She knows the whole family have seen this, but it's only her mistress who seems concerned by it. She is sure it is not typical, though tries not to cause any further alarm by speaking of every occasion.

It is a beautiful hot summer's day, as the last loaf goes into the stove, moisture clammy on her face; streams of it running down her back. It is hard work this weather, though the light breeze coming through from the scullery cools her ankles. The children are happily playing, running in and out, round the garden, stopping only for cold drinks to keep them going.

'Come on Freddie! Follow me again,' says Maud, as she runs out of the kitchen.

Rebecca takes little notice as they play.

'Rebecca,' Maud calls.

'What is it Maud?' her face still to the stove.

'Rebecca, look at Freddie.'

When she turns to see him, he is shaking and jerking, his arms rigid and his mouth a little red with blood.

'Maud. I want you to go and fetch your mother quickly,'

'It's alright Freddie,' she says softly, trying to hold his shoulders while his stiff body shakes. By the time Alice comes from the parlour, he is on the ground. Rebecca tries to stay calm but her belly churns and thoughts of what to do flood her mind.

'Oh Mrs. Tyler... I turned from the stove and he was shaking. His arms were all rigid... then he fell down and started this jerking. There's some blood round his mouth.'

'Fetch the doctor please Rebecca... and go for Mr. Tyler on your way.'

She runs so fast to number eleven she almost trips up the steps. 'Mr. Tyler, come quickly. It's Freddie. I'm going to fetch Dr. Sayer.'

Rebecca arrives with Dr. Sayer who asks for space to administer to Freddie, talks to him in a low voice.

'Did he behave in any unusual manner before he fell?'

'I didn't see Doctor Sayer. I was at the stove with my back to him and when I turned round, he was just standing there, rigid... and then he fell forward,' Dr Sayer puts a cloth to Freddie's mouth as soon as his jaw slackens, and stands to face Mr. and Mrs. Tyler. He pauses before speaking.

'I think he may have had a convulsion... and this blood you see is because he's bitten his tongue. That's fairly common in convulsions, as the teeth clamp down hard. He's beginning to come out of it now. His muscles are relaxing... he's coming back to us. It's nothing to worry about. Many children have these and grow out of them with time. Freddie will too I'm sure.'

He lifts the child gently, takes him through to the dining room, where he lays him in one of the large armchairs, Maud running to be with him.

'Rebecca, will you fetch a blanket and cover him well. He might be feeling cold after this. Now, you're not to worry. He may have others but as long as you stop him biting his tongue, he'll be fine and as I say, he'll grow out of them. Do you have any questions?' Alice and Alfred look at each other but neither says anything. 'I'll be on my way then.'

Rebecca is not sure how she feels as she shows Dr. Sayer to the door, wondering if this might have been avoided had she not had her back to Freddie, and when she returns to the dining room, Mrs Tyler is watching over him, her eyes red, her cheeks tear stained. Rebecca stands there not knowing what to say, thinking she is guilty of something, without knowing what.

'Are you all right, Mrs. Tyler?' She looks up at Rebecca with such forlornness, she can hardly bare to hold her mistresses gaze. 'I'll make a pot, shall I?' It's stupid, but the only thing she thinks to say.'

15

Dr. Sayer turns left from the house, towards the sea. He needs fresh air, to ponder on what he has just done. It is one of those decisions made in an instant, without thinking about it, without even the notion of consequences. It disquiets him and before he knows where he is, finds himself in Lewes Crescent and almost outside the Hargreaves' residence. Still unsure of what to do, he lingers by the door a long moment before steeling himself to ring the bell.

'Good day. Is Mr. Hargreaves at home please?'

'He is Sir.'

'Then I'd like to speak with him if it's convenient.'

'Come in Sir. I'll let him know you're here. Can I take a name?'

'Dr. Sayer.'

The house appears lavish, if the main hall is anything to go by, its ornate ceiling looking down over plush chairs and beautiful carpets, all matching in colour and design. He is so engrossed in taking it in, he has not heard Mr. Hargreaves approach.

'It's good to see you,' Mr. Hargreaves says, holding out his hand. 'Please, this way,' and he leads the doctor into a vast sitting room, even more splendid than could be imagined.

'What can I do for you?'

'I'm in a bit of a quandary, and as it concerns our godson, I thought we might discuss it… I would really appreciate your opinion… and possibly your help.'

'Well. It sounds rather intriguing, so tell me the cause of your quandary.'

'I've just come from seeing Freddie… I was called to the house… He was fitting but… I've kept it from Alice.'

'What did you tell her it was then?'

'I said he'd had a convulsion and that there was no reason to be concerned.'

''I see... What might be the difference between the two?'

'Well. Many children have convulsions, mainly with high temperatures... perhaps when they're on the cusp of a childhood illness. A fit however, is an entirely different matter.'

'How so?'

'Fitting is what occurs with epilepsy.'

'I'm not a doctor, dear fellow, so don't fully understand the implications of what you're saying. Please, explain what you think is going on and why you've chosen not to tell the family.'

'I delivered Freddie, as you know. At birth he didn't take a breath for many minutes... I worked on him... on his tiny body... he was limp and beginning to turn blue, but I kept going. I didn't want to lose him you see. Eventually he breathed.'

'I'm aware of this, but without any medical knowledge, I still don't know what you're trying to tell me.'

'Forgive me. There are times when a doctor holds life and death in his hands... times when it's better to allow nature to take its course... and times when a doctor will intervene to secure life. With a baby, not breathing for a long time can cause great difficulties as the child develops'...

'So, are you saying it's not always good to save such a life?'

'I've thought for some time that Freddie may have epilepsy... or at least Petit Mal... that's where the patient has lapses of memory due to the brain not functioning properly. When there are full fits, like the one I've just witnessed, it's highly likely that this is Grand Mal, as it is often called, or to give its correct name, epilepsy. It's much worse. The brain is somehow interrupted of its common function, causing the body to behave uncontrollably, and the patient to have no idea what has happened.'

Mr. Hargreaves thinks about this for a long time, while Dr. Sayer searches his heart for confirmation that he has done the right thing, and not simply of omitting the truth, but whether it had been the right thing, to have worked so long with the child at birth, that he survived. His heart is leaden. He feels a great weariness flood his body. He has doubts about sharing the secret, but whether it is right or wrong, it is done and cannot be undone.

'I can see from your face and posture, that you are much distressed by this, and I sympathise with the predicament you've clearly carried for a long time. How sure are you?'

'Quite sure now.'

'How have you arrived at such a conclusion?'

'I've seen it.'

'Then why not tell them the truth?'

'Ah. Mr. Hargreaves, I've seen patients with the condition at the asylum. I know what it can do and how it can lead people to a life of misery away from their families… isolated. I know how society views such men and women… as lunatics held in an asylum… as the lowest of the low… as lesser beings. They're often shut away for lifetimes, when in reality, they could lead perfectly good lives, with help. Is that what we want for Freddie?'

'It most certainly isn't. But is it fair to Alice and Alfred, to keep it from them? How will they manage the condition?'

'I'm a doctor… you're a gentleman. Would it be impossible for us, together, to do the best for him? And if it is epilepsy, he may still grow out of it. Many children do.'

'Well. I must say I'm rather shocked by the news… I do feel for your position… I truly do, but now that I know we must decide on a course of action. We could tell Alice and Alfred, support them through the troubled times… or… you and I could maintain the secrecy… It's not an easy decision!'

'Do you understand now why I needed to confide it?'

'I do, but before the two of us decide, I'd like to bring Mrs. Hargreaves in. She's his godmother… she has a sensible outlook on life and I believe she wouldn't thank me for keeping it from her.'

'I can see that.'

Mrs. Hargreaves sits silently listening to her husband and the occasional remark from Dr. Sayer, and continues in silence when they are finished. She is not the sort of person to make rash decisions, rather she needs to think through the news, to consider the implications of each course of action. The two men watch her, wait quietly for her to speak, Dr. Sayer feeling the situation closing in on him somehow, as though by telling it again, he might have lost control of it.

'Do you have a favoured position, Dr, Sayer?' She asks at last.

'I do.'

'Have you had sufficient time to conclude anything?' she asks, turning to her husband.

'I believe so. I'm inclined to say that we should keep this knowledge to ourselves, for if, as Dr. Sayer has said, Freddie may be free of the condition when he's older, it would be cruel to give Alice and Alfred cause to live in fear. Wouldn't you agree?'

'Oh, I do,' says Dr. Sayer, 'I was rather hoping for that outcome.'

Mrs. Hargreaves sits quite still for a while before realising that the men are looking expectantly at her.

'I see this as a mother would… perhaps wondering if I'd rather know, but ignorance is bliss, is it not? If he grows out of it, all well and good. If he doesn't and… there are consequences, we must be prepared to take them. Are we prepared for that? Are we sure we're doing the right thing by keeping such a secret?' She waits but there is no response from either of them, so goes on. 'How will we be able to watch over him… to support Alice and Alfred… how will we feel if, God forbid, the condition worsens?'

'Well,'… says her husband, 'visits from Dr. Sayer may well raise suspicion… but we can visit and ask as much as we like… watch from a distance… talk to Alfred in the shop. What do you think?'

They watch her face as it forms a quizzical frown, look at each other for some reassurance, hoping they will not have to persuade further.

'You both seem to have come to the belief that it's better they don't know… so I suppose I should go along with it, but I don't feel entirely comfortable. It's a dark secret,' she says.

'Aren't all secrets dark my dear?'

16

Alfred's brother, Harry, whiles away time, waiting for his father to tell him about his morning errands, so does not at first see the pain on his father's face, until he turns at the sound of his voice.

'Harry would you take this list and manage these jobs today, please,' he says.

'Of course. Father, what is it? Are you in pain?'

'Oh. It's only a bit of indigestion son. I hurried breakfast this morning and now suffer for it. A lesson to you young man!'

Before he leaves the house, however, Harry finds his brothers, lets them know their father is not his usual self. He will be gone most of the day and at least wants them to be aware. After lunch, Alfred and David take furtive looks towards their father, having noticed that he finished his lunch rather quickly.

'I'm not surprised Father's getting indigestion,' says David. 'He needs to slow down and give his stomach a rest!'

'I've been watching him, and you're right. He's not doing his constitution any good at all.'

It is about two-thirty when William experiences greater pain in his chest, almost the whole way round, and his arm hurts. He slips quickly into unconsciousness and dies on the floor of his workshop before the ambulance arrives. Lily flies to him, hugs him, weeps for the man she loves, for the man who is not old, who has never had any medical conditions, who should not be leaving her. When the ambulance departs, and she is once more upstairs with her children, the shock takes over and no amount of comforting can sooth her. Lily is deep in her own grief. The boys are profoundly affected, but Lily does not seem to care that they have lost a father. There is no compassion, no comfort for her sons. Her own grief has no room for them and they have to find solace in other members of the family until

Lily is ready to leave her room. After the funeral, the shop reopens. David, Alfred and Henry decide to continue as normal for the time being, and eventually the two older men make the business their own. For her part, Lily is happy for them to do as they wish. She has no desire to know of the business now, any more than she had when William was alive. For almost a year her attire is black, as though she sports her grief among the neighbourhood, but gradually she begins to return to the woman they know, and takes more of an interest in her family. Her love for her children and grandchildren, make her realise that life must go on. Never once, however, does she comfort any of them for the loss of their father and grandfather. 'I've lost my husband,' she cries, and even though Jonathan reminds her that they have lost their father, she cannot, or perhaps will not, acknowledge it.

There are good times to follow though, while mixed with further sadness. David and Harry, are married giving rise to great pleasure and merriment, but Alice has two further pregnancies, resulting in a miscarriage and a still birth.

'This is all just life, isn't it.' states Lily. 'There's birth and there's death, my dear, and only Our Lord has the power to give and to take life away.'

'Yes Mother. It is so, but knowing it doesn't always help salve the loss of two children. I often wonder what they would have been like, who they'd have taken after, and it grieves me still, that I'll never know.'

'You're not the first woman to have lost children, and you won't be the last. It's the way of the world. It's time to let it pass and look to the future.'

With Rebecca's support, Freddie grows in stature and character, although he continues to have convulsions every now and then, with absence moments in between. These come to be known as Freddie's 'nowhere times' because when asked where he has been, he says nowhere. He becomes less clumsy, enjoys short walks each day and gradually begins to show facial expressions and good eye movement. He is a loveable little boy; with a sense of humour and appreciates the attention this draws from his family. Alice begins to cultivate their small patch of garden, creating one part for flowers and one for vegetables. She finds this therapeutic after the daily chores and dressmaking, and whenever she goes outside, Freddie follows.

'Here you are Freddie. Have this little trowel and dig some of the soil, like Mama. That's right. Turn it over and chop it up so it's nice and fine. Then I'll show you how to plant some seeds. It can be your own little garden.'

'Look Mama,' he says as earth flies upwards and over his head.

'Not like that! Gently, so that we don't get covered. The seeds need that soil. Now scrape it up and make it nice and smooth… That's better. Hold out your hand and keep your fingers really close together.' She puts a few seeds into his palm and shows him how to spread them over the dug patch.

'Will they grow?'

'Oh yes. They'll grow into beautiful colourful flowers and have a lovely smell.'

She shows him how to pull a carrot, wash it clean and scrape it, then gives it to him to eat. When his flowers grow, she shows him how to pick them and arrange them in a vase. Even at such a tender age, he seems able learn these practical activities, waddles inside to find Maud, Rebecca, his Grandmother, or indeed anyone who will share the joy with him. Alice watches him sometimes; listens to his giggling or simply plucks him up and holds him close.

One spring they watch a pair of starlings make a nest in the eaves. The birds find a small hole which they chip away at until it is large enough to pass through into the roof space. Each day Alice takes Maud and Freddie to watch as the pair fly backwards and forwards with bits of straw, stick and all manner of things, until at last they see only one of them foraging.

'Soon we'll hear the new baby birds cheeping', she tells them. 'They'll make such a noise because they'll be hungry all the time.'

'Will we see the baby's Mama?' Freddie wants to know.

'I hope so. We'll have to wait for a while though until they've grown enough to be able to fly.'

Freddie waits patiently, watches the hole in the eaves, until he is able to announce that a miracle has happened. There are babies in the hole! He claps his hands with glee, goes to tell everyone he can find, the good news. A few days later while he stands gazing upwards, he sees one of the adults return with a long worm in its beak.

'Mama, Mama. Come and see. Come and see,' he shouts appearing in the scullery. They follow him outside to find the starling on the roof with the longest worm ever; so long it is curled round in a loop with its two ends hanging out either side of the beak. It looks like one of Maud's skipping ropes. The starling squawks really loudly, turns in all directions as he warns predators not to come near the nest, and from inside comes the sound of high pitched cheeps. Alice thinks the noise is enough to wake the dead. Maud and Freddie laugh so much they are unable to stand still and Maud has to rush to the privy in her excitement. Freddie's eyes are alight with wonder.

'Mama they'll have a big dinner today,' he says looking up at her, and she, looking down at him, wonders how she could ever have been so worried for him.

One day as Rebecca takes the washing to hang out, she sees Freddie stooping with his hands on his knees, his bottom high in the air and his head buried in the flowers.

'What are you doing Freddie?'

'Smelling the flowers,' he says indignantly. 'They smell like Mother. I want to smell like Mother.'

Rebecca picks a sprig of the Lily of the Valley and secures it in the buttonhole of his jacket.

'There, you smell just like your mother now.'

Freddie kisses her cheek while she fixes it, goes as fast as he can, through the house into the parlour where Alice is busy with a customer.

'Mama! Look. Becca says I smell just like you now.' She scoops him up, hugs him, and introduces him to her customer, who tickles him under the chin and declares him to be an adorable child!

Freddie's sense of smell continues to be a source of amusement. He loves being by the sea drawing in deep breaths of its saltiness and whenever Rebecca takes him to the fish market, he marvels at the smells as well as the shapes, colours and sizes of the fish laid out before him. When he sits by the fire, he likes to smell the wood as it catches light. His time in the scullery on wash days, breathing in the soapiness of the suds, has become a source of amusement for the whole family, and if Rebecca is not watchful, he might even pull the clean linen towards him, risking the necessity of having to rewash it. His favourite aroma of all, however, is to be found in his father's workshop. He smells leather as soon as he opens the door of his grandmother's house, and follows it all the way down the narrow steps. He never tires of this, asking often if he can go to help his father.

'I'm not sure you're such a help my man,' his mother tells him, but he is happy to do no more than sit and watch Alfred fashion the shoes, as long as he can have a small leftover piece of leather to hold.

In 1866, Alice gives birth to another girl, Harriet, and Freddie soon discovers a smell he cannot bear. Whenever she needs a nappy change, he calls for someone to 'come and take Harriet'. He is not terribly amused by this little bundle that does nothing all day but sleep, cry and eat. Even when it is explained to him that he had once been such a tiny baby he cannot believe that he had been anything like that! More importantly he is still the only boy in a house that seems full of females and sometimes it would be much better if he had someone like himself to play with. In truth he takes no real notice of Harriet. Maud on the other hand, has always been there for him. He loves her; he looks up to her; he cries every day when she first starts school; waits at the front door to greet her when she returns. Maud in turn loves her brother, has an enormous amount of patience with him, often stopping what she is doing to help him or play with him. As they get older, she begins to dress him in the mornings and encourages him into his nightclothes at bedtime. The best of all times for Freddie is when she cuddles him in their shared bed at night and sometimes, he will force himself to stay awake a little longer to feel her arms round him.

17

I help prepare my son for school, speaking of it positively. He does his best to stand still while I try to fit his new clothes, but he's not used to standing still unless he's in church and often becomes frustrated so I abandon the task. I worry about this inability of his, knowing that sitting still in a classroom all day will be alien to his nature. He starts very soon, going with Maud to the church school which is only just down the road, and he is really pleased to be going with his big sister. He seems to look forward to it, listens when Maud tells him about the teachers and the fun she has, sensibly omitting anything that might just make him feel differently.

As the day draws close, Freddie begins to talk about all the things he does now that he will not be able to do at school and I can see that he has started to think more about this change coming to him. His excitement for a great adventure wanes discernibly and when it arrives, he comes down stairs slowly in his new clothes, fiddling with the collar, scratching at his legs. Maud follows, pushing his back gently to increase his pace. She is a good girl, getting him ready as well as herself, which takes considerably longer, but they both sit and have breakfast. My two adorable children so grown up already.

'Can I have my raggedy clothes on Mama?'

'Not today, Freddie.'

'But they scratch me,' he whines.

'No child of mine is going to school in what you call your raggedy clothes. You'll get used to the new ones and in time they'll soften and scratch less. Now… Let me take a look at my two schoolchildren!'

Rebecca wipes his mouth and hands, takes him up for a hug. She is almost in tears to see her little charge leave for school. 'You're such a big boy now,' she says, 'you have to be like all the other boys and look as fine as them.'

They leave the house hand in hand and wave. Freddie looks backwards as he walks. I close the door and turn to see Rebecca wipe her eyes.

'It's like losing him,' I say.

'That's how I feel too.'

'He'll be fine, you'll see.'

'I don't know Mrs. Tyler. He's not like other lads. He seems defenceless. He can't sit still unless he's drinking smells,' she says, and we both laugh. 'I'm sorry. I shouldn't be saying such things, to you of all people.'

'It's all right. You're with him all the time. You know him better than most people and I suppose it's as natural for you as it is for me.'

Freddie keeps looking backwards as he walks, no longer excited to be grown up enough for school. He knows the school building for he has walked past it many a time, but really, he has no idea what happens in that austere looking building and is only now beginning to ask himself what Maud does all day! From outside it looks just like a large posh house and indeed was built as such before being taken over by the church to be used as a Voluntary school for the poorer children of Kemptown. When Maud and Freddie arrive at the front gate, she kneels down beside him and points,

'You see that door over there? That's the door you have to go through and after school, I'll wait for you here.'

'But I want to go with you. I don't want to be on my own.'

'Have you forgotten Freddie? I told you that boys and girls aren't taught in the same room. You have to go that way and I've to go this way. Look, there's Harry and Nathaniel, your friends from the beach. Go to them… they'll help you.'

He watches as she moves towards her door and speaks to other girls, the building swallowing her up. He wails in despair, heads slowly towards the crowd, everyone seeming to be much bigger than him, and when he gets closer, he loses sight of Harry and Nathaniel altogether. He knows he should not be crying, nobody else cries, but in his distress, a great fear of what lies inside takes hold of him so that the noise he makes grows even louder. Two older boys run towards him laughing and pretending to cry, but as soon as a very tall man appears, striding towards him, they run off, filing into school with their friends. Freddie is quite frozen to the spot as he looks up into a face, full of moustache and anger.

'You boy! What's your name? Mr. Roberts shouts.

'Freddie Maurice Tyler.'

'Sir!' he yells, now almost stepping on Freddie's feet.

'Freddie Maurice Tyler, sir.'

'What are you making all this fuss about? Have you not been brought up to know that boys don't cry?'

'Sorry... uh... sir.'

Mr. Roberts takes him in behind the other boys who are to become his classmates. Inside the door he finds himself in a hallway remarkably similar to the one at home, but this is lined on one side with pegs, already the space almost full of coats. One is found for him at the end, closest to the room he is being guided into, by the hand on his back, so that he almost misses the peg, his legs going faster than his reach can manage. He is in what looks to be the biggest room in the world, full of tables and chairs, in long rows stretching from one wall to the other, with only a couple of lanes to walk between them. Freddie cannot really count well at all so he thinks there must be at least a hundred rows which gradually fill with boys. They stand behind chairs, upright and silent. Mr. Roberts marches him through one of the lanes to the foremost row, finds him an empty space, and stands at the front on a box, the better to see his 'flock'. The day begins with a prayer, which Freddie thinks is good. He prays silently that this day will not be too long and that he will learn enough to prevent a return to this awful place. What follows, however, is by far the longest day of his young life.

A cane points to numbers on a black board and almost immediately a chorus of chanting is heard, but Freddie's tiny voice is just a beat behind all the others, until about the third time round, when he is able to recite some of them on time. It seems to go on for hours; he is bored; his bottom hurts from the hard wooden seat; the noise is almost too much for his sensitive nature and then, when he is beginning to understand what is required of him, the cane points to a different set of symbols. New chants begin without a second between them. Once more his rendering of the letters is not in time with the other boys.

The headmaster becomes aggravated by the trailing voice and tells Freddie, crossly, to keep up. Close to tears now, and fearful that he might actually cry, Freddie listens for a while attempting to learn some of what is being chanted, before trying to join in again. He is miserable. He does not want to be in this place, his body does not want to be so still. His mind simply cannot focus. He wants to be by the fire to smell the wood, out in the garden between showers, smell the fresh salty air, in the scullery with Rebecca. In fact, he wants to be anywhere that is not in school. When he fails to join in, the boy on his right pokes him in the ribs. He has never been poked before and decides that after this is over, he will tell Maud for she will surely make things better. Tears fall silently across his cheeks which only serve to make the poking more frequent and more painful.

By the end of the day, Freddie has been reprimanded three times. Once for crying, once for getting up to attend the privy without asking and once for not paying attention. To make matters worse, Maud is not outside the gate when he arrives, as she said she would be. He has to wait while boys run past him, some almost knocking him over. When she does arrive, he flings his arms round her waist, buries his head in her skirts and sobs.

'I'm never going to school again Maud,' he wails.

'Oh Freddie, the worst day is over. It'll never be that bad again.'

'It will. I already did three things wrong and was told off.'

She takes him by the hand and leads him home. The fire in the stove is blazing when they step into the kitchen. Rebecca makes a pot of tea which they drink between chewing on slices of bread and butter. She wants to know how his day has been, but Alice comes through. His mother gives him a tight hug, before Maud takes him upstairs to change their clothes. Freddie is delighted to be able to put his 'raggedy clothes on and runs back to the kitchen yelling 'raggedy clothes' at the top of his voice. Once he has settled down again, Alice asks,

'What did you do in school today?' He says nothing, just stands there looking at the floor.

'It's all right. Tell Mama,' says Maud, encouraging him with a smile. When he finishes, it is hard for Alice not to look at Rebecca and laugh, but she manages a furrowed brow and says,

'Oh Freddie. You must behave at school. You must sit quietly to learn your numbers and letters and always ask Mr. Roberts if you need to leave your seat.'

'But I don't want to go back,' he cries. 'There are too many boys. They laugh at me and prod me when I get things wrong. You and Maud can teach me.'

Alice feels her heart quicken for him, her child who is not like his sister and who she knows will not likely do well at learning.

'I'll speak to father when he gets home from work. I'm sure he'll have something to say on the matter.'

Later in the evening Alfred takes Freddie into the parlour and sits him on his knee. Alice watches quietly with Maud beside her. Freddie settles into his father, nestling his head against his shoulder.

'What do you want to be when you're all grown up, Freddie?'

'I don't know Papa. Can I be in the shop with you and learn how to make shoes?'

'Well now. That would be a nice thing to do with your Papa, but you might decide to be something else. How do you think you will pay for the things you want?'

'I don't know.'

'When you become a man, you'll need to work to earn money, to buy the things you want and if you don't go to school and learn to read and write… to learn your numbers and how to add them up… Well, you might not get work… then you'll have no money… and you won't be able to buy anything. Now Freddie. Will you promise me that you'll go to school with Maud every day and be a good scholar so that Mama and I can be really proud of you?'

Freddie makes the promise, for to go against his father is the worst of all misdemeanours.

As the months pass Freddie settles into a routine and behaves himself as much as he is able, but is not happy. His days are filled with a mundanity that makes him melancholy and live only for the evenings when he can be free to follow his real love of the outside world. He begins to experience severe pains in his legs, making walking any distance even more difficult than he had been used to. There are nights when he cries for his mother to rub them better, and the mornings which follow always leave him deprived of sleep so tired and sluggish. Mr. Roberts complains that he is not concentrating and soon word spreads that Freddie spends too much time daydreaming or simply staring for ages at what appears to be nothing. The family accept that he is making progress in his learning, but nothing that equals his sisters. Alice wants him to be seen by Dr. Sayer but Alfred is firm in his response.

'He's a boy Alice. He'll grow out of all these things. I'm afraid my dear that you fuss too much after him. He needs to be left to make his own way in school as all the other boys are. Now, we'll not speak of this again.

18

At the age of seven, Freddie is introduced to a new baby. 'A boy, just like you,' his mother proudly announces. Pleased, though not overjoyed at what he sees as another stinky bundle, he does not relate to his brother David, for many months. He does, however, help Maud and his parents with Harriet when it is asked of him, and gradually he begins to share with her all the beautiful things in the garden and about Kemptown.

Maud is by this time allowed to take both Freddie and Harriet to the beach, where they spend most of their summer days. If they ask politely, Rebecca packs a lunch for them. They always return home covered in sand.

'Brush that sand off before you come into the house,' Rebecca orders, though she can never stop herself laughing at their little grainy bodies. 'I've got the tub ready for you in the garden. 'Come on, quickly now, before it covers the floor.'

'Becca, can I go in first this time,' says Freddie in a rather pleading voice. 'Maud always has the fresh clean water and I get her sand!'

'Well. Don't you think it's polite to let girls wash their delicate skin before you get in with your rough and tumble play?'

'I spouse so. Can I do some gardening while I wait then?'

At dinner that evening, Freddie asks,

'Mama. What's polite?'

'Where did you hear that Freddie?'

'Becca said it was polite to let girls go first.'

'Freddie we're having dinner and you should be quiet as usual. This is the time for adults, not children,' says Lily sternly.

Alice looks at Alfred whose head stays low over his food.

'It's alright Mother. He can ask. How will he learn if he doesn't ask questions? And maybe this is a good time, when we're here to answer them,' says Alice.

The look on Lily's face says everything, but Alice continues.

'Polite means that you know how to behave, Freddie. If you're polite, you're nice and kind to people.'

'But why can't boys go first sometimes?'

'Girls are not as strong as boys. They're delicate, so boys need to look after them and open doors for them; let them sit on the chair if there's only one left. That sort of thing. Do you understand?'

'I think so. But sometimes then, I wish I was a girl.' Lily does not join in with the laughter, such is her stringent adherence to the way children should be raised.

Being by the sea and bathing when they return, is a ritual played out day after day during the hot months. Freddie may not have been doing too well at school, but he knows how the tides move backwards and forwards; he knows the sound made by receding waters; that wet sand is heavier than dry sand; he knows how creatures, like crabs and tiny fish, move across the beach and in the rock pools. He drops stones in water and wonders at the concentric circles produced. He begins to want to know about all these wonders he sees, so Maud takes him to purchase books whenever they are affordable and reads them to him. His Uncle David shows him how shoes are made, and when he is old enough to go to the blacksmiths, Uncle Stephen shows him how iron is wrought and he adds the smells of burning metal and intense heat to his cache of loved aromas.

Freddie becomes acquainted with deep sorrow and grief over the following years. His Grandfather Rowe dies the same year his baby brother is born, and the house is full of sadness and mourning, which gives way to a period of tremendous activity he is not old enough to understand. It is explained to him that his grandfather has gone to heaven to be with Jesus, which he knows from when his other grandfather died, but now he is seven and better acquainted with Grandfather Rowe, so it takes time for him to appreciate that he will never see him again. He misses the visits to the mill across the Downs, watching his uncles drag the large bags of flour across the mill floor, for they are not able to maintain the mill after this and it is sold.

When Freddie is eight, his beloved Maud becomes ill with muscular pains that over a period of just a few hours cause her to collapse at school. It is the middle of January with snow on the ground and chill winds blow in from the sea. Mr. Roberts carries her home and Dr. Sayer is called for. He thinks she has a bad case of flu, but as the days elapse it is clear that she is unable to move her legs and he judges this to be more like polio. She will require careful nursing in isolation as polio is extremely contagious. Alice is carrying her fifth baby. She is ordered not to nurse her daughter; not even to enter the sickroom and so it falls to Rebecca Lily and Emily to ensure Maud is cared for. The third bedroom, by then being Freddie's and David's room, is rearranged to take a third bed for Harriet, while Maud's room becomes a self-sufficient sick room.

This room, so long in Freddie's memory the cosy comforting place he inhabited with his sister, will from that time onwards become his most hated room in the home. He is not able to be with her. He can only ask the women folk daily how she is and listen outside her door to her laboured breathing. He feels at a loss to know what to do without her. He has never been without her and he finds the days long and so full of sadness. To keep him occupied, he is encouraged to help more and more with household chores and look after Harriet and David, now aged four and two. Gradually he comes to understand that he is growing up and that as a result there are expectations of him; that he can no longer spend his hours in the garden or by the sea, marvelling at their magnificence. He prays for Maud every day, watches the comings and goings of the sickroom as often as he is able.

In helping with his younger siblings Freddie comes to know them better, and much of the love he has known from Maud transfers from him to them. He is, his father often remarks, still clumsy. Slowly, with Rebecca's help, he learns the most appropriate ways of doing things and when his legs are good, he is allowed to take them for walks just as Maud did with him.

By the middle of February, Maud begins to feel better, having come through the worst of her illness. However, she does not regain full use of both her legs. At ten years old she has become an invalid remaining physically weak and in need of much support.

'I've managed to get a pair of crutches for Maud,' says Dr Sayer, on one of his regular visits. 'They should help her walk. Where is she? I'll need to show her how to use them.'

'She's upstairs Doctor. Shall I fetch her down? asks Rebecca.

'No. That's ideal. I can show her how to manage the stairs. Shall I go up?'

For the first time Maud feels a mixture of anger and thankfulness. She is glad to be alive but often becomes angry at her condition, though her patience and perseverance allows some degree of independence. Later, Dr. Sayer helps further by designing, with Alfred and Stephen, a set of shoes and callipers, and though these latter are not the best, they give Maud much more support and over the coming weeks, she learns to walk again.

'I don't know which of us has the worst legs, Freddie,' she says, as they wobble together down the garden.

'Oh. I think it's you today!'

19

I'm in the kitchen with Rebecca, talking of the morning chores, when I hear Lily calling as she comes through the front door,

'Have you heard? Kemptown's going to have mains water! There's talk of it all round the town. Everyone's hoping they'll be the first to be connected.'

'Oh Lily. What fantastic news. Do you hear that Rebecca?' I say, and the three of us sit round the kitchen table with tea, ruminating on all the wonderful days to come without the arduous task of having to fetch the most precious of our daily needs.

When Rock Street is finally completed, our taps are turned on to fill all manner of vessels, so ingrained is it that vessels have to be filled! Mr. Hargreaves, takes no time at all to arrange for both our properties to be fitted with modern stoves capable of heating tanks of water. This is a luxury I could never have dreamed of. I buy new washstands and jugs for all the bedrooms and Rebecca spends hours cleaning from top to bottom. Life is so much better. For many days I marvel at the sweeter smells, the cleaner walls and floors, and Rebecca can't quite get over the time saved by the mere fact of having running hot water.

I give birth to our next child in March 1871; a tiny little girl we call Mary, after my mother. She's so sweet, my smallest baby, so that she looks more like a doll than a baby. It's an easy birth, and it's not long before I'm back in my usual habits. I'm getting used to this birthing now. Alfred tells me I'm a good mother, which I rather think he should believe anyway. Maud's gradually growing strong again, fiercely independent in her ways and Freddie makes lots of effort, if not at school, then in our home. Harriet and David have become good friends, playing together most of the time and therefore less demanding on poor Rebecca, whose work increases dramatically with each of our children. We have five now, from just a few weeks old to ten years, and there is added pressure on our space.

'I go back to school tomorrow Freddie,' Maud says one afternoon. 'I'll need you to help me now.'

'I will. We can walk slowly and I'll take you to *your* door,' he says with a gentle smile that lights up his face. 'And if you need me, you can ask for me. Mr. Roberts won't mind, will he?'

'We'll have to wait and see Freddie.' I listen to them, sounding all grown up and my heart swells.

Our peaceful life does not last though, for we're beset with further illness. It sweeps through town until it lands with severity here. David's the first to catch scarlet fever, and Freddie has to leave his bedroom while it becomes the new sickroom. I carry my sixth child, feeling like a donkey again with all the extra weight and am mortified to once more be ordered not to enter the room. I'm anxious for David who's extremely ill, but he begins to recover as each of the others contract the deadly illness and in turn are isolated from the household. I make sure Mary is never too close but can't prevent her from the disease. She's the last of the children to succumb and still so young, she's not as strong as her siblings.

'Alfred. She's raging with the fever. And look… the rash has begun all over her little body.'

'Give her to me Alice.'

'Not yet. I want to cuddle her first. She needs her mother's arms round her.'

'Alice! Please be sensible. You're with child. Remember how it's been all through this wretched illness. You mustn't risk yours and the baby's health.'

Alfred prises her away from me before taking her to the sickroom where Rebecca's looking after the other children. I hear her cry constantly with the pain in her small limbs. She's unable to eat anything and very quickly loses weight. I'm beside myself with fear for her. I want to go in; to look at her; to hold her, but am kept away, always, they say, for the sake of my unborn child. Dr. Sayer visits daily and Mary's never left alone. She's been ill for a week now, and Alfred comes to me with news of her fading. I cannot believe it. The gravity of it doesn't reach my head. I watch the bedroom door and wait in hopeful vigil, pray to God every day and when she cries, I'm thankful, for she still lives.

It's only days before my baby is due, and Alfred stays at home. I know it'll not be long; the mood is sombre, with little activity downstairs, save the occasional sound coming from the kitchen as Rebecca works quietly. Upstairs I hear Lily and Emily as they go in and out of the sickroom; across the floor; sometimes I hear them talk soothingly as they settle Mary. I'm listless and yet can't remain still. Alfred cautions me against becoming overanxious as it may harm the baby. I do not heed him, for how can I even think of a baby not yet in this world when Mary's about to leave it. I see the children playing on the kitchen floor and stoop to kiss them on top of their heads. I want to pick them up; to hold them close for I know it'll comfort me to feel their small warm bodies next to mine. I go back upstairs to sit in silence.

Dr. Sayer comes mid-afternoon, goes straight upstairs, and we follow; wait outside the room. Alfred draws me close before guiding me into our bedroom, where we sit side by side, our heads bent; neither of us knowing what to say to comfort the other. It feels like hours we sit there, before Dr. Sayer knocks on the open door and comes to us.

'Alice. Alfred. I'm sorry to say that Mary has passed away'.

I know he's spoken; I see his lips move and I hear Alfred murmur thank you, but my body freezes, and as Alfred takes my hand, I lift my head and ask, 'How is Mary now?'

'Alice my dear. Mary has died. Do you understand what I'm saying?' he says.

'Mary has died.' Alfred repeats softly, tilting my face towards him. 'The doctor did everything he could for her but her little body wasn't strong enough to withstand the illness.'

'Noooooooooooo.' The sound, when it comes, is a shock to me, as though it belongs to some other person a long way off. I hear guttural words come all in a rush between sobs - 'I want... my uh daughter. Let me... hold her. I want to... see her,' and yet it's not me for I don't sound like that.

'I can't let you near her Alice. There's still infection which even at this late stage could harm your baby,' says Dr. Sayer and he turns to Alfred. 'You may go in though, while I give Alice something to calm her.'

Reluctant to leave Alice, Alfred goes into the sickroom with his mother, unable to believe the change in Mary's features. For the first time in many days however, she looks peaceful, but it's as he picks her up that the true horror takes hold. Her body is limp and the colour almost drained from her. He puts his arm around Lily who weeps silently, for has she not spent weeks nursing her grandchildren. She's tired, bone weary and suffering this loss equally. He does not want to leave his baby but gives her into Lily's arms.

'Mother will you please make the arrangements with Dr. Sayer, for me? I must be with Alice now.'

'Yes dear. Of course, I will.'

Alice, is at least calmer and no longer sobbing. Alfred listens to the bustle in the next room, overhearing instructions to burn all mattresses and bed linen that have been used, followed by scrubbing of walls, floors and furniture. He watches as Dr. Sayer leaves the sickroom with Mary wrapped in blankets, and follows him down to the parlour.

'Where will you take her?'.

'To the hospital mortuary,' he says. 'She'll be taken care of Alfred. You may rely on that.'

It breaks his heart to hear such words spoken aloud. He is a philosophical person. He accepts death as a necessary part of life and is sure that God takes Mary as part of His Great Plan but what the meaning of it is, he cannot begin to understand in this moment. Alice's faith is steadfast also – but he thinks a mother's bond with her child is far greater than that of a father, and wonders how he will find the strength to console her.

Something snaps inside me. A cord which no one else can see; can know of. This morning I had a little girl. Now I have not. How to explain it? I've not even been able to see her or hold her. She disappeared in an instant, like a puff of wind has blown through our house and taken our daughter with it. I know Mary will be with God and will have everlasting life. I have no doubt of it, but in my heart, there is an enormous chasm, a Mary shaped chasm in which she fits beautifully. I know too, that the death of children is never far away, nor few in number, but my loss is made more unbearable by separation. I can't understand what's happened today, much less how He can have done this to us. We tell the children, comfort them as best we can, and I go to bed in hopes of sleep.

Over the next few days, I go about in a sort of dream, the baby inside me kicking, and I think it's doing it only to remind me of Mary. Maud makes herself busy to curb her pain. David and Harriet are too young and after shedding tears, seem to accept that their sister is in Heaven. Freddie though has a different reaction. He simply can't believe that he'll never see his sister again. He's unable to cope with the death of creatures, never mind Mary. He wants to see her, asks for her, doesn't believe it can be true. His thoughts seem to muddle; for he says God is cruel, that he didn't love Mary. He says the church tells lies, and flies to Rebecca who holds him tightly. I can't bear to see it. Less than a week later, Dr. Sayer is again at our home delivering another boy, Walter. He says for every baby who dies there is another born, and we're lucky to have another so soon after, but I have no desire for this baby. I don't want a replacement for Mary but am at least glad that it's not another girl. That would have been too cruel indeed.

20

I walk quickly home from school, wanting to enjoy the summer evening. I'm twelve now, mother and father insisting that I stay longer than most other children, so in the last two years I've been the oldest boy. This, though, is my last walk from that place, the beginning of a different life. It's been the longest I've ever spent anywhere; the longest; the hardest and the most hated of all activities. I think of it today as rather like a penance for being a child; I've feared the cane lashing on my open palm; the headmaster's wrath when I can't remember where I've been; the boys I once thought of as friends, laughing at the way I walk; the way I disappear into my own head without knowing it.

I've learned some things. My numbers are quite good. I can add together and take things away from each other. I read simple words with ease, but stumble over long ones, so that the way they're said is beyond me, and sometimes, if a sentence is long, I can't understand the different parts of it and have to go back and try harder. Mr. Roberts nearly always gave my writing back to be done again. He used to say it was neat, but he could hardly read it because all the spellings were wrong or I hadn't used that punc… word. But I've learned more than that. I've learned to be stronger, come to know what it means to hold my head up. I've accepted that I'm not like my brothers and sisters, who're all clever, and it doesn't matter.

I reach the house which stands tall and narrow, like a shelter I crawl into to forget. Becca meets me in the kitchen with a cool draught of water and one of those smiles that light up her eyes.

'Hello my man,' she says. 'It's all done Freddie… no more school! I've buttered you some bread and there's cheese if you want it.'

'Thank you. Where's Mama?'

'She's out with grandmother, but I think she'll be back soon. She'll be eager to see you.'

When I've eaten, I walk down to the sea's edge, take off my boots and socks, and paddle in the cool blue water. Waves lap over my feet and tickle between my toes. I scoop up handfuls of sea to splash my face and arms, bare in the day's heat, and drink in the saltiness. I delight in the soft, gritty sand, the roundness of the pebbles made smooth by the sea, and listen for them rustling as the tide moves away. This's where I belong, not in a closed building, unless it be home, but out in the fresh air, among God's amazing creation. A westerly blows gently, so I turn to it, my face drying quickly, feeling tight with the saltiness. There's a cloud on the horizon; a small baby cloud all fluffy and pure white, and it drifts slowly towards me on the wind. I watch the line between sea and sky and wonder what lies beyond that watery cliff.

I know there is France and then way down, Africa is somewhere round there. But I don't know what lies in those places; what the people are like; the weather; how they live, and I wonder if I'll ever know of people from far away, if I'll ever move across the sea. I'm completely happy, quite relaxed, ready for whatever lies ahead, for I know that now I must begin to be a man, just as Mr. Roberts has told us. I must make choices, earn a living, and put this time behind me. I take the walk home more slowly, not wanting to be out of the sun, but it disappears behind the houses as I cut up Chesham Place and into Rock Street. The smell of dinner reaches me as soon as the door opens and David and Harriet run to meet me, bundling into my body as I try to close the door. I bend to kiss them both on the top of their heads, a welcome we always exchange.

The table clear of our meal, I sit and look through one of the books Maud bought me. It's about the seashore and all the nature to be found there. I often look at it, sometimes adding to my list of things already seen. I fix the pictures of new ones in my head so I can look for them. I'm concentrating so hard I hardly hear what father says and ask him to repeat it.

'Get your boots on Freddie... I'm taking you out for a walk.' I look at him a moment before I register what I'm to do, and see mother with a thin smile... she knows what this is about. I don't though. Father and me... well, we've never gone out in the evening... on our own. I hurry to be ready and we leave the house, walk up towards Brighton and father says not a word. I'm thinking I must have done something to displease him, but when I search my mind, find nothing. As we get nearer to the town, he guides me through narrow streets. These streets I know, but only in the day time. Here, now, there are far less women than is usual, and many more men, who I suppose would be at work during the day. They huddle about, talking in loud voices, so I wonder if they are mostly deaf. They are thickest about the entrances to taverns and inns, and most have large beakers of drink in one hand, tobacco in the other. Suddenly there's an uproar of rowdy laughter from one of the groups.

'It's a different place at night,' father says, and I don't know if he wants me to say something, but if he does, I can't think of it.

We round the next corner where a group of men are closed round two women, and it looks as if there's an argument, or something. I see one of the men raise his fist to one of the women, hold back a second and then punch her chin. She falls to the ground and I start forward to help her, but father holds me back.

'No son,' he says.

'Why are we here Papa? I don't like the noise or what these men are doing. I'd like to go home.'

'All in good time', he says. 'All in good time.'

The evening draws in as we walk, lamps are lit and the warmth of the day slowly fades. I wonder how long these men have been here and why they meet in such large crowds. But I wonder more what this is all about; why father brings me here; why he stays so silent. It feels suddenly like a punishment so I say,

'Papa… I know I've not done as well at my schooling as you'd have liked'… but he cuts me off.

'It's all right Freddie. This isn't about school. I know you did your best.' And we go back to silence. I almost walk into a big pool of vomit right on the path, the sour smell of it getting to me just in time. As I step aside, I bump into a huge man, but before I can apologise, he turns on me and yells words I haven't heard before. Under the lamp light I see his ugly face. A cut lip runs red down his chin. His eyes roll about and his head wobbles. I move quickly to stop any more bumping, father steadying me.

'I think we'll go home now son.' I'm so pleased I decide to take any punishment due to me when we arrive. The walk has taken an hour or more, my legs wearying so that I can't reach the blessedness of home fast enough.

There's tea and a cake laid out on the table and father bids me sit. It's just the three of us, the young ones in bed and though the strangeness of the evening is still with me, I delight in this treat. When father leaves for the privy, mother says,

'Did you enjoy your walk Freddie?

'Uh… not really Mama… I don't know why father wanted to take me… it was truly horrible at times.'

'Ah…' says father returned. 'There was a reason my son, though perhaps my way of demonstrating it has been a little harsh, but you're going out into the world where you'll be faced with all manner of new things which will seem exciting. What you witnessed out there tonight is the behaviour of men turned to drinking alcohol. Most of them are good men who work hard for their families during the day, but lose their way as soon as the drink touches them. Alcohol is the scourge of the devil Freddie. It addles the mind and lets the devil in… and there's nothing can be done about it. You'll need more than ever to keep your faith in God and allow Him to guide you through. He's been a great guide in our lives and we've been blessed as a result. Your mother and I ask you today to take the pledge that all our family have taken in the past, which is to never drink alcohol. Will you take this pledge son?'

'How does it happen Papa?'

'I confess to not knowing how. I do know that it gives rise to behaviour that's both improper and unseemly.'

'I'll take the pledge father. I want you and mother to be proud of me and I surely don't want to behave like those men we saw. I won't have the devil taking over my mind!'

'Good boy Freddie. You'll not regret it and it's surely God's way.'

21

Following father down the steps of the cellar on my first day at work, he smell of leather rises up and I breath it in deeply like so many times before, only now it'll be with me every day. We greet my uncles, David and Harry.

'Welcome to the business Freddie,' David says and Harry taps me on the shoulder; asks if I want a tea. Father sits me down on a stool at a high table and tells me what I will do. He starts going through all the tools, naming them. David tells me it will take time and hard work. I tell him I'm not afraid of hard work. There are so many that. by the time father reaches the seventh one, I've forgotten what the first is called, but I dare not say anything. By lunch time my pleasure is already fading; nerves flutter in my belly; my head's too full and I'm flustered. Father sees it though, and when we've eaten our bread and cheese, he asks me to put them all away. I can do this, for I can see the shapes clearly and don't need to know what they're called, and when it's done, I'm pleased to have done something useful.

The months and years after that are hard, though I do my best to learn the trade, but after a while, even with all their help, it's decided not to let me try any more making. I keep the workshop neat and tidy, making sure the leather's always in good condition, and put the lasts together at the end of the day. It's not what I want but at least I earn a small wage, and the smell of leather greets me every day. I know I'm failing. Just like at school, I don't seem able to keep things in my head. It's as though they're there one minute but float away the next. As soon as I try to remember what's gone before, I can't find it. There's no room in my head for everything I need to know and it begins to press hard on me. There's a knot in my chest when I'm shown something new, so that my head feels full up even though it's not.

The only time I'm at peace is when I look at my books or go outside. Whatever the weather, it doesn't bother me. I'm free then. Air washes me of all I can't do. I know father loses hope. He never gets angry, but his patience runs out and I'm feeling so miserable. I'm frightened of getting things wrong so my fingers fumble and my head hurts with the worry of it. Maud's gone into service and I hardly see her. I miss her. She'd say kind things, but she only gets one afternoon off and spends it with mother. I start to believe father doesn't want to sit with me of an evening, after managing all day, so I'm alone mostly, either in the bedroom, the garden or by the sea.

Our meal tonight is one of my favourites but I can't eat. I apologise to father and go to my room. The outside draws me, but it has been raining all day, and I can see from the window how the earth is puddled. It shines in the lights from other windows and from lamps in the street behind. I stop myself from drawing up the sash, breathing in the sweet fresh air, and instead take a chair to watch the goings on.

'Freddie… Freddie, it's Becca,' she calls from outside the room. As I let her in, she says, 'Your mother and father would like you to join them in the dining room.' She's smiling so I think perhaps it can't be too bad.

'Freddie… we've seen you become so miserable lately. We'd like to understand why and help you if we can,' says mother. It's not a question so I don't know what to say and stay silent until father says quite roughly,

'Lift your head son. Look at me.' When I do, I see his face soften a bit which makes me feel worse, because it would almost be better to be scolded. 'Tell me what's ailing you,' he says, but I don't know where to start, or how to say what's in my heart. I look at mother and she takes my hand, says, 'It's all right son. Take your time.'

'I can't do it.'

'Can't do what?' mother asks.

'I can't learn… can't make boots… can't make you proud of me,' and I feel my eyes prickling. I don't want to cry… I'm a man now. Men don't cry.

'You don't need to do anything to make us proud of you my dear. Father and me'… she looks at him as she says, 'we're proud of you just because you're our son.'

'We don't want you to be so unhappy,' father says, 'You've been with me for nearly three years Freddie and I don't think it's for you son. I think you might be better in another trade, doing an apprenticeship. It's not that I don't want you to work with me, it's that I want you to be successful and independent as a result of what you're good at. Do you understand?'

'I think so. But what can I do?'

'Why don't we look in the papers for something? There may be work with the council, or some company who need people to garden… or look after the parks. Would you not love to be outdoors with nature?'

'I would Papa. To be outside would make me happy. We'll look, shall we? You'll help me?'

I must have been smiling because mother laughs, father laughing too and my heart already feels pounds lighter. I try to be helpful in the house, running errands, helping Becca, looking after the babies. Walter goes to school with David and Harriet, Edward now two years old is growing fast and loves me to take him to the sea. There's a new baby too, Lily, who is about four months. I had a birthday a few days ago, and am fifteen now, almost ready to take another chance in life. I've applied to join the Royal Navy training corps as a boy, on the 'HMS St. Vincent' and have been accepted. I'm looking forward to it, but also scared of failing again. Becca tells me to stand tall and be confident. She tells me I can do anything I want to, and I want to believe her so much, but it does not get any better for me.

22

It was a miserable wet and windy day on January 9th 1878 when I arrived at the training ship, at Haslar on the South Coast, ready to become a navy boy. The ship was huge. When it was in service there'd been one hundred and twenty guns and I couldn't imagine so many large metal things side by side on the deck. I couldn't find the words to say how it felt being surrounded by sea, air, and birds. I loved every day as I woke up to it but it was only a few weeks after the start of great activity, standing for hours and walking up and down, when I began to feel pain in my legs again. They'd been better and I'd not had any of those convulsions since I was eight. I did still go somewhere and not know it, but nobody ever said anything. I thought it was over, that I wouldn't have these problems then. I began to slow down. I couldn't keep up with the other boys and they said I was lazy, but really, I was trying so hard. Sometimes I had to ask to be spared from my duty and by the end of February, the officers were a bit short with me. On March thirteenth, I was dismissed as unfit for navy life. My misery returned.

I cursed my legs. I knew I'd done nothing wrong. My discharge papers said my character was excellent, but what good was that to me if I couldn't earn a living. I didn't want to go back to father's business, where I'd failed so badly, so instead, found work as a general labourer. After a while Father said I'd become quite a well-known figure in Kemptown. His customers talked of me saying they recognised my plodding gait, which father explained was the way I walked. Our local police stopped and talked to me, PC Tuppen often sharing his time. He said I've a cheerful nature and I was pleased he thought so. Working outdoors made me happy. Even on the coldest mornings, or when the air was thick with haze, little drops of water misting my face, or the crisp snow crunched under my feet, I know I smiled to myself with the sheer pleasure of it. Sometimes I'd notice things that drew me, and rather than pass by, I'd stop to examine them. One day there was a tiny robin on a hedge so close to me I could see into his eyes and watch as he turned his head this way and that, bobbing it up and down and my heart was full of love for the creature who stopped to greet me. I remember that so well.

I never complained at going to work, but my legs still hurt when I walked far. I couldn't sleep at night for it sometimes, wishing I was a small boy again so that mother would come and rub them better. I still had those nowhere times too, not remembering where I was or what I'd been doing, but I've heard my friends and work mates say, 'It's just Freddie. Give him time and he'll be fine.' I think they must have understood somehow.

One evening, at dinner, Father asked me if I'd thought about joining the forces. I was eighteen by then, and wondered if he'd forgotten my months in the navy? I told him I didn't think such a life would suit me; that I could only see barracks with small spaces, lots of men and no air, but Mother asked me to think about it. She said it would set an example to my brothers. I didn't want to, but after they kept talking of it, I applied. It was 2nd February 1881 when I enlisted into the 48th Brigade of the Queens Royal Regiment at Aldershot.

Training was like nothing I had imagined. Every minute of time was controlled and checked with the sergeant yelling at me to pull my shoulders back or stand up straight. He even said I was a disgrace to the Troop, which hurt me a lot. I couldn't write home because I didn't have anything good to say. I missed seeing the outside world. Even out on the parade ground, I couldn't look up to the sky to watch the clouds and birds fly by. I couldn't look down to see the patterns in the grass and the soil, or the little creatures that made me happy. Eyes always had to be ahead, on the sergeant; on the soldier in front; on the flag; on whatever was demanded of us. Five months went by while gradually the physical pain in my legs and the worry of letting the troop down, made me visit the doctor. He asked lots of questions, ran his hands over my thighs and legs. He squeezed as he got to the lumps and bulging veins. He told me I had varicose veins and I spent twenty five days in hospital.

I thought a lot while I was in hospital, but still couldn't write home. It was as if everything I did ended in failure. I was sure that if I'd been able to march, I would have made a go of it, perhaps even been more than a private. I prayed all the time for God's help, but the bed rest didn't make things better. The army doctor said that an operation was needed. Then he gave me the worst news. He would recommend a discharge on grounds of disability. Ten days after that I was brought before the Board at Aldershot. I left that room with such a heavy heart, I believed it would break.

After that, however many times Mother and Father said they were not disappointed, I couldn't settle. Failing again played on my mind. I wanted to hide away somewhere, take my heavy body and lay it down with my head buried. When I remember it, I can see myself in my room, sitting on the floor with my knees up, head down, crying. Maud tried to talk to me. Usually, she would be able to make everything better, but I told her there was no future I could see for myself. However hard I tried, bad thoughts crept into my head. It was like standing at a deep pit. I saw its edges crumbling with the weight of my feet. I didn't know how to step back from it. It was like being between bright sunlight and a deep dark hole. One day, when the heaviness in my heart was too much, I fell into it. Covered in its darkness, I didn't notice how time passed and afterwards, I learned that Maud had come every day, after work, to sit with me and though I don't know how she did it, I began to feel things again in my body. I could think about life outside the pit, of what I used to enjoy, of my family. I began walking along the beach again, smelling the freshness, feeling the wind, and realised I was alive.

23

When I get to the kitchen, mother and father are both eating breakfast. I ask if there is any left, and they both look at me with surprise.

'Freddie! says father, 'what a change in your mood! Come… sit with us.'

'I've made a decision father. I plan to go to Canada for a new life.' It comes out in a rush, their faces turning from surprise to frowns. Mother makes a stifled little noise.

'But why Freddie?' she says. 'There's life and work enough here for you. Canada is so far away from us. Is this not a rash decision?'

'Mother, I've tried to do things to make a living… to make you proud of me and I've failed'…

'Now Freddie,' father interrupts.

'No father. Please listen. I know it's my condition which makes me fail and not anything I've done… but it's hit me hard. I feel useless. The Army doctor said I'd be fine with light work and there's plenty in Canada. It'll be a great adventure for me and I don't intend to be there for good. You'll see. I'll soon be home again.'

I think they are shocked into silence, so after a few minutes I ask for their blessing. They give it. Of course, they do, but I see mother in a miserable mood for the next few days. I don't want to ask her if it's because of me… I don't want to hear the answer, but I know it is when I hear father tell her she coddles me too much and that they have other children to care for who need them just as much as me. He tells mother that she has to let me go sometime. I don't know how it makes me feel, but it makes me more determined to go.

'Freddie! Where have you been all day?' Mother says as I walk into the kitchen.

'Is father home.'

'He'll be a little late tonight. He has to complete an order for tomorrow. He won't be long now though.'

'I'll tell you all where I've been while we eat. I'd really like a good hot cup of tea and then I have a little something for you mother.'

'Well. Tell us then. I think we're all wanting to know where you've been.' Father says as we sit round the table for our meal. I finish my mouthful and watch them watching me.

'I've been to London, Father.'

'London! But why son? Did you go on your own then? How did you manage?' Mother asks all the questions at once.

'I've been to Pitt & Scott's ticket office at St Paul's Churchyard, and bought a ticket to Manitoba.' Mother looks at father, while all my brothers and sisters look at me, their faces puzzled. 'I went on my own and I think I managed well,' I say between trying to eat the food on my plate.

'I'm astounded Freddie. Why didn't you tell us you were going?'

'Father. I wanted to do this myself. I thought that if I could go to the city and buy my ticket without any help, I'll be sure to manage emigrating.'

'Well.' says Harriet. 'I applaud you brother,' and she claps her hands, making me smile.

Nothing else is said for a little, all of us finishing our meal, but when Becca takes the dishes away, mother says,

'I'm proud of you Freddie. Tell us something of your day.'

'Well, when I got to the place an elderly man asked I if I needed help, so I told him what I wanted. He was very good, telling me of the things I should know, and the best way of making the journey... all that sort of thing. The ticket I bought is from Liverpool straight through to Manitoba via Halifax, on the Allan Line of steamers,' I say taking out the ticket and reading the names. 'I did think of taking steerage, which is a pound or two less, but decided I would feel safer having a cabin.'

'Very wise Freddie. Did he advise you to do that?' father asks.

'I suppose he did in a way. The fare includes all transport, an overnight lodging before sailing... being taken care of by an employee of the steamer as well, and help at each stopping place... And as Liverpool is a long way, I booked an extra night's lodging so

I'll go a day earlier... oh... and I bought a copy of *The Emigrant's Guide to Canada.*'

'Can I have a look?' Harriet asks and I hand the ticket to her, which she passes round the table. 'I never thought I'd see such a ticket brother... it's so colourful too. Make sure you look after it.'

'Freddie...' father says. 'How did you pay for all this?'

'I had some savings from work and the army paid me five pounds. It wasn't quite enough, but it did pay for most of it. The rest I can pay at the steamer office when I get to Liverpool.'

'What's it like?' David asks.

'What do you mean?'

'London.'

'It's full of people and carriages. I saw St Paul's Cathedral. It's in the middle of St Paul's Churchyard, where the offices are. It's such a beautiful building, I've no words to describe it... it's so big with a huge dome. I heard someone call it that. Wealthy folk walk out in their fine outfits... there were young men and women wandering about in groups and families with children. I went to Fleet Street, where the newspaper offices are, and there are shops, public houses, coffee houses and homes which seem to go on forever. It's narrow and the buildings tall, so there's a darkness about the place... and the buses, are followed by collectors of horse droppings who bend low behind each bus, before following. Their buckets and shovels make such a noise. My head was bursting with it all.'

'It sounds as though you've had a grand experience Freddie,' says father and when I look at him, he's smiling.

'I've never known anything like it before... but you know... I'm glad we don't live there... I felt the pull of Brighton's open spaces, its Downs and seafront, its peacefulness... and I'm pleased to be home.'

24

Rebecca sees a renewed vigour in Freddie's mood and though she will miss him terribly, takes great pleasure in witnessing him as he'd once been. She notices too that Mr. and Mrs. Tyler are much relaxed and that Alice enjoys her time away from dressmaking to be with Isobel. Freddie loves the little ones. He does much to look after them at home, so that she is able to complete the household chores more quickly. Lily's with them most afternoons now, sometimes a happy soul, but at others, Rebecca thinks she might have taken a misery potion before leaving home. She is sixty nine now, and while she looks younger, her temperament is often that of an older lady with a grievance. They never quite know which one will be here, and often share a knowing smile when the old lady appears.

She is loved though, and mostly just fits in with what's happening in the home. Rebecca observed however, over the last few years, that Lily takes issue with Freddie. She might not realise it, but is rather critical of him, even when he is in the room. He says nothing to her and she doubts he does to his parents, but it must hurt him. He takes these things in so deeply. After breakfast one day, he asks Rebecca to go to Brighton with him to buy a trunk. They take the bus into town to save Freddie's legs, knowing that they will have to walk home with it. It's a bright day and people jostle to get on the bus but they manage to get a seat. The town is busy too it being the beginning of Christmas preparations. People gossip in small groups, and children play around their mothers. The shop is in the centre of Brighton, and sells all manner of bags and travelling cases. An extremely pleasant young man serves Freddie, making sure the trunk he selects is suitable for his purpose, and he buys the largest, affordable, and well-made trunk he can, with handles on both sides and a good lock. The portmanteau he buys is small enough to fit inside, so they only have one large piece to carry.

It's a difficult walk with the cumbersome purchase and people seem to have been blinded while they have been in the shop, for they move little to let them by, so they are forced into the road and stumble.

'What do you think Canada will be like?' Rebecca says.

'I don't know. It's a big country and I think there's lots of space for people like me to work... I read from the book I bought that it's very cold with long winters but the summers are hot.'

'Do you think it'll be like England?'

'They say some of it's covered in huge mountains with really tall trees and there are lots of lakes.'

For most of the walk they laugh, deciding it is better to be in the road dodging carriages and people coming at them from all directions.

'Look out!' yells Freddie.

'That was a close one. We'd better concentrate more or we'll risk not getting home.'

Autumn is glorious as they make their way, with its colours and crackle of leaves under foot, and they feel the extra heat generated by an ungainly walk. There are lots of, *'Do you remembers...'* and they both secretly know how the coming separation will affect them, for they have always been close. Short periods of silence fall, both in their own memories. They struggle to get the trunk through the front door when they arrive and collapse onto kitchen chairs, fully worn out by the day.

'Thank you, Becca,' says Freddie, his voice low and full of heart.

'Thank you, Freddie,' she says, 'for letting me share the day with you.'

The following day, Alice wakes in bright humour, so once the little ones are ready, sets about making some clothes for Freddie to take; shirts, waistcoats and jackets mainly as he already has good trousers. As always it sooths her to sew, and she will feel closer to him knowing what he's wearing. It is her contribution to his new life. She can picture him, not in the country he is going to, for what does she know of that, but at least dressed and ready to work. Alfred is busy making sure Freddie has good boots and shoes to take as well.

As Autumn turns to Winter, there are many celebrations to organise, beginning with Walter's ninth birthday. Alice wonders how those years could possibly have gone already. Then there is Edward's fifth before Freddie's nineteenth, with Alfred being forty-one just before Christmas and New Year. In January Maud will be twenty-one, which must be a special day. The bustle, and at times frenzied activity, keeps everyone's spirits high, so nobody cares what the weather is doing.

Towards the end of February, Freddie visits his godparents to let them know of his impending departure. It may be that he will not see one, or even any of them again. They are ageing; there are always accidents and, in his heart, he knows that he may never return home for one reason or another.

'Ah! Freddie,' says Mr. Hargreaves when he is shown into the room. 'How are you? Come. Come and sit down.'

'Good day to you Mr. Hargreaves. Mrs Hargreaves. I'm well thank you and hope you are too.'

'Yes, dear boy. We're both very well having got through the winter without any flu!'

'I've come to tell you that I'm soon to be emigrating to Canada and would like your blessing. I'm so very thankful for everything you've done for me… it means a lot to know you're happy for me to go.'

'Well!' says Mrs Hargreaves. 'You've certainly brought us some different news and you certainly have our blessing. What sort of godparents would we be if we didn't support you in your mission?'

'Thank you. I may not see you again before I leave, so I want to say goodbye and God keep you both well.'

'Wait. You can't go without a little something to help you on your way,' says Mr. Hargreaves, getting up and going to his bureau. 'Here,' he puts a crisp £5 note in Freddie's hand with an even crisper £10 note.

'Oh, I can't accept it, sir. I didn't come here for favours.'

'We know that. But please take it. We can afford it and you'll need it. It's our way of helping you over the coming year.'

Freddie colours at their kindness as he stows the money in his breast pocket.

'Thank you both. I'll write as soon as I can and I'm sure you'll get to see the letters. I think Mama will show everyone!'

Waving Freddie goodbye, Mrs. Hargreaves says,

'How will he manage, dear?

'I don't know any more than you, but perhaps he'll find what he yearns for. As long as he comes back to us safely.'

104

Freddie's next port of call is Dr. Sayer. He stays longer there, because as well as giving the news and receiving the doctor's blessing, he listens to advice, to heed the words of the army doctor and gain employment which avoids long hours of standing or walking. The doctor is at pains to ensure that Freddie knows what to do if he should have prolonged or increasing episodes of his absence seizures, or indeed those convulsions.

'I know you haven't had any of these for many years, Freddie, but they can always return and may be caused by anxiety. If this should happen you should seek medical help without delay and I'm asking you to promise to do so.'

'I will Dr. Sayer,' he says. As he says it, he is not sure at all how he will cope with nobody to look after him, but has no choice other than to manage as best he can if such a time comes.

'I'd like to give you this to help you on your way,' the doctor says, as he offers a £10 note.

'Oh no. I can't take it from you. I've just had the same from Mr. and Mrs Hargreaves and I only want to say goodbye and wish you well.'

'Well now. I hope you accepted it from them and will do so from me! I know all three of us would be truly unhappy to have you leave without the means to look after yourself. So please, put it away.'

For the second time that day Freddie is deeply embarrassed although grateful for the help that has been given. He tells his parents, who are delighted, and give him a further sum of £20 they had all saved. He will be comfortably able to cover all the daily necessities during the trip, and buy the land he secretly hopes to have. He keeps his money in a leather draw-string purse his father made for him, his ticket safely stored in the jacket pocket he decides to wear on the day.

By the end of February all arrangements are complete amid a gathering fretfulness in both his parents. At the end of a particularly difficult day for Alfred, he retires to the parlour, sinking into deep thoughts and quite oblivious of the movements around him.

'What is it Alfred?' says Alice. 'you look far away.'

'I don't know really my dear. I feel so worried these days. How can I come to terms with my deepest fears that Freddie may fall into sinful ways?'

Alice is not sure how to answer him. Her forehead wrinkles in deep frowns, and though she is unaware of it, her eyes become fierce. Her response when it comes however, belies her soft expression.

'Alfred. Our son is a gentle kind person. He may not have great intelligence. He may not have the words or confidence to outwit would be persuaders'… and here she pauses to choose her words wisely… 'but he has as a strong faith in God to guide him. He has a deep seated sense of right and wrong. Remember how he is with all creatures. Think about how he has managed his physical problems'… feelings overtake, as she raises her voice to her husband, in a way she has never done before…

'He's stronger than you think Alfred. If you're not able to trust him, it's your weakness and you must pray for the strength to combat your feelings.'

She releases a long slow breath, shocked at her own sharp expression. She is not used to speaking so abruptly, but she will defend her children; she will let it be known that she, at least, trusts them. In the stillness of the parlour, she hears only the clock ticking and Alfred breathing heavily. Looking towards him she sees his head bowed. She knows by his face what he is thinking, wonders if she should step in immediately and apologise, but allows the silence to continue anyway. She waits. They rarely have cross words, these two. They are both gentle natured; persuasive; unconfrontational. They love each other dearly.

To hear his wife, speak so vehemently; to hear the accusation in her tone and her criticism, leaves him shocked and at a loss for words. How should he respond? Other men, he knows, would chastise their wives for daring to speak out so. Will he allow it? Is he not master in this home? Then perhaps… is Alice right in this matter? As he continues to think, Alice feels the atmosphere within the room thicken. She becomes uncomfortable, not simply due to the mood, but in feeling that she has been disrespectful in her forcefulness. She has been foolish, has over-reacted. But she will not be the first to speak now. She has said it. It truly pains her to think of Alfred having so little trust in Freddie it causes him such fear. No. Now it is for Alfred to make clear his mind.

When she can no longer sit quietly, all conversation seemingly at an end, Alice rises, makes for the door, believing that her husband will prevent her from leaving, ask her to stay. He says nothing, allows her to go, and make her way upstairs to bed. She is, at the very least, perplexed. She cannot think of any time in the past when stubbornness has crept between them. Now it seems to have done, she does not know how to handle it. Sliding between the sheets she attempts to find a comfortable position, but her body is far from sleep and her mind will not rest. She questions her words knowing them to be unreasonable. She questions her obstinacy. When her thoughts turn to what Alfred said, she begins to discern a different motivation from her first understanding of it. Is it perhaps not so much a lack of trust in their son, as she thought, but rather more of a genuine fear for him?

Alfred climbs into bed sometime later, just as she manages to relax and let sleep take over. He gathers her in his arms and kisses her cheek, watches her eyes flutter open to reveal their beauty, glistening with tears.

'I'm sorry Alfred.'

'I'm sorry Alice. I've been mulling it over, and I know you're right to reproach me. I know my fear is unfounded but I worry about him nonetheless. What manner of things there might be to unsettle him; to provoke new feelings in him; to turn him away from the path he pledged to follow? It's not that I have no trust in him. He just has no one now to protect him. I can't help feeling… that it's only a matter of time.'

'He has God… And do you not think that I worry about him too? Do you not consider that I feel loss and disquiet also?... We mustn't be against each other Alfred. We must instead be together, support one another, for how else will we stay positive for our children?'

'I shall ask God to help me,' he says shyly.

'And I shall pray for calmness.'

On the Saturday before leaving, Freddie walks down to the sea for some air and a final look at the shoreline, east towards Rottingdean and west towards the town of Brighton where, even at this time of year, people gather for walks and entertainment, especially on this day, as they hope to see the royal family riding out. He searches a few rock pools for those little creatures he loves, and when seagulls screech above him, he knows he will miss home terribly. The sea is not the true blue that it will be in summer but nevertheless is a rich colour, with rolling waves edged in white, landing on the beach in those glorious musical tones he is so familiar with. As he stares out towards the horizon, he thinks of all the places beyond it, and believes he might understand something of what makes men go in search of them. He wonders if everyone leaving for new lands feels such a contrast of emotions, for he is full of excitement, fear and hope all at the same time.

25

Freddie sets out with great excitement, towards the train station, accompanied by the whole family. He proudly wears his best clothes. His hair is well cut and he is close shaven.

'You look very handsome Freddie.' Alice says as they ride along. 'Fit for travel anywhere.'

'He certainly does.' agrees Lily, altogether the proud grandmother.

Thankfully, the day is cold and crisp but dry, a very weak sun shining on them. With a mixture of joviality and tears, advice of do's and don'ts ringing in his ears, his excitement is dulled somewhat, partly replaced with a deep sadness. On arrival at the station, he goes to purchase a ticket thinking, *There's no going back now. It really is full steam ahead.* He turns to find his family and though the station is busy he has no problem seeing the large group bunched together by the platform gate. His trunk having been stowed, he says goodbye to his brothers and sisters, his grandmother, and uncles, before turning to Alice and Alfred. He hugs his mother tightly, kisses her tear stained cheek.

'Be safe son. Look out to avoid trouble and take the good paths God offers you. I'll pray for you every night.'

Freddie shakes his father's hand, holds it for a while to carry with him its warmth and love and then boards, drops the window to lean out for a final long look at the faces of his beloved family. The whistle blows. The train begins its journey. When he can no longer see their faces just a blur in the distance, he takes a seat inside the carriage, the final words from his father in his head. 'Remember the pledge Freddie. Remember the pledge and God will keep you safe.'

I remain on the platform long after Freddie disappears from view, and even when the last carriage has turned the bend in the track, I don't want to leave. My body feels rooted to the platform; my heart heavy; my loss unbearable. I've said goodbye to my son before; of course, I have; when he went to the navy school; when he joined the army; but this is so, so different. Then he'd not been far away; still in England and easily found. Now he'll be quite out of reach. He'll be in places I can't imagine; doing things I know nothing of. What if he needs me? What if he can't manage alone? What if... I can't bear to think.

Slowly I turn and walk out of the station to join the family. Alfred takes my arm with a comforting squeeze. He says nothing. For what is there to say on a day when our son, who is kind and loving, but in no way a worldly man; a man whose reading and understanding of most things is less than it should be; our son who's trusting and scared all at the same time, has left so completely.

'What is it Alfred?'

'I can't help but worry about him, my dear. I've said so before that he may yet be easily swayed into an unchristian lifestyle, that he might break the pledge and fall into intolerable sin. Does it mean I don't trust my own son to make wise decisions?'

'Surely his kind heart will endure and keep him safe, with God's help,' I say, praying silently for it.

We make our way back through the town wordlessly. I register nothing of the daily business around me, so locked am I in our tiny familial world, and when we arrive home in Rock Street, we gather in the parlour, where Rebecca brings tea and cake. The sombre atmosphere lingers, until Lily says she ought to be returning home as the day has worn her out. She bids us all goodbye, a single tear visible at the corner of each eye.

26

The motion of the train helps to settle his growing sense of apprehension. He has read as much as he can about emigrating, but wonders if the reality will live up to the advertisements and reports he found. He enjoys travelling by train though, and soon relaxes enough to watch the beautiful Sussex countryside flow by, marvels at the engineering of the tunnel he passes through as well as the viaduct he passes over. Smoke from the engine drifts by the window in ever changing shapes, as they slow down and accelerate. The rhythm soon relaxes his body enough to allow his mind to sleep. He dreams weird and wonderful scenes where the faces of his family appear in fantastical images. They flit past his eyes quickly, sometimes just one, then two or three together. Some have beautiful smiles, while, by contrast, grimaces are displayed on others. They are waving him away, beckoning him to move towards them, shouting loudly and then whispering in unrecognisable voices. 'What do you want?' he shouts at them. 'Can't you be happy for me,' he pleads. 'I don't understand you,' he cries out.

He is woken when the train comes to a jolting halt, opens his eyes quickly, thankful to be released from the awful dream. He is sweating, beads run down his forehead, onto his nose, so searches for his kerchief to wipe his face. The dream unsettles him, he tries to remember who was waving him off so happily. Was it Grandmother, glad not to have to worry about him anymore? At once the carriage door is flung open and a host of bodies appear, traipse through, take vacant seats with a clatter of luggage and chatter. Freddie makes sure the smaller of his two bags is tightly wedged between him and the side of the seat and his portmanteau is still on the luggage rack above him, as a young couple fill the two seats opposite.

They acknowledge his presence with small nods of their heads, to which he politely reciprocates. The remainder of the journey is consumed with little peeks at them, so comical do they appear. They are clearly gentry, he being on the portly side with long legs that stretch out across the divide and almost under the seat next to Freddie. He has a very round ruddy face, quite bulldog like in shape, sporting a wide moustache which he fiddles with frequently, and dark brown hair that is quite long at the neck but obviously beginning to recede at his forehead, leaving a blotchy expanse of skin to the eyebrows. She is quite extraordinarily the opposite. Her thinness and the pallor of her skin together with the blondness of her hair make Freddie wonder if she is ill. While her clothes are evidently of a high quality and, Freddie thinks, rather beautiful, the pale colour she has chosen to wear seems only to exaggerate the whole effect. While he toys with his moustache, she plays constantly with her purse; twisting the cord; repositioning it on her lap; placing it beside her on the seat; returning it to her lap. *She's nervous,* he thinks, and wonders where they might be going. As though at that minute, the man has read Freddie's mind, he turns to his lady, saying,

'You're restless my dear. There's no need to feel anxious. After all it's a holiday were taking. It'll do us the world of good.' His voice is a full baritone and as he speaks the plainness of his face instantly softens into a broad smile which reflects in his eyes. She pats his hand lightly, tells him she is fine and that it is not the holiday itself making her nervy, but the getting there. It being such a long journey. Freddie is fascinated by this couple who seem so far removed from his station in life, but display such similar fears and emotions.

Within the hour they arrive at Victoria Station, the first part of Freddie's journey done, and having collected his portmanteau from the shelf, his bag and eventually his trunk from the guard's van, he manages to secure a porter. With the aid of a carriage across the city, another porter and good fortune he soon finds himself settled into his second train of the day. This journey will take several hours and he is thankful that he had set out from Brighton early that morning. He eats a little of what Rebecca packed for him and opens the newspaper he bought before boarding. Freddie accepts he is not a good reader, like his brothers and sisters; words on the page not coming easily to him, but he usually manages to understand the sense of the text without worrying too much over every word. At first, he flicks through, passes over all the adverts on the first pages. His eyes alight on an advertisement for Sunday trains to Brighton from London as a day visit, no less with the Pullman Car available on cheap tickets. He has seen these trains arriving, full of wealthy folk

112

desirous of a day by the sea. He has watched them sometimes as they promenade along the pier close to his home, with their refined dress, fancy bonnets, and parasols, often vying for space at the side railings with local children and their parents. It pleases him to think of Brighton making the London newspapers even if it is such a simple advertisement. Looking further into the paper he comes across an article about Jumbo the elephant whom he knew to live at London Zoo, but is about to be sold to Barnham's circus. Like many of the population, Freddie is not in favour of such a sale, for it means a life of hard work for the poor creature. In the article the newspaper begged Barnham to agree to a clause that will allow the elephant to be returned to London. It states that he is kept in chains, and is to remain tied for the time he has left here. *How terribly sad*, he thinks, *to be tied for no wrongdoing*.

Freddie notes the train is already quite full as it departs London, but even so it stops frequently on route to take on passengers. Some are individuals like himself; some are couples; some are, what appear to be, whole families with parents, grandparents, and children of all ages. Since very few people alight from the train, he wonders if they are all heading for ships out of Liverpool and with no concept of the town, its docks, or its streets, it occurs to him that there might not be room for them all. He passes most of his time dozing, checks every now and then that his bag is safely tucked out of sight and eventually he feels the jolt of the buffers as the train arrives at its destination.

27

I want to stand to relieve my body's stiffness, but with such crowds doing the same, think it better to stay where I am. There is so much pushing and shoving. When most people have gone, I leave the carriage and stand on the platform, which is full of people and I am afraid to move in case I step on someone's feet, or even worse, kick a child. Most people face the guard's van at the back of the train, where they hope to find their luggage, but my ticket includes mine being moved for me. Beyond these people, others try walking in the opposite direction towards the exit. I feel stifled and with tiredness creeping upon me, I want nothing more than to be in open space by the water. A further three quarters of an hour passes before I am on the docks, and daylight has faded. I stop for a moment to look about me and after a while an agent from the Allan Line is by my side.

'Are you Mr. Alfred Tyler?'

'Yes. I am.'

'I'm Henry. Pleased to meet you,' he says, holding out his hand.

'So many ships. Is it always this busy?'

'Oh yes Sir. Every day it's the same. Shall I take you to your lodgings now Sir? I expect you'd like to be free of your bags and have a good meal before sleeping off the day's journey.'

'I would that and thank you.'

Just a short walk and we arrive at 66 Old Hall Street to be met by the patron a Mr. George Hunter, who manages the house for the shipping company. He smiles warmly, and shakes hands with Henry. He takes us to a room where we talk about the business of the house, and not long after Henry gets up to leave.

'I'll take my leave now, Mr. Tyler. I'll be back here to collect you first thing in the morning, so you'll need to be sharp.'

'Thank you very much for all your help Henry, and please do call me Freddie. Mr. Tyler seems so formal.'

'Goodbye then Freddie.'

'I expect you'd like a good hot meal,' says George.

'I don't think I do. I'm tired by the days travel and would rather just retire and sleep. I would like to take a coffee with me though if that's all right?'

'I'll fetch it straight to your room, young man. I hope you find everything to your liking.'

I'm awake early and smell breakfast, hearing voices from the dining room downstairs. The smell and emptiness in my stomach tell me I need to eat, so after a quick wash I go down and meet George who brings me a large bowl of porridge and lots of good hot toast. He asks me if I want beer but I say tea or coffee is enough. Henry arrives and I make to get up but he says there is no hurry, so we share coffee together.

'When you're ready sir, we'll make a start. There's a lot to be done today and the sooner the better, before the crowds gather.'

'I need to fetch my bag. I won't be long.'

The streets are busy as we walk to the docks, the morning cold and grey, with fog on the water. A breeze blows it toward land where it mists my face. I smell the salty air. It feels like home, but there is so much activity along the way, that I don't feel lonely. Colours, smells, and sounds, all add to my hope of adventure.

'My first call must be to the Allen Line Offices,' I say. 'I've a small balance to pay on my ticket.'

'That's fine. Let's get that out of the way before we do the next job.'

'And what will that be?'

'Oh. It's the most important thing we'll do today. We have to see the medical inspector at his office. If we're too long we might find a queue. Sometimes these go half way round the docks and back!'

'I knew this would be needed but read that there would be a doctor on board too.'

'There's one on board every ship with full medical supplies should they be required, but every person travelling has to be vetted as to any ill health or need for medication before they board. If the officer finds them medically unfit, they are refused travel. In steerage,' says Henry, in his broad local accent, 'it's crowded and becomes extremely hot so that any illness taken on board soon becomes a grave problem.'

'Yes. I can see that, but what about those poor souls who've already paid their fare? Do they get it back?'

'I think it depends on the shipping line.'

I think about my legs. Although this morning, after resting, I'm walking well, might the doctor see my varicose veins and say they'll stop me from working? Might I be forced to tell him of my nowhere times and convulsions? I'd not thought about these before, and feel nervous as I wait in the queue, wonder what I'll do if I can't go to Canada after all. I feel myself shifting from one foot to the other and I become hot. Thankfully, I only have a short wait and hear the doctor say I'm healthy enough to travel. My ticket's stamped as proof, and I leave the office with huge relief.

I buy food for the journey, for although the meals are said to be good, I think it wise to have something for in between times. When all the necessary last minute things are completed, Henry takes me to Waterloo Docks to see the Polynesian and where I'll need to be in the morning. All around there is movement and loud noise with the loading of goods, people like me checking to see where they will need to be and ship's crews making ready. The mood is of joy and hope. People laugh and point, greet each other and say their goodbyes. The ship is a fine vessel, its funnel painted with red, white, and black stripes and she rises out of the water to a great height. Though the early mist cleared and left a watery sunshine, the day has chilled now that darkness falls, so after a last look round, I head back to my lodgings which are close so, I won't have far to walk in the morning.

28

It was the best of times, it was the worst of times, … we had everything before us, we had nothing before us, ….
Charles Dickens: A Tale of Two Cities (1859)

Wooden gangways are fixed to most of the steamers, busy with porters loading trunks, and companies delivering goods, as I make my way along the quayside. About the docks are a great many advertisements for the different lines, all with bright colours to catch the eye and information in giant letters to attract people to buy tickets. Men, women, and children hurry along to find their passage, most with large amounts of luggage and for some, more than they can handle. Porters perhaps too much to afford. Children run to catch up with mothers; mothers look back urging them to hurry up. Names are called, shouts of 'where are you?' Workmen overflow on the quay and not all it seems to me go about a righteous business, for among the porters, delivery men and agents, are those who urge people to buy tickets for a particular line. I'm told they earn for themselves a princely sum from the ship's company if they succeed. Police are present also, for there's always much theft from travellers' pockets and bags. Passing ships as I go, I hear the music of pipes, fiddles and voices coming from most of them.

'Why is there music everywhere?'

'Are well' says Henry, 'steerage passengers are allowed on board the night before sailing. I suppose it's because they can't afford lodgings. Most of them are Irish and they sing and dance all night long... They must be so happy to be leaving the hardships of home. It's rather good, don't you think?'

'I do.'

At Waterloo Docks, the Polynesian's gangway is already full of people making their way on board, with an agent waiting below to scrutinise tickets. I take my turn, thank Henry for his help, and am waved into the queue. On deck are large numbers of people who stop to gaze up at the steamer's refinery. The rigging rises high into the sky, a clear blue, the day being calm and peaceful. Above the main deck is a small, covered promenade which Henry told me all steamers have, but until 1882 they'd been open to the elements and had been the cause of accidents and even deaths as passengers fell over their railings. He said the Allan Line was one of the first to install such protection. The Polynesian is also a mail carrier and so time of departure strictly kept. There's no waiting for those who are late.

I watch as the gangway is drawn up and look at all the people waiting on the quay to wave farewell. All along the ship's railings emigrants crowd to see the last of those they're leaving and I see the sun rise above the buildings of Liverpool, thinking it a good sign for my adventure. Before long though, I'm struck by a sudden sense of loss as I realise my loneliness. I've nobody to see among the crowds and feel tears prick the corners of my eyes, so move further in to make space for others. I go towards the bows as far as I can, to watch the tugs make ready, but the pain of not seeing my family; the fear of what lies before me drives me to find an out-of-the-way seat where nobody can witness my distress. Then I stand, take some deep breaths of air, the salty sea cheering me, and think, *The Atlantic beckons me.*

A cry goes up 'let go for'ard; let go aft,' and the steamer begins a slow move away from the dock, and without pause, passengers are called onto the front deck for a roll call, for none of us are able to take our cabins until a further check of tickets is complete. As we gather, sailors carrying poles, hammers, spiked sticks, and the like, make their way to cargo and steerage decks, searching for stowaways, who would put themselves in much danger to flee to Canada without paying a fare. Many people, including women and children, are brought up and put onto small boats for return to the docks. Crew members stand about on high ground, searching the crowd of hundreds for whoever might dodge between, in an effort to escape. And dodge they do, pushing and shoving those who wait patiently. When caught, no amount of begging changes the decision to have them returned. Others are found to be crippled or unwell and they too are refused passage, even though the full fare might've been paid. I see this and stand still, so my walk does not give me away, the thought of being sent home now too much to bear. It near breaks my heart to see these poor people beg and cry to be taken to Canada and I know, if I were a wealthy man, I'd pay their passages.

'Why must they be taken back to Liverpool when they've paid the fare?' I ask of a sailor standing close by. 'Is it just the Allen Line that does this?'

'It's every line, young man,' he says. 'If they carry passengers who can't pay their own way when they arrive, the companies are charged seventy five dollars for each one of them. That's a great deal of money and it would make everyone's passage much more expensive.'

'What will happen to them now?'

'Oh. I don't know. Some of them may be able to make it back home, but I suppose those that have no money will fall on the poor houses in the town.'

'That's so sad. To think they're trying to escape such terrible lives and now they may be the worse for it.'

'You could say it's part of life.'

For over three hours we stand on deck becoming colder as each hour passes, for although the sun shines, there is an onshore chilly breeze. I find this difficult, my legs causing me great pain, but as soon as the Captain is satisfied that all is in order we're shown to our quarters.

29

My cabin's a double. It's neat and clean and is quite suitable, having all I'll need and bathrooms just a short distance. I try the bottom bunk which, though narrow is unexpectedly comfortable and being the first to arrive, make it my own. It's not long before the door opens and a rather well dressed gentleman comes in, holding out his hand.

'Good day to you. My name's William Trout. It looks as though we'll be fellow travellers across the ocean.'

'Hello. Pleased to meet you. I'm Alfred Tyler but have always been called Freddie'.

I hear the education in William's voice and wonder how we might manage together for it's clear we come from quite different places.

'I've taken the lower bunk. I've a little trouble with my legs and will find it difficult to climb atop. I hope you don't mind.'

'That's fine with me. I'm taller than you and can easily reach. Will it be alright if I take the furniture on this side Freddie?' He says, pointing to the bulkhead.

We busy ourselves in storing away belongings, the strangeness of being so close to someone unknown reminding me of my first few days in the army, when conversation did not come easily and was unnatural. I'm aware of this other body moving round me, the two of us doing some kind of dance between furniture, bunks, and trunks, trying to pass each other in the narrow space. We go the same way, me to my right and him to his left, then back again and yet once more, before William holds up his hands and says,

'Stop. I'll go this way and you go that way.' We both laugh, and I'm less anxious afterwards.

I have my things away first, my trunk being much smaller than William's and I wonder what things he's brought with him in such fancy luggage. I stand out of his way, at the porthole to watch the tugs gently pull the steamer from the quay and towards the harbour mouth. There's little movement in the still waters of the dock, and it's easy to see all the comings and goings on shore, many people waving as we pass.

When the engines begin to drive, there's felt and heard a great rumbling. I go atop to witness the smoke billow from the funnels, seagulls floating above in the warm air, their screeching calls seeming to fill the space. The salty air fills my nostrils. It's such a sight, the ship passing through the narrow harbour entrance, and I wonder if it's wide enough to take us. I think of my family as I stand there, of home, the seashore, the wonders I found there in years gone by. I think of this new land I'm heading for and see myself as though in the centre of the world, neither here nor there, just afloat on a journey with no man that I know and no knowledge of how it will be. I long for the warm arms of mother, to hear Maud and the young ones laugh, to sit at the kitchen table with Becca, play games in the parlour with my brothers. I know I can't let myself think this way, so look out over the rails towards the sea and remind myself of this great adventure I hope will make me successful, and my parents proud.

I don't hear William approach, and his arrival by my side makes me jump. I wonder if I've been in one of my nowhere times.

'My dear man,' exclaims William, 'I didn't mean to startle you. I think your thoughts were far from here.'

'They were... but it's alright.'

'I was lucky to find you among the crowd. You're the only person I've spoken to since we came aboard, apart from the crew, and I confess to finding introductions and social chatter difficult these days.' This surprises me for I see a confidence in William that I surely do not have. 'Shall we find somewhere to sit awhile before the cold drives us below decks?'

When we're seated, William asks,

'Do you make the journey alone Freddie, or is there someone you wait on deck for?'

'No. I'm quite alone.'

'Where are you making for, Canada or America?'

'Oh, Canada. I have a through ticket to Manitoba.'

'That's an incredible coincidence, old chap. I travel alone on the same ticket. I wonder if that's why we're billeted together?'

'Maybe. Or maybe God really is looking after me,' I say with a nervous laugh.

'You believe in God then Freddie. I'm afraid I don't, but have no problems with those who do.'

'I do William, but will not try to convert you,' and it's William's turn to laugh. We look at the water for a few moments, before he says,

'I'm twenty one and the oldest of seven, four sisters and two brothers. I was born in a little village in Surrey called Abinger Hammer... went to Cranleigh School... a private school. We all went there, well the three boys... then I worked in my father's accountancy firm.'

My body stiffens as I listen to him, my first thoughts about him surely being right. I wonder what he'll make of my story. I'm not in a hurry to tell it. He's an agreeable man but is bound to become less so when he hears of my background. As we sit there, the cold seeps into my clothes, finding its way to the flesh on my back, so I say,

'I think I'll go and find the dining room. I'm quite cold now.'

'May I join you?'

'Of course.'

The Polynesian has first class, intermediate and steerage quarters. Those of us in intermediate and steerage are not allowed anywhere close to those in first class. Our dining room is comfortable and clean, and we settle to eat heartily of soup, roast beef and potatoes, then plum pudding with sauce. Stewards serve us, chatting easily as they move between tables to offer coffee and other refreshment. Now full and quite warmed through, we go back on deck to make the most of this fine weather. After a little search, for it seems most passengers are out to take the air, we find a place to sit and let our meal settle, but my thoughts turn again to the difference between us. We're not of the same class; we're worlds apart in our learning; we're not men who would normally meet, much less form a friendship.

'Tell me about yourself Freddie. Where do you hail from and what cause do you have to be on this steamer heading out into the Atlantic Ocean?'

I say nothing to begin with, but he doesn't turn his face from me, so I have to say something.

'Well, William. I was born in Brighton. My father has his own boot and shoe making business and I worked there for a little time... I hated school and have little education save what my sister Maud has helped me with.' It is all coming out now in a rush; my uncertainty of this moment growing swiftly. 'I have a slow mind... but I love all things that I find in the hedgerow, on the beach, in my garden.' I tell

122

him of my time in the army, the condition which caused me to be discharged, about my feelings of uselessness and being unable to see a future for myself. I rattle on because I've no idea how to stop this pouring out of all that's been hidden in my mind. I'm so embarrassed, I can't look at him. I walk away, turning as I do to say,

'We're so different, aren't we? You're of the upper class, and I'm not far from the lower class... It's not normal for people like us to be together, never mind share a cabin.' I look to the ground, feeling shamed. Silence, but for the background hum of others and the rumbling of engines. A silence that says so much. A silence I want to escape from. William follows me. I hear his steps close behind and then stop, but I keep on ahead.

'You think I judge you Freddie?' William shouts. I turn to look at him, walk back to where he is.

'I fear you will and I'm sorry for my outburst... I've never spoken like this before. I fear you'll think of me as being lower than yourself.'

'But by believing this you judge me!' Not loud or angry. Just firm with a hint of hurt. 'We're surely both the same Freddie. We've had different lives only because of our parentage and their situations. Neither you nor I had any part in that, and I for one don't believe either one of us to be below or above the other... We both have desires, regrets, hopes, and fears. We're both making this passage to escape something and find better. You've been honest, and I think that took great courage, something I know I'm rather short of... May we not come together in our differences and perhaps we'll find our strengths and weaknesses will support us. At least while we remain on this voyage.'

I try to take in what he says, unsure of its true meaning. 'You think we can get on together?'

'I'm sure we can.'

We find another seat, and there's an atmosphere I feel unsure of, until William carries on.

'I want to share with you my reason for being here... I was engaged to be married to a wonderful girl.' I'm not surprised to know this, for he's a handsome man, of the sort I think many young ladies would fall for. His hair's very dark and curly, his eyebrows also dark and quite full, and his brown eyes have a light in them when he smiles. His face is altogether kindly.

'We'd been walking out for just over a year, but... I knew almost immediately that I wanted her to be my wife. Her name was Anna. She was beautiful Freddie.'

His voice becomes soft and the corners of his mouth turn upwards as he thinks of her.

'She had the deepest brown eyes with lashes that seemed to go on forever. Her long dark hair framed a surprisingly pale porcelain like face, and in the middle was a little button nose… Our wedding was planned, and we were so incredibly happy.'

As William falters, I feel my own body's stillness, my breath shallow, my attention solely on what this man must be going through. The longing, the softness, the love in his voice is truly powerful.

'One day Anna went out walking. She loved the countryside… went out every day, arriving back home with all manner of tales; eager to tell me what she'd seen or heard… She sounds a bit like you Freddie!' he says with a gentle smile and breathy sound. 'She crossed the railway line… like many times before… but that day she was too close to the bend in the track… She lingered too long in her crossing… didn't hear the train travelling at speed round the bend… She was killed instantly.' A deep sigh. 'My world fell apart Freddie. I couldn't work… couldn't sleep… couldn't rise from my bed… I lost all interest in life. My parents didn't know what to do with me and eventually father filled my position in the firm. I thought I'd die from the loneliness… I knew I had to get away from everything that was Anna.'

He looks up with tears in his eyes, a frown across his forehead. It's the saddest face I think I've ever seen.

'One day I got up, went out and bought a ticket to Manitoba.'

Tears fall across his cheeks, dripping from his chin and the tip of his nose as he comes to the end of his tale. I watch with an ache in my heart for this man I've only just met, but somehow feel closer to than any other. I put my arm across his shoulder, try to say he's not alone. It feels like we're in a bubble, our own tiny world.

'I'm so terribly sorry William,' is all I can say.

After a while, we move to sit with a group of people, and chat and laugh, so I think we're ourselves again. The talk is of hope and fear, the same for most of us, and I begin to feel more settled knowing I'm not on my own with these feelings. It's late in the day and it stays fair, but the cold is biting now. I excuse myself, for I'm suddenly very tired, go down to the cabin, and watch from the porthole to see the sun dip into the sea on a golden skyline, as day becomes dusk. I eat bread and butter with cold meat for tea and then about six o'clock, go back outside, where I'm always happiest. Lit up through all the rooms, the ship feels homely, welcoming, glowing with warmth, and from the starboard side I can just see the faint outline of the coast with the Calf of Man Lighthouse shining faintly like a lowly star.

The sky darkens as I watch and stars begin to pop out until, after only a short time, the heavens are filled with tiny lights twinkling as though they talk to each other. Although our speed is fairly slow, being still in the Irish Sea, I hear splashing against the hull as it ploughs through, see little white horses on the crest of the waves. The moon is new and so gives little light to the skies and I feel that I'm in a huge space, just a tiny speck in the world and strangely close to God in this moment. I want somehow to capture this time; to keep it to share with Maud; to have it safe in my pocket for those times, which I know will come, when I need the comfort of it.

30

I climb up to the top bunk, but not being sleepy, watch Freddie as he kneels by his bed and prays silently, for which I'm thankful. It has been one of the strangest days of my life, arriving on board this vessel. I don't know what I expected to find in the man I would share the journey with, but I suppose it was somebody like myself, of the same class. Not so. I lie here on my first night, above someone who I'm instantly drawn to, but whose life is so far removed from mine, I can't begin to imagine it. We're different, he's right in that, but I think we see different differences. I see a young man who folds his clothes neatly, taking care of the garments lovingly made for him by his parents, beautifully made to withstand time. Mine, on the other hand, mean nothing to me... made by the tailor; easily replaced; now in a heap on my trunk where they will crease and spoil... nobody now to take them to press, to deliver them back to my room ready for another day. I have a lot to learn.

I see a man with a nervous disposition, afraid to speak of himself, to hold his head up... so unlike me... one who has no belief in his own worth, for did he not assume I would cast him off once I knew of his family position? And yes, I believe in that moment he did judge me. He saw a type, a class and not me at all. I wonder at the cause of his demeanour... I can't think it the result of his upbringing. I think there's some deeper reason. Even in our short acquaintance, I've seen him close down, as it were, somehow slip inside himself as though the world disappears. He's not well educated and yet he has not the rough edges I associate with those like him. There have certainly been positive influences in his life.

I see also a man who has not yet succeeded as he wishes to, and yet has the courage to make this journey, alone, wanting to know what's possible. A man who doesn't prevaricate, who is driven to be something, to outwit the hand he's been dealt. Beneath our different exteriors, we're more equal than he's able to realize, and I want to know more of him. I want some of his kindness, his humility, and yes maybe even some of his godliness. I think he's a man in need of friendship, true friendship that is born of understanding and shared experience. In that we are quite the same.

31

I wake to the sound of retching, before the smell of vomit reaches me, not one of my favourite smells. I wait a few seconds for the retching to stop and sit up, the space between the two bunks only just enough. William kneels on the floor, his head over the ewer. The smell is unbearable, and as I climb out, I see why. It's everywhere, over his covers, the floor, himself, so there's hardly anywhere I can step to miss it. Poor William. Brought low before a stranger, something I feel sure will embarrass him. Being sick is one of my fears in life. The feeling before, the lack of control in the act, the smell, the taste in my mouth and nose, the afterward, all work together to make me dread it, and for all the troubles my legs give me, I'm thankful now they're at least seaworthy. It's dark still. The steamer sways, disturbing the rotten mess before me.

'William. How long have you been like this?' He sits back on his heels as I hand him water to drink.

'I don't know. It feels like hours but it's probably not that long. I'm sorry old chap... taken by surprise I was... and so fast I had no time to reach the ewer.'

'I'll see what I can do, but will try for a steward first. Don't drink too much. I'll be as quick as I can.'

Before I go, I wrap all his covers in a bundle and haul them out with me, the alleyway outside our cabin telling me that many more have been taken with it. I go down to the bathroom, drop the bundle, and make my way along. I'm up one staircase before I see someone, bucket and mop in hand. We find William sitting on the floor shivering, so I put one of my blankets round him, that too becoming smeared in the filth, and set to work with the steward to do what I can.

'Is there much of it?' I ask.

'Yes Mr. Tyler. Steerage is overrun and there'll be more before the day's out.'

We clean the cabin; backwards and forwards with fresh water, clean mops; topping up the drinking water for William before I make a start on him. He's weak now. He allows me to go through his trunk looking for clothes, wash and dress him. I do it without thinking. It's new to me, working like this with a grown man, never mind one so much above me. Maybe he's used to such care, having had servants all his life. For me though, the undressing, the closeness would normally fill me with a kind of horror, but I do it for it's necessary. The steward, Edward I learn, brings fresh blankets, and even makes the bunks for us. I think he must have so many others to attend, but when I say so, he shrugs his shoulders and says there are enough stewards to manage tonight. When all is done and he leaves, William looks much better, or maybe it's that he's clean, and I give him my bunk, just in case. Not being able to reach the top one, I sit for a while, listen to the rumbling of the ships' engines, before falling asleep on the floor.

Daylight breaks my dreams. The floor is hard and my back pains me as I sit up. William still sleeps though, so I wash quietly and get dressed. The smell remains, but now I'm not needed for it, it turns my belly and I think how strange it is that I can do something so horrible when it's needed, but not when there are others who can do it. I step outside to the same smell but many times stronger, and now I really retch, feeling for my kerchief to cover my face. Stewards pass me towards steerage. I press the kerchief hard up against my nose and try not to breath, all the way to the dining room. By the time I get there, there's little hunger left in me, the smell of cooked food almost too much. I manage to eat bread and butter, drink plenty of good hot tea and head for the top covered deck.

I see from here, our passage is between the coasts of two lands, so ask someone what they are and am told they are Ireland and Scotland. I never knew they were so close. It's not long before we pass the northern point of Ireland and begin full steam ahead into the Atlantic Ocean. The weather's changed. Gone are the beautiful blue skies of yesterday, now filled with cloud and there's a strong breeze from the starboard side. I think of the thick warm jumpers Maud made me and wish they were not in my large trunk in the hold, for I would be glad of one now, though the deck covering helps to dull the wind a little. I lean against the railing to watch birds follow us, grabbing whatever they can from the scraps thrown overboard. They soar on the warm air over the funnel, dive down from great heights, then flap their wings quickly to climb up again, their beaks full of something good. With each display I find a different comfort.

The day passes in looking after William and being atop as much as possible, for each time I go below, the stench catches my throat and nostrils again. I can't eat in case food refuses to stay in my belly, but I'm hungry still, either that or there is sickness brewing. By late afternoon I find William sitting in a chair with his head laid back, his eyes closed. I try to make little noise but bump into furniture, which wakes him.

'Sorry William. I tried not to disturb you, and wouldn't have but for my clumsiness.' When he looks at me his face is pale and drawn, his eyes less bright, as though all his breeding has been vomited up with his food.

'I wasn't deep in sleep. I rather think it's me who should apologise to you, old chap, for having to manage me all night. I'm sorry Freddie. Not many would do for me what you did… I can't thank you enough. In truth, even though I was awake, I don't really remember much. Was it really awful?'

'It was the worst I've ever seen. It was so bad, there was nowhere to stand. A steward helped me… I'd rather not have to do it again!'

'You gave me your bunk too.'

'I thought it best for both of us.'

'You're a kind man Freddie.'

William takes up his book and I'm happy to stay here in the cabin's warmth, now the smell is less and I'm used to it. I watch him, the concentration on his face shows how involved he is, and I'm taken back to my time learning to read, struggling even with Maud's extra help. I don't know why learning is so difficult for me, when it's not for my brothers and sisters. I can hear father telling me I must keep going to school if I want to make my way in the world. But I wonder what school has really done for me. All those hateful years, and I still cannot read or write properly. Perhaps God has other skills in mind for me. I can only hope so. My empty belly rumbles so loudly it breaks the spell for William. I apologise and we both laugh. We try the biscuits from the shop in Liverpool, which now feels so far away. William has one and manages to keep it down, while I have several and he goes back to his reading.

Freddie thinks I read, but my eyes are on him, sneaky almost. I don't know what to make of him, so unlike any other man I've known. My friends at home are like me, the same upbringing, the same schooling, so we tend to think the same things, have the same opinions of the world. And though I've known men from his class, I've never had any inkling to want to get to know them. They've been servants, groundmen and the like. A quick 'good morning'; 'how's the family?' that sort of thing being the only interest I've shown. There's so much more to Freddie. I admire his courage in traveling so far on his own. It's been only two days and yet I feel a kind of kinship with him. Perhaps it's because he cared for me in my sickness, but I don't think so.

As I watch, I notice him stare at something, a half biscuit in his right hand, but he's not moved for a while. He must be deep in thought again, and I can't imagine what those thoughts might be for such stillness. I wonder if I'll ever know. He blinks, looks at his biscuit, almost a questioning look.

'Where have you been Freddie?' he looks at me with knitted eyebrows.

'Just here, I think. Have I been gone long?'

'I don't understand. You haven't actually been anywhere, just sitting there holding your biscuit, old chap. Is something wrong?' He looks away and I know in that moment, he's keeping something back, something he can't tell me, or perhaps, doesn't want to tell me, so I wait. Eventually he speaks,

'In our family we call it my 'nowhere time' because I don't know anything of it… I've no memory of it… sometimes I don't remember what I was doing before it… it can last a few seconds or a few minutes.'

'What causes it?'

'They tell me when I was born I didn't breath for quite a long time, so my brain does funny things.' He smiles as he says this, a sort of 'I'm used to it' smile, but one that doesn't reach his eyes, a sad smile.

'At school I was told off for day dreaming… staring out of the window. Some of the boys made fun of me… poked me… laughed behind their hands… and I've had the cane for it too. I was lazy they said. But, you know, William, I don't think I'm lazy. I know I can't learn sitting still… from books and copying. I learn more when I'm shown something. I've pictures in my head when I do things. I always try to work hard.'

'I'm so pleased you told me. I've noticed some moments and wondered about them. Does it not make you afraid of doing things?'

'Oh no. What am I to be afraid of? I live with it... can't shut myself away... what sort of life would that be?'

'You're a brave man. I'm not sure how I'd manage.'

'You would... and I'm glad you know. Maybe you'll stop me falling overboard if such a situation arises.' He says this with a smile that now reaches his eyes. 'I'm rather tired now. It can make me that way, so I think I'll go to bed. Goodnight William. Thank you for listening.'

32

In the early hours of Friday morning, I wake to a different sound. Waves crash at the steamer's hull and a strong wind lashes the porthole, as if begging to be let in. I swing my legs out of bed and sit up slowly, feel the sway of the ship before making my way to look out. It's still dark, there being no moonlight. I touch my forehead to the glass, peer from side to side, see nothing but dark shades of cloud blowing about. Sometimes they're briefly lit by the lights on deck and I can tell that we're moving slowly. William stirs, sits up quickly, bumps his head on the deckhead before clambering down to join me.

'I'm extraordinarily tired but I think my stomach may have repaired itself Freddie. Thank you, for taking such care of me yesterday.'

'I hope it has, for this swaying will start it up again. It doesn't look like a good day ahead.'

'It definitely doesn't. What did you do all day while I was in bed?'

'I watched the birds diving for scraps. I saw them float above the funnels. The sickness below decks is terrible and gives off such a stench a kerchief is needed in hopes of lessening it. You'll need yours today. You must be ready for the worst.'

After about thirty minutes of tired chatter, we try again to sleep, which I do. It's almost daylight when I next know where I am. I hear and see, the strength of the wind, feel the Polynesian buffeted on its slow course. Being hungry I ready myself for breakfast, make sure to pull on as much warm clothing as I have, and with kerchief at the ready, open the door.

It's even worse than yesterday, though I can hardly believe it possible. Not simply sickness now, but bodies and effluent, such that

I've never experienced, and I retch again and again as I make my way quickly to the dining room. Once there I steady myself, take deep breaths of somewhat sweeter air, and find a table. This morning's menu is herrings. I can't. I simply can't bring myself to look at them, much less eat them. I settle instead for coffee and buttered rolls knowing that I should line my stomach with something. William arrives as I'm almost finished and I wave him over. He gets to the table and all but falls into the chair beside me, his legs clearly weak and his face deathly pale.

'I'm glad of your warning, but hadn't expected what greeted me to be quite so bad. I had to force myself to continue. Then I tripped on something in the alleyway almost falling to the deck. If I had, I'd probably still be lying there awaiting rescue.'

'I think it would be better for you to be up on deck today, where at least the air will be fresh, if we can find some sheltered place.'

'I think you may be right Freddie. I'll fill my lungs with it.'

We manage to find somewhere protected on three sides, not many passengers being out, so it feels sheltered as we watch stewards going about their dreadful chores. Buckets and mops fly everywhere in the strong wind. The ship's doctor scuttles to and fro from bow to stern. He's a small man, almost as round as he is tall, his medical bag dragging on deck as the ship sways. His long grey hair seems to float, as it's caught by the strong wind, sometimes falling over his eyes so he has to hold it back.

'I do believe he'd take off if he were thinner round the middle,' says William, and we look at each other, laughter turning to comical howls. Towards lunch time we're joined by others desperate for fresh air and shelter. Since fish is on the menu for dinner, we decide to forego this and make sure we eat a good tea, but part of the reason is that we're unwilling to give up our places.

During the afternoon, with skies remaining black, and wind continuing to beat about our feet, as it funnels round corners, we learn of worse to come. Even at this early stage of the voyage, there's more than just sea sickness in steerage. Rumours come to us of some poor souls having cholera, and by the time evening draws in, the weather showing no signs of fading, cholera spreads so rapidly, the doctor's unable to minister to every patient. Notices go up over the ship warning us to remain in our own areas, in an attempt to slow the contagion.

'We need to return to the cabin, Freddie,' says William. 'This is bad news.'

But before we have time to clear the deck, we see three passengers go down with it. They are taken by surprise at how quickly the sickness and diarrhoea fells them. In no time at all, their eyes sink into their heads, before they drop to the ground. We hurry on to reach what we hope will be the safety of our cabin. Silent thoughts fill the space between us. I see my family, my parents perhaps wondering where I am. I pray for them, ask God to look after them all, to keep them safe until I might see them again. I pray for all those with the sickness, that they be returned to full health and that if it was not to be, that they should not suffer, that God will guide us into the unknown, spare us an early death, help us to help each other.

33

Come the morning we are in a bad position. The wind's changed direction, coming now from the south, and bringing with it a storm which we're heading into. The engines are reduced to their slowest speed. I go atop. I need the air, even while I know it's not safe, that I'm putting myself at risk of either the weather or the sickness, that the best place to be is in the cabin. But I feel desperate for the openness, everything the cabin shuts out. I watch the sea, mad with crashing waves. Those that are closest breech the deck in places and water rolls towards the stern of the ship. All about is darkness even though the night has passed, and the lights still shine from the steamer's rooms. Strong wind carries rain which lashes about me. Sharp flashes of lightening make bright displays and there are thunderous noises all about. As the weather worsens the Polynesian battles its way through. Along with others who have braved the outside, I cling to anything that is strong, and watch as stewards bravely try to carry out their grim tasks.

I shake off my wet clothes and lie on the bed for a while, though sometimes almost thrown off as the gusts cause the steamer to lurch. We pass a reasonable day, chatting and playing cards, before fumbling our way to the dining room. When we're back, full and comfortable, I say,

'William, do you think it's safe for you to be on the top bunk during this storm?'

'I don't know, old chap. I think we may find out!'

'If you were to be thrown out, you might do yourself harm. I'm happy to share my bunk with you, if you'd like. It's as close to the deck as anything.'

'Will you not feel compromised Freddie?'

'I'm not sure what you mean. I've shared my bed with my brothers before.'

'Well… if you're sure you don't mind, then I think I'd be considerably safer.'

'It's narrow, of course, but we can lie back to back and head to toe.'

We're tired. We're down at heart. We're afraid for our lives. I think my journey might end here, in the Atlantic Ocean, alone, without my family, my precious Maud. I wonder if I'm strong enough to stay afloat should the steamer capsize. I see worry on William's face. He frowns. His skin is pale and drawn, and I wonder if he sees the same on mine. All I can do is pray and try to stay busy until the storm passes.

'At least we're not sick,' I say, after one enormous roll of the ship, and after a pause, William says,

'If we don't make it old chap… well I want you to know that I'm thankful to have met you… to have had your company for these few days at least.'

'And I yours William.'

Each time we leave our cabin, we hear of the cholera spreading. People die hourly, it now being rife in our quarters as well as steerage. If the storm doesn't wreck us, we might still be taken by this terrible disease. A kerchief's no longer enough to keep the stench at bay. It seems to creep through the ship like a ghost, and there is so much crying and wailing for lost loved ones, that the noise is always with us, and sometimes keeps us from the briefest of sleep. The last three days have been the worst of times. Fear makes us feeble, stops us from thinking, so at times we are bad tempered, reacting to the slightest thing with harsh words, and are uncaring with each other.

Two further days pass without any lull. Days of such grief we find it almost impossible to stay positive. William has his reading but I haven't found anything on the shelves that makes me want to try and read.

'What do you have in mind to do when we reach Canada?' William asks.

'I don't truly know… I have money to buy land. That's what I'd like, but I'm not sure I'll manage on my own… I think I'll have to find some labouring… I've done it before… the only problem is my legs. To be honest William, I don't want to work for anyone… you know, be tied to hours… that's why I want to have land… to work for myself. What about you?'

'I will buy land. I want my own space to develop and make good… so yes I'll definitely do that.'

Our talk is not the bright chatter we mostly share. It's dulled by the greyness, the wind and rain. It's unhappy talk trying to be happy, but even while the ship throws us about, threatening our bellies, we're thankful that the illness has not come to us yet.

34

When eventually the storm abates, Freddie and I are horrified to find it's been replaced by a dense fog which brings the ship to a complete standstill. The engines are shut down, for fear of what might be lurking unseen and dangerous within it. This fog invades us, a grey blanket stifling our senses. Stillness, a new fear and going nowhere. On the day it descends the rumours are of hundreds taken by the illness and of burials at sea once the weather eases. With all provisions in our cabin consumed, we make the unsavoury trip to the dining room, but such remains the disgusting odour, that sometimes having reached our destination, appetites have deserted us. We manage with buttered rolls, cold meats, and plenty of liquid for much of the time. I see that Freddie has lost weight and suppose I have too. We're once more ensconced in our small space with no intention of venturing far for the rest of the day.

'Would you like to read 'The Immigrants' Guide to Canada'?' I ask, holding it out to show him.

'I don't think so, thank you. I bought it for myself when I went to London, but as I said before, I'm not good with reading. There was so much I didn't understand... Too many long words! I left it at home in the end thinking it wouldn't be any use to me.'

'I'll read it to you if you like... and I can explain those bits you don't understand. All you have to do is let me know.'

And so, in the unusual atmosphere of tranquillity we share information about the country we're heading for, becoming more acquainted with what to expect. I'm pleased Freddie stops me for clarification. He's become less self-conscious of his difficulties with me, and I'm infinitely more patient than I might have been before I met him. I'm wary of sounding like the teachers he hates, but persevere and praise him when he understands. It becomes a joke after a while which he laughs at, and then we stop for water and talk about what we know.

'This country is surely one of hope and opportunity for us with its vast lands just waiting to be worked,' I say.

'Do you think a hundred and sixty acres is a lot of land?'

'I do Freddie. Most people seem to emigrate as whole families with strong sons and even grandchildren to share the load.'

'Only I've been thinking while you read... about my legs and not managing.'

'Perhaps it will be the same for me... I might be stronger than you but who's to say I'll manage it alone?'

I read on a little, pause,

'We're getting on well aren't we Freddie?'

'I believe we are.'

'Well, how would you feel about going in together?'

'Um... It would be good for me but we're so different. What if you come to find me too simple? What if I hold you back?'

'Just think about it. We can stay together for the rest of the journey and purchase one plot of land between us. It'll halve the work and halve the cost... We'd be company for each other... Freddie, whatever happens in the future, it'll give us a good start to this new life.'

There is silence again and I almost see his brain working, so say,

'Don't feel you have to. Take some time to think about my suggestion and we can talk about it more later.'

'It's not that I need time William. I'm just a bit shocked that you'd want to do such a thing.'

'Look old chap. You must have more confidence in yourself. Why wouldn't I want to? Why wouldn't it be a good idea?' I hear my voice rise and become tense. This lack of assurance in himself prevents him from flourishing, and I'm sure he can.

'Yes... Yes, it is. If you're sure you can put up with me.'

'You can be sure of one thing. I'll soon let you know if I can't!' I say, smiling now, for it seems to me to be a perfect solution for us both, that fate has played a hand in billeting us together. But there's something else in me that wants this. I like Freddie. I like him a lot, though there's still much to learn about him, and I don't want to say goodbye... to watch him go to fend for himself. I believe I'll always worry about him without knowing why.

We're quiet for some time, perhaps both taking in what we've just agreed to. I hope he's as happy as I am in this moment.

'William, there's something I've been thinking about… I hope you don't mind me asking, but why didn't you travel first class… a gentleman of your standing?'

'I was going to. Then I thought about what I was embarking upon… not a holiday… a new way of life… away from family… I was looking for something else in life. So, I changed my mind… and am pleased I did.'

'Me too,' he says

35

The fog lifts as quickly as it had appeared, and the sky, though dark, is pricked with starlight. The calmness of the water, the suddenness of it all is as eerie as the storm and fog themselves, so they wonder if they had imagined it. Most of the passengers are on deck now appreciating space that had been afforded them during the previous few days. At full speed the rumble and throb of the engines are welcome, as is the black smoke billowing from funnels. There is general hope for a period of good weather to make up for lost time. They look up at the sky and see the beauty of it sparkling above, far too many points of light to see in one view. Two men stand close by them.

'Isn't it marvellous?' one of them says, looking at William.

'It's quite difficult to describe such a sight,' he says.

'I'm John,' the man says, offering his hand, which William shakes before introducing Freddie, 'and this is David,' he adds.

They talk for a while about the stars, John knowing much about them and afterwards, go for some refreshment. William, John and David take a beer, but I favour coffee.

'You don't like beer?' asks David.

'I don't know. I've never had it. I took the family pledge never to touch alcohol when I left school, and intend to keep it. It would fair break my father's heart if I went against it.'

'Oh,' he says, a bit surprised, and they continue getting to know each other.

They learn from a steward that there have been no new cases of cholera, the best news they could have. Two hundred and twenty four people died. It stills Freddie's heart and he thanks God they have been saved.

'What happens now? Asks William.

'All belongings are burned in case they carry germs, and the bodies are sewn into blankets and anything else large enough to cover them completely, ready for burial.

Dawn breaks into a cold but gloriously sunny morning. It is still and calm in the Atlantic, almost as though the weather itself is paying its respects. The captain is there, his men lined along the starboard side, and in front of them, bodies lay side by side, some so small it takes their breath away. Relatives wait to say their final farewells, the air full of wailing and crying. All on deck seems brown or grey, dull and colourless. William and Freddie find a place among the crowd. People pray silently, only lips moving; others pray loudly for the souls of their folk. Words mingle together so that no one prayer can be heard.

The ship's priest raises his hand to silence the noise and being satisfied, begins.

'The Lord is my Shepherd.

I shall not want.

He maketh me to lie down in green pastures:

He leadeth me beside the still waters.'

As he goes on, each body is laid to rest. It takes four men to heave them over the side, and each time, a huge splash is created, salty tears rising high above the side of the ship.

'He restoreth my soul: he leadeth me in the paths of righteousness for his name's sake.'

'Yea, though I walk through the valley of the shadow of death, I will fear no evil'.

'For thou art with me; thy rod and thy staff they comfort me.'

'Though preparest a table before me in the presence of mine enemies; though anointest my head with oil; my cup runneth over.'

'Surely goodness and mercy shall follow me all the days of my life:'

'And I will dwell in the house of the LORD forever.'

Each splash is another dead person, lost to the ocean. Freddie imagines them like chrysalis, lying head to toe at the bottom of the sea, food for hundreds of creatures, their bones lying naked in the future, telling the world of this terrible tragedy.

Everyone joins in with The Lord's Prayer, saying it over and over as the bodies on deck grow less. Freddie can't hold back tears, for though he had not known them, he sees their lives cut short for want of better for their families and themselves. He says a silent prayer for God's graciousness, because one of those bags could have been him. William's face is pained, his shoulders slumped. He winces as each body is let go, and Freddie knows he's thinking of his fiancé. Moving towards the stern Freddie joins others unable to manage such sadness and grips the rails firmly to steady himself. The ship's wake stretches out behind, topped with white foam. Nothing lies between the Polynesian and the horizon, so vast is this ocean.

'Are you alright Freddie?'

'Yes. Yes.'

It is John. They stand together for a while and then go to find a warm drink., after which, Freddie goes on deck to look for William. He finds him back in their cabin, sitting with his head bowed, his hands over his face. William looks up as Freddie enters, turns towards him, his eyes red and sore looking, his face tear stained and his hands trembling.

'William!

'Oh, I'm sorry. I've just been reminded so forcefully of my darling Anna's funeral... her coffin being lowered... the sound of the soil as it was thrown in... the final realization that I would never see her again... I think I've not had time to grieve for her and today seemed to bring it all out.'

Freddie kneels beside him, lays a hand on his shoulder.

'You're not alone now. No need to apologise. You can share whatever you want with me. I'm a good listener.'

Their journey is like a see-saw, pleasures and miseries taking their turn. Stomachs, hearts, and minds sway daily between events, so they never know what the next high or low may be.

After a stroll on deck, they return for the evening, glad of the cabin's warmth. William takes up his book while Freddie tidies up a little, and his mind turns, as it so often does, to his family.

'Do you think much about your family William?' Turning his book over, he takes a moment before saying,

'To be truthful... no, I don't.'

'Don't you miss them?

'Not really,' he says and seeing the look of surprise on Freddie's face, he goes on. 'You see I was never really close to my parents. Being sent away to school at a young age and not having spent much time with them as I grew up, I suppose I didn't get to know them properly. Mother was always out at lunch or those ghastly women's' afternoons. Father worked long hours and didn't want to

144

know me when he returned late and tired. It was the same for all of us. We always felt in their way; loved far more by nanny and the servants. Now I'm older and know what it is to love someone, I can see that we were the products of duty rather than anything else.'

Freddie thinks for a moment, finding such a childhood hard to believe before he realises William is holding out his hands in a 'now you' way.

'I miss my family very much.'

'Please… tell me about them.'

'I've only ever known kindness and love. I thought all families were like ours. You know what trades my parents are in. Maud's my oldest sister. We were young together before any of the stinky bundles arrived…. that's what I called all the babies! Maud's clever like you William. She reads; goes to the library to find things out…. many times, she's taken me with her. She looked after me; read to me…. helped me understand things. I love her very much. Grandmother is lovely too but she can be a bit sharp sometimes. I think you know everything about me now… If you want to change your mind about going in together… Well… that's alright.'

'I think you're a very brave man… you haven't run away from life as I have… you've told me your deepest anxieties. I admire you for that old chap. Why would I not want such a companion?'

Like many who suffer lack of confidence, or whose minds harbour thoughts which cannot easily be put into words, Freddie had felt for such a long time, a great dark weight in his chest, that same weight he had known after being discharged from the army, and that heaviness now seemed to lift.

36

Their ninth day is favoured with more fair weather allowing the Polynesian to travel at full speed, a light wind from the west sending long rolling crestless waves towards the starboard side. All passengers came to understand that day why this steamer had been nick named the 'Rolling Polly', for she rode each wave side to side; rising and dipping; port to starboard and back again like an inescapable rollercoaster. It makes walking on deck awkward, people bump into each other as they attempt to move forward, young children unable to play safely, so that eventually families begin to sit huddled together wherever they can. Those who began their journey with families but are now alone wander aimlessly about, drawn to each other, away from those unaffected by disease. They are raw; in need of a space in which to share and voice their emptiness. As he watches them, Freddie thinks what brave souls they are, and wonders if he would have been able to carry on, as they seem to do.

Cold air refreshes them but also brings about hunger for they have eaten so little recently. Their meal of soup, stewed beef with vegetable sauce, followed by bread and butter pudding, fortifies them well enough to venture into the cold again. As they emerge from the steps, they hear a cry go up... 'Come and see... Look... out there.' A whale is spotted, not too far from the ship, its black upper body visible above the water, its fin shining in the sunlight. It is a huge beast. The largest creature Freddie has ever seen, even while its head and tail fin are under the surface. As they gather at the railings to watch, it disappears briefly, only to surface without any warning, nose first, high up into the air it sails above the sea, dives back into the depths, rises again blowing an almighty spurt of water.

'What a wonderful thing to see,' says William.

'It's enormous, isn't it? I never knew there were such large creatures in the sea. And how can they jump right out of the water like that? I'd have thought they were too heavy,' says Freddie as he watches in awe and admiration.

The whale is not all they witness that day. A flock of storm petrels flies above them; tiny birds about the size of the robin which Freddie knows well. Seamen call them 'Mother Carey's Chickens', though nobody can tell them why. Later in the day a group begin to fish with lengths of string and bits of old food they find, and are surprised to land a cod or two. William and Freddie wander towards the bow where they see fancifully attired folk in first class. While women sit around tables, being waited upon, wrapped in heavy coats, with hands in muffs, their men stand together in groups, guns at the ready. The two men watch as birds are shot, each one falling to the sea to join those buried the previous day.

'I know some of us have killed fish today,' says Freddie sorrowfully, 'but that was to feed themselves. These people are killing for the fun of it.'

'I have to admit to having taken part in a few shooting activities. It was the only thing my father would let me accompany him to. He used to say it would make a man of me, but I never enjoyed it. I only went to spend some time with him and even then, he didn't really notice me. Now I feel inclined to see it from a different perspective Freddie. I agree with you. It seems to me there are enough pleasures to be had without killing for killing's sake.'

They turn away, not wanting to witness any further death. As dusk begins to turn to night, darkness now enveloping the ocean, they grow cold, until they are chilled to the bone. But they, and everybody around them seem happier than they had been for many a day. For the next two days the weather remains fair with only a smattering of cloud and a gentle wind from the north. Stewards can still be seen with their paraphernalia, backwards and forwards, for although most passengers have found their sea legs there are those who have been wretchedly seasick for the entire journey, confined to their quarters, missing whatever pleasures there are to be had. The steamer continues to travel at full speed, but has yet to make up the time lost, and just when Freddie thinks they have done with the merciless perils that have beset them, a shout goes up from high in the crow's nest. Out in the middle distance a large white shape looms before them.

'What is it?' someone calls.

'An iceberg,' another voice shouts.

'We're going straight towards it!' a third worried voice now.

There are gasps and frightened calls before a hush descends across the deck. They feel the steamer slow drastically as it draws closer than is comfortable, realising the white giant is actually in the middle of a much larger ice flow. Another dangerous situation; another fear; another sway in their fortunes. They can only trust in the captain and his crew to navigate them out of this ocean's torment.

They slowly move around the nearest ice and growlers, but the enormous berg dominates their view. It is several hundred feet high and about half a mile in length. As the ship slowly ventures further round, other smaller bergs become visible and even though each one is capable of their ruin, Freddie and William find it impossible to turn away, for there is such beauty in them. Their whiteness is almost blinding, made even more so as the sun glints from them, shining through the thinner parts, with blues and greens emerging then fading. It is a long afternoon. Many people pray, or chant and some even sing their morose invocations. Worried faces search for comfort from any quarter, all the while staring as they draw perilously close.

'Is this normal?' asks a man standing close to them, but nobody knows, until a sailor comes through the crowd and stands beside him, he asks again.

'What causes them to be here?'

'Normally they'd be up by New Foundland but it seems that the ocean current has driven them south. It's likely a result of that storm we had. If we manage to skirt them, we'll be fine, but it'll take us a long way off our route and add days to the journey. It's not what we wanted after all the time already lost,' he says, his voice quite dejected.

By the following day, however, they have made good speed and are heading north again between ice and land, towards their destination; one which they all now concede they will see, and the morning after that, brings with it an excess of cheer. Even though a foul wind makes headway difficult, it is on this day that the faintest outline of land is sighted. Passengers sing and dance again, the end in sight. During the afternoon most of them start packing their belongings and in the dining room the noise of chatter is greater than at any time since they left England. The service that day, it being a Sunday, is better attended than it has been all voyage. They have travelled a distance of two and a half thousand miles across open ocean, many of them never having gone further than their own small towns before.

On Monday March 20th 1882, four or five days later than expected William and Freddie step from the gangway of the Polynesian and set foot on the island of Nova Scotia, Canada. The docks are full of steamers, each one disgorging its passengers onto the quayside where they are met by agents and government men. Most stumble on dry land, needing to find their land legs, and there is much laughing at those who find it almost impossible to move forward. The two companions stay close together as they are pushed forward from behind, being directed towards a building where tickets and money brought into the country are scrutinised. Then a medical check is carried out before they are allowed to leave the main dock area. Porters carry luggage to trains, help those who struggle, and direct those lost or bewildered. Wagons loaded with goods have to be negotiated, but eventually they find their train. In the carriage, rows of wooden seats stretch behind them, and Freddie thinks it is quite like Liverpool docks only much colder and very much busier. Their relief is palpable. Tired bodies sink into listless oblivion. Children fall asleep hugged by parents and Freddie beams. They have made it.

The Intercontinental Railway with its enormous steam engine and hundreds of thankful people, leaves the port in Nova Scotia and in the morning, they change trains for the journey west. It takes several days to make the long haul, but there are many stops for taking on wood and water, and they are able to take advantage of a comforting meal and liquid refreshment for just a few cents. They warm themselves by fires beside the track, the weather being bitterly cold.

The train passes through a wonderland as if made for giants. The lakes go on as far as they can see. Deep valleys of forest, where the trees grow up the mountains on either side, often blocking out the light. Snow from mountain tops reaches the valley. Everywhere the scene is white, the little ploughs on the front of the train clearing it away.

When they arrive at Winnipeg, capitol of Manitoba, they are sore from the hard seats, their bones and muscles ache from sitting in one place for too long. Freddie's legs hurt trying to keep up with the crowd, as they follow the guide to the immigration shed, a large wooden building in open land, surrounded by forest and in the distance, mountains. This is their home now for at least a week, but it does not rock so is a blessing.

149

37

I open my eyes, close them again, open them. Freddie still sleeps. For a few seconds I'm unsure where I am. Everything about me is strange. Most noticeably all is still. No noisy engine, no rocking motion, no voices in the room. Though reluctant to move from the warmth and comfort of my bed, I gradually raise my stiff body and sit up. I discern growing chatter from other rooms and outside. I reach out and shake Freddie's shoulder.

'Freddie, old chap. We're here. No more boats. No more trains… Come on… Wake yourself… We've work to do.'

'Ah… I was having a beautiful dream…'

'I'm not leaving you here. We need to eat and see the agent. We're in it together, remember.'

He rolls out of bed to a kneeling position on the floor, stands slowly, stretching each limb as he does so, runs his fingers through his tousled hair and looks about him.

'Have we really made it? '

'We have. We're here in Winnipeg. Can you believe it?'

'Not really. It seems so long ago we left Liverpool. There were times I thought we'd not get here,' he says as he washes and dresses quickly.

We make our way to the kitchen, where breakfast is provided for us this first day, and stop to read a notice.

MEETINGS TODAY
THOSE INTENDING TO PURCHASE LAND – 11AM
THOSE INTENDING TO LABOUR – 2PM

There's already a queue when we get to the meeting room. We're mostly among families as we find spaces, and I see John and David not far behind us, so turn and wave, nudge Freddie who joins in.

'We should see them afterwards,' he says, 'find out what they're doing.'

'We shall, old chap. It would be good to get to know them. They're buying land so we might even end up as neighbours.'

There is an air of expectation, the atmosphere convivial as the agent stands to speak. He's a tall man of about forty, straight backed with wild auburn hair, but a neatly trimmed beard as though the two belong to different people. A moustache worms its way over each cheek ending in points which he accentuates by twisting them often with thumb and forefinger.

'Good morning. My name's Finlay Duff and you may be able to tell that I hail from Scotland.' Gentle laughter runs about the room. 'I came here as a youngster about twenty years ago and I'm proof that any one of you'… and he points across the crowd… 'can make good lives here. Not only can you develop this land, but you can also become its businesspeople… its leaders; its future.' Someone in the group claps loudly, others join in, until the sound is ringing all around the room. It's precisely the sort of message we need to hear.

'Before you aspire to such opportunities, however, you face hard work. Make no mistake, the way forward will not be easy… but if you're willing… you will succeed as many before you have done.' There's a buzz of agreement, which stops abruptly as Finlay holds up a hand.

'Now, for a small sum you can secure a quarter section of land in a township… but… there are three regulations you've to abide by if you eventually want to own it. So one, you're required to cultivate the land or make improvements to it, within three years. Two… You're to build homes on that land and three… You have to occupy those homes. Now… if you manage those three rules, you'll be able to apply for a land tenure.'

I take notes as we listen, although 'The Immigrants' Guide to Canada' has informed us of much of it, but Finlay goes on to tell us how and where land can be secured, the tools we'll need and of the next part of our journey.

We go to Winnipeg to change money. Freddie has $220, I have a little more. We agree to put together $150 each which we hope will cover the cost of land, tools, and provisions, leaving us with something for ourselves. We believe we're well off, there being many among us with no funds, and going in together means we have reserves. The land office is crowded when we reach it, so we've a little wait. There's a great deal of discussion among those purchasing as to where exactly they want to go, and we witness an argument between two families who want the same piece of land. I'm unable to believe that in this huge country, with so much space, such a dispute can occur, but we're all different. I look towards Freddie while this goes on and see a broad grin appear. His face is the epitome of excitement. I think he might burst if we're not seen soon.

When it's our turn, the land agent shows us a map of Manitoba, covered in a grid. In each square there's a set of numbers and letters. I realise how it works, but am at a loss to see what's already taken and what's still free. He shows us the available pieces of land, some south of here, some west. We choose ours to the south, towards the border with America, but not too close. When the transaction is complete, the agent writes the address and hands it to me. I hold it tightly, not wanting to drop it in the crowd, and look at Freddie, who's still beaming. We're overjoyed. I can't think of anything but this, our land, and we're not the only ones. Outside the office, are others who've just realised a dream; fought their way to it; suffered untold miseries to get to it. The air's charged with a new energy as families go in and emerge laughing, crying some of them, shaking hands, clapping, singing. We don't care in that moment, what the natives think. The prize is ours to hold, our new address:

Township 2 Range 3W
Section 2 South East Quarter
Altona
Canada

'Freddie, old chap, look,' and I show him the paper on which it's written.

Taking my hands, he jumps up and down with joy. We dance around the street together, bumping into others who're also dancing to the fine voices raised in song. It is madness. People gather in groups, numbers swell, the pavements too narrow to hold us all, so some dance in the road. An agent appears from the office, asks us to move on because we're blocking the entrance, so Freddie and me, well... we just dance down the road until he stops, groans, and says,

'My legs William... I can't dance anymore'...

'Let's have a sit down before we look for tools and things.'

'I'm so excited, I don't know what to think,' he says.

'You're not alone. Look at all these happy folk. I bet none of them can think further than the paper in their hands.'

'It makes it real, doesn't it? It means the misery of getting here was worth it. But I can't help thinking of those poor people who lost all their families and the dreams they had. Alone now. I wonder what they'll do?'

'That's a good question Freddie. I suppose they'll be helped to find work, for work they must under the terms of travel. It won't be easy for them though. Well... it won't be easy for any of us... there's so much we have to achieve in three years. I can only see extremely hard work ahead. Are you ready for it?'

'I am. Let's go and buy those what we need,' he says, taking my hand again, squeezing hard. I'm so thankful for this friend I've made. I feel a tear prick the corner of my eye, turn away. How much my life has already changed... I know it to be for the better.

We take a cart back to the shed, stow away our tools, and begin to make some positive plans, as we have two days to wait until leaving. I read the advice to immigrants about what should be done first, how to approach things and the animals we'll need and can have on our land. Then I read it to Freddie. He makes some good suggestions, his skills far outweighing mine.

38

It's more than a month since I left Brighton, to find this New World. We wait ready beside our cart. The overseer's checked to make sure they're all stable and safe. On top of many loads, children make themselves seats, some of the older ones hanging their legs over the sides to get a better view. It's cold, in the early morning, not much above freezing, but the skies are clear, so with warm clothes the sun feels good. There's a murmur of voices as the first cart is led away, and the air is mixed with excitement and unease. I think none of us thought to hear such a blood curdling squeal from the Red River carts, even though Finlay had told us about it. William puts his hands to his ears and pulls a face so unlike him, it makes me laugh. We're fourth in the train, and by the time we move off, the sound is already deafening. With the wind against us, I can't imagine what it's like at the back. Many carts before have laid the trail, so there are deep ruts in the ground. It's easy to slip into them, perhaps even sprain an ankle, but as oxen travel about two miles an hour, it's comfortable.

Most of our journey is through high grassland, so we can't see the river, but sometimes the trail takes us close and when it does, we rest. The water's cold and we bathe naked. It soothes our sore feet. We have no choice but to put on our dirty clothes, but it doesn't matter. At most stops, settlers meet us with food and drinking water. They give advice, tell stories of how they managed, and while they're not always happy ones, they're still helpful.

'I remember when we were on the trail, just like you people now. It was winter though and the ruts were filled with water... our feet were wet all the time. No camp fire was big enough to dry all the shoes and stockings... We had to put them on again still wet from the evening,' says one old man.

'I remember it too,' says a woman. 'Everything we wore was soaking wet... right down to our skin... and the cold... well it got right into our bones so we shivered and shook all the time.'

'But you know what'... the old man went on, 'we didn't mind. Yes, we were cold and we shivered but we didn't forget what we were heading for and we didn't forget the hunger we'd come from, because here at least we had food in our bellies. We had good people around us and sometimes we were even able to laugh at ourselves. You'll see... all of you.... Whatever hardship you feel on this trail, just remember what you'll have at the end.'

For two days it rains non-stop, making us shiver miserably as the temperature drops towards evening. Many catch coughs and colds. No-one laughs and jokes now. Children and sometimes women cry in their misery. Those who are older suffer most. They ride on the carts when they can't move further. They bathe their feet at every stop and wrap them in torn bits of fabric from women's petticoats, but for most it's only a brief relief. William has holes in his shoes, his feet always wet and he has many blisters, but he says he's used to the pain now. I've a few blisters but no holes. I'm glad of father's boots as I watch the poor folk in front of us.

We go to see John and David, who are behind us, and share refreshments offered by the settlers, sitting by a fire to dry as much as we can.

'I don't think I've ever been so cold,' says David, rubbing his hands close to the flames. 'How much further do you think?'

We look at each other, shrug our shoulders.

'It can't be far now, surely,' says John. 'We've been walking for days and I'm sure I heard someone say a day or maybe two more.'

The weather has slowed us, and the ruts are full of water so the tops of them are slippery with mud. Illness slows us too. Several older men and women cough violently and we stop for them until the fits have gone. As we near the border with America, the train stops. We watch as a driver comes down the line, frees an ox behind us somewhere, leads it with its cart and family, along one of the wide passageways between settlements. We wave to them, and wish them luck. There's a thrill now. We know we're nearing the end. Four stops later, we see John and David leave.

'We'll come and find you,' I shout. 'It would be lovely to be close to them,' I say and William agrees. The train comes to another halt, and a driver comes to us, unhitches our cart, leading us away. I

155

look at William, his face full of joy, his wide eyes shining, but we say nothing, for there're no words to explain what we feel. It's about one thirty in the afternoon when we arrive on our land. The day has been calm, a little overcast, but no rain has fallen.

'Here you are lads,' says the driver, turning the ox to the right onto a patch which seems to go on forever. 'Your new home! Take your time to unpack, we'll be back tomorrow to collect the cart.'

'Thank you,' we say together, shaking his hand. And then I wonder about the ox overnight, for there's no fence to be seen. 'Will the ox be safe through the night?' I ask.

'Oh. Yes. He's tired, won't wander far. They're used to it. Let him roam about for a while and then see you can tether him with something if you're worried. Well… goodbye to you both and best wishes for your future.'

39

'We made it Freddie,' I say in a hushed voice, as though there are others hiding, listening to us. 'We're where we want to be… on our own land in a new world with the rest of our lives ahead of us.'

'I don't know whether to laugh or cry. Where's the boundary? How much of this is ours?'

'I have no idea and I'm not worrying about it now. All that matters is this,' I say stretching my arms out to take in all we can see. I take hold of Freddie's hands now, jump up and down, making him join in, and we laugh like little children who've been promised something extra special.

'If my father could see me now, he'd die of shame! His son standing in the middle of a field, in the middle of nowhere jumping for joy.'

'I think if my father could see me, he'd be proud that I made it. I know he thought I wouldn't do it… though he never said as much, but I could tell by the way he said things.'

We run through the tall grass, leap over it, land awkwardly, fall into it.

'This is ours,' I say. 'All the land we can see, the grass, the sky, everything. Oh, Freddie, I'm so happy, I could cry.' There's no response so I look round. He lies on his back, the grass almost hiding him, the space a man shape on the land, and as I lean over, he's crying. He tries to hide it when he sees me looking. I tell him not to, his cry turns to sobs. I hold him, offer my own sounds, let them mingle with his, until all emotion is washed away.

'How long have we been lying here?' asks Freddie.

'I don't know, but I think we need to start some work, or we'll waste what's left of the daylight hours. And by the way… do you know you stink?'

'Of course, I do. I've been in these clothes for days! And do you know you stink too?' We laugh at ourselves and I'm happy to see he's become relaxed enough with me to make such comments. We unload the cart quickly, letting the ox wander while we do it. By the time we finish, our belongings are spread across the grass in two piles, things we need now and those that can wait. The cart we leave where it is. We think we'll need it for shelter tonight.

'Can you remember how to start the sod house?' asks Freddie.

'Sort of, but I've got the guide somewhere... in one of my bags... it explains it. See if you can find a large flat space we can use as the floor, and I'll find the book.'

We have the floor, instructions, and the right tool for cutting the sods. Neither of us moves... the task is daunting... doing something so much more difficult than knowing how to. I take up the spade, try to cut a slice of sod the right length and width. It's heavy going. The land, never worked, is hard, the grass never cut is tall, and in truth I have no idea how to use this tool.

'Perhaps we should turn the spade round and use the side rather than the end,' says Freddie after a few tries, which produces only scraps of turf and holes in the ground.

'I don't know. But at this pace we'll never have a roof over our heads.' We're laughing so much we double over, shaking with it, eyes streaming with tears. Somehow, it doesn't seem to matter if we have shelter, so happy are we. We hear voices in the distance, and see a group of people amble towards us, calling and chatting, laughing among themselves, no doubt at seeing two raw immigrants.

'We heard you as we drew near,' said a man.' We've come to meet our new neighbours.' Freddie shook his hand and introduced himself.

Our neighbours are two families who have settlements to the north of ours. Violet and Henry Walters have four children, Robert, George, Anne, and Thomas. Eleanor is Violet's sister. The other family are Ethel and Harry Miller who have a little boy of two called Charles.

'You must have a poor opinion of us,' I say, 'behaving like children.'

'Believe me there's nothing we haven't seen before!' Henry says, 'We're here to help.'

Before long, the men, women and older children begin to do with ease what we could not.

'There's nothing like being shown how to do something,' says Freddie. 'We'd never have worked it out on our own!'

158

We watch how they use the spade, and suddenly it makes sense. They brought their own tools with them, obviously prepared, maybe having helped others before, and then we join in. We work late, under the light of lanterns, to make a start on our first home. Violet, Ethel and Eleanor, bring us refreshments to quench our thirst. Each morning we add more sod bricks, and because it's slow work, our neighbours help us towards late afternoons. The external part of our sod house is complete in record time, including a shed for storing tools. Each night we light a fire to cook on and keep warm by, playing silly games that make us laugh, and find rest after each hard day's work. Sometimes we wonder what we've taken on, but the inside of the house takes shape. Blankets between walls, separate rooms and with a proper stove and some straw bedding, we're content. When the weather is dry soil falls from the roof while we sleep and we wake up with grit in our mouths and nostrils. When it rains the water drips through, so we wake up wet. Henry and Harry show us how to avoid these unpleasantries, by stringing fabric under the roof and sealing holes with clay.

Mostly we are so tired, sleep comes easily and we always wake fresh and ready to start again. Only when we both feel we have a home to call our own, do we write to England with news of an address.

It's a long time before our many acres of land are fenced, but as soon as they are, we buy oxen for the plough and make them a paddock, for it's time to start working the ground. A strong man can plough an acre in about six days, and while I'm able to manage this, Freddie has great difficulty keeping anywhere near the same pace. His legs prevent him from moving quickly much of the time, and I've noticed him over the previous few weeks, standing in the field, sometimes hands on plough, sometimes having let go, staring into the distance. I know of his 'nowhere times', and I witness it more lately. We usually split tasks to work in different parts of the field. I make sure to watch at intervals, my main concern being the possibility of accidents. Alongside the ploughing, we begin to lay the foundations for a permanent home, which we plan during the evenings, often taking it in turns to work the fields and the house. We're doing well and making good progress with the cellar. In the fields, the first seed of Indian corn and potatoes are almost ready to sow. They'll make good crops for feeding ourselves and the animals.

The start of summer is warm and mostly dry and since there is less to do in the fields, we work on the house. Our neighbours offer much help and we get to know them well. Eleanor has a little business, making mattresses from straw covered with fancy cotton fabrics, which she sells to the settlers. She brings one each for William and me, and stays a while with her brother-in-law, watching us work. Ethel and Harry entertain us for dinner at least once a week. I think Ethel feels a little sorry that we don't have a woman to look after us. She often talks of marriage, which we make light of, and Harry reminds her gently not to interfere.

As the season moves on, we make more pens, build shelters and fill them with straw and troughs. At market we buy two cows, two pigs and two sheep. The sheep we leave to graze the grasses and hope they will not stray too far! As the sun fades, the sky turns red and orange. We enjoy the warmth, take in our growing crops, our home, and our newly settled animals.

'Freddie old chap… these are good times. The best times,' says William.

It's late summer now, the day bright and cheerful, the sky cloudless and the wind just enough to create a gentle cooling breeze. I work in the cellar while Freddie tends to the livestock and ploughs a little more land. It's unusually warm in the cellar and though shaded from the early morning sun, by lunchtime, I'm rather clammy. Stopping to make a drink, I'm surprised to see no signs of Freddie having come back for refreshment, so go to find him.

A fair acreage of land is already ploughed and I've to walk quite a long way to where I think he'll be. The breeze cools me, so I don't hurry, but enjoy being outside, listening to the constant drone of bees as they fertilize crops. The pungent smell of animals and corn on the air, add to my desire not to hurry. As I near the edge of the prepared fields, I see the ox in the distance, wandering along, plough dragging behind, but it's moving in the wrong direction. I can't see Freddie anywhere, so I run through freshly tilled earth and across untamed grass, to manage the animal. There's no Freddie.

'Freddie. Freddie. Freddie! Where are you?'

Shielding my eyes from the sun's brightness, I scan the area but see nothing of him, so follow the shallow furrow left by the unmanned plough. I find him lying on his back among tall prairie grass, his face ashen, blood seeping from his mouth and there's a trickle of deep red blood by his head. I kneel down to him and see the whites of his eyes. There is a heartbeat, so my first fears recede

160

but as I kneel, it feels as though we're the only two people in the world, that we're invisible among the half ploughed brown soil and green prairie grass. *What would I do without you Freddie?* I think. Until now, I'd not realised precisely what this man means to me, that in the short time we've been together, this stranger, should matter so much.

'Freddie?'.

He's bitten his tongue badly, and it hangs half out of his mouth, the ugly red cuts oozing, his teeth crimson. I wipe it gently and talk to him of silly things, anything that comes into my head, but there is no response.

'Arrg,' says Freddie, his voice raspy, and slowly he opens his eyes, takes his hand to his head.

'Stay still for a while, old chap. Don't try to move yet. You've had a fall Freddie… a nasty one by the look of it, It seems you've hit your head on stones as you fell back. A good headache in the making.'

When I think it's safe, I help Freddie to his feet, but he's weak and needs support. His legs wobble, his shoulders droop, and the cut on the back of his head is clearly visible. He looks up at me.

'You're crying,' he says, his face showing the pain he is in, as well as puzzlement, his eyebrows almost meeting in the middle.

'Never mind that. Let me help you walk and we'll go in for tea.'

'Now, that sounds lovely. I've a dreadful thirst… have I been away William?' His voice is achingly sad.

'Where you've been, I really don't know. Can you tell me?'

We walk back towards the house, and I note the oxen are stationary so decide they can wait for a while. Freddie says,

'I'm sure I was ploughing, so where are the ox and plough?'

'They're a way down there.'

'I must go and get them back.'

'No. I think you must get home and sit for a while. They'll be fine. I'll take care of them when I've taken care of you, old chap.'

Summer rolls into autumn which moves swiftly into a very cold winter, deep snow covering the land. Fires burn through the day and sometimes through the night. In January, Freddie receives a parcel and letter from home with wonderful items, coffee, tea, and soap, a new pair of boots and two more thick jumpers with matching scarves. There is also money, which is most welcome, for it will be a long time

161

before they do not have to plough most funds back into the farm. His letter is full of good news too, which he shares with William.

'You're a lucky chap Freddie, to have such a loving family… to be so cared for. I honestly don't know how that feels,' says William, his voice trailing off. While he is happy for Freddie, he feels a deep sadness for himself, knowing that neither his father nor his mother would take up the pen for him; too busy with their socialising to concern themselves with a son they never really noticed.

'Thank you, William.'

40

The years pass quickly while Freddie and William work hard to cope with the requirements of the Canadian government and succeeding, they apply for a land grant. Fattened animals sold at market, enable them to grow their stock. It is a miserable March morning when they deliver milk to the local shop in Altona, arriving wet through from the fine drizzle, and stop a while to shelter. William picks up a 'T Eaton' catalogue, full of wonderful things for the home, and they borrow it, choosing several things, they need, and a few to add to their comfort. They are doing well, about half the land having been ploughed and sown, and spend much time with their neighbours to the north. Eleanor comes most days once her chores are done, Freddie always looking forward to seeing her. Even when they are too busy to sit with her, she seems not to mind, and he becomes fond of her. They laugh, see to the animals together. Sometimes when the work is done, she eats with them. Tonight, William's cooked lamb with potatoes and beans, the smell filling the house and their plates are clean in no time.

'What brought you to come and live with your sister here?' William asks.

'Violet and I were the only girls with five brothers. We lived in London and when she and Henry married, they came out here almost straight away. Then the boys gradually left home to make their own lives and I was the only one left to look after my parents.'

'That must have been hard for you,' Freddie says.

'Not really… My parents were really young at heart and truly kind, even though they weren't always in the best of health. The lady I worked for was understanding and whenever she could, let me stay to care for them, so I was fortunate… Then… one winter they both caught the influenza. It was a bad year for it, many losing their lives. Dad died first. He couldn't breathe with the chest infection and one morning he just seemed to give up… I suppose his body couldn't fight it anymore.'

They see the pain she feels, but after a brief pause, she carries on.

'Mum died the next day.'

'I'm so sorry Eleanor,' says Freddie. 'It must have been an awfully bad time for you.'

'It was worse for Violet because she wasn't able to get back to see them. I think she's never quite got over that. She doesn't speak much about it… Of course, I had to arrange for the burials, but my brothers helped a lot. If it hadn't been for them, I don't know how I'd have managed… After that I came out here to be with Violet and Henry.'

'It must have been awful for Eleanor to have gone through that on her own, don't you think?' Freddie says when they are alone.

'It must've been. I can't imagine having to cope with it, old chap… You like her, don't you?'

'So, do you William!'

'Yes. Of course, I do. But you really like her,' he stresses the 'really'.

'Truth be told, William, I think I do.'

'Then why don't you ask her to take a walk with you? I believe she'll not hesitate.'

'Ah… I don't think she likes me that way.'

'Why do you think she's here so often?'

'She likes being with us I suppose.'

'She likes being with *you* old chap!'

'Well… I don't know… I'm afraid she'll say no… then she won't come anymore.'

'Look Freddie… where's the courage that bought a ticket for half way round the world? Honestly, old chap… sometimes you frustrate me!'

A week later, Freddie and Eleanor begin walking out together, for short distances at first and then further afield. Eleanor spends more time with them. Freddie develops a small garden round three sides of the house. It reminds him of Rock Street when he was a small boy on his knees, planting seeds or picking flowers to take to his mother, and he tells Eleanor about it. In the evenings, the three of them take tea in the garden. Life is good, for all the hard work it took them resulted in a flourishing farm and wonderful home.

41

I watch as Freddie pushes his breakfast round the plate. I watched the same action over the last couple of days. He's not eating well at all, so I know there's something on his mind. I say nothing, waiting for him to start the conversation, but am plagued with bad thoughts, bad for me at least. I think maybe he wants to go home, or set out on his own… wonder if I've done something to upset him? This morning my patience wears a little thin and eventually I say,

'What's on your mind Freddie?'

'Oh… Nothing much,' he says, without looking up. I'm uncomfortable that he doesn't look at me. I must be the problem. 'Spit it out old chap!'

'Well… William… I've been thinking a lot lately,' and he stops, as if such a statement is all that's needed. When nothing else is uttered, I begin to feel the first little shivers of real fear travel down my legs. *What can be so hard*, I think. *What will I do if he wants to go home?* In a slightly faltering tone I say,

'Come on old chap. It can't be that bad surely? Just say what's on your mind and whatever it is we can sort it out.'

'Oh! It's nothing bad William… I'm a bit embarrassed is all.' Blushing heavily and beginning to sweat he blurts it out…

'I want to ask Eleanor to marry me!'

So relieved am I, I can't stop the laughter that seems to leave my body involuntarily, but Freddie misunderstands and turns on me.

'You think it's funny? You think I'm too simple for her? You think she'd never want someone like me for a husband. You think she's more *your* type, with your education and fancy ways.'

With each statement his voice rises in volume until he shouts out the last one, flings his arms about, red faced. I'm mortified, but at the same time angry that he still, after all this time, judges me wrongly. I stand quickly, my chair falling back and my drink spilling over the table.

'No Freddie. That's what you think! I'm going out. Perhaps we can finish this later.'

I run across our land as though my body wants to escape. Tears flow down my cheeks and I know I'm being stupid to cry over this, but somehow, I simply can't help it. My fear of losing Freddie, of losing all the good times we've shared, is just too much. It's in that moment that I realise I love this man, who's more a brother than all my brothers have ever been and would ever be, but I'm stronger of character than Freddie, so shouldn't I be the one to have more understanding? Shouldn't it be me who encourages Freddie out of his lack of confidence, and not behave in such a way that makes him worse? As I think, I wander back towards the house and find him still sitting at the table, unmoving.

'I'm sorry Freddie. I thought you were going to say you wanted to go back to England or something. I really thought I was going to lose my old friend… It was selfish but…' I didn't know what else to say.

'No. It's me who needs to apologise. I don't know what made me say those things. I sat here and tried to pull myself together. I know I've hurt you William… Haven't I said things like this before?… I don't know why I don't learn from them… I hurt myself too, knowing you think I don't trust you… Surely, I should've buried all those feelings by now. I don't understand what got into me… all my feelings seem to be mixed up… for Eleanor… thinking that you would mind… William… I'm sorry.

He speaks with his head still bowed, almost as though he's not addressing me, but voicing the words in his head just to let them go. I pick up the chair, sit opposite him, ask him to look at me.

'Do you think I haven't seen you two together? The way you look at each other; the way you pine if you don't see her for days? I was like that once… remember it well… recognise the signs Freddie… Yes, I knew it was coming one day and I'm truly happy for you dear friend,'

'Will you help me… you know with asking Henry and Violet and with all the arrangements?'

'You bet I will. I'll be there every step of the way! No more doubting please Freddie. I'd never knowingly do anything to upset you. Now. Isn't it time we had a small celebration? Fancy a good hot cup of tea?'

166

42

I'm nervous but William helps me, so I arrive at the door of Eleanor's house, knock rather gently, wanting to run away, but plant my feet firmly on the ground and knock again loudly. Violet stands there but says nothing. I suppose she's not expecting me. My mouth dries.

'What is it? Is something amiss?'

'Nnno,' I stumble. 'Can I see Henry please?'

'Of course. What am I thinking of? Come in Freddie. He's in the parlour.'

They're all there. There's no escape. Six faces look at me, wondering what I'm doing here.

'Henry. Freddie would like to speak with you.'

I see her raise her eyebrows and tilt her head. Henry sees my need for a private meeting, so we go into the kitchen. Afterwards Violet is called in to hear the news and Henry asks when I'll talk to Eleanor.

'Oh, not just yet for I need to buy her a ring. I didn't want to get one in case you or her should refuse me.' I feel my face become hot and know I'm blushing.

'There's no need. She was always going to have this one,' says Violet smiling, while attempting to remove a ring from her left hand.

'It was our mother's engagement ring, passed to me when it was my turn and now, I want it passed on to my sister. It's been the tradition to pass it on from mother to daughter for three generations now and I've only got boys. I hope one day, Eleanor will have a girl of her own to give it to.'

My body shakes, my mouth dries, sweat trickles down my back, and I laugh out loud as I cross the fields, run along the path and into our hallway. William waits for the outcome, a nervous look on his face, but the look on my face must say everything he needs to know. He is so happy for me, he hugs me for ages.

'This's just the first hurdle old chap. Now you've got to go through it all again with Eleanor!'

We're exhausted. It's been an emotional evening, so we take ourselves to bed. I didn't sleep well though, the memory of asking Henry still too raw.

Eleanor comes to the house the next day and has morning refreshments with us. I'm nervous, not wanting to wait to ask her and cannot stay in any one place for long. I see William watch me, a big grin on his face.

'Freddie. What's the matter? You seem to be on edge today. Won't you sit with us for a while?' she says.

'Err... I've got something to do in the fields. It's quite important and won't wait. I'll see you back here in a moment.'

'Oh. Alright. William will entertain me I'm sure,' she says, with the hint of a smile.

'Don't be too long Freddie, or your tea will be cold,' says William.

I leave them. Walk out into bright sunshine, I feel the perspiration on my neck. The ring's in my pocket, where it's been all night, and now I play with it, turning it round and round, feeling the gems on the top and the smoothness of the gold band. *Please God*, I think, *let her accept me as her husband, for I don't know what I'll do if she refuses*. I make my way indoors and ask Eleanor if she'll come into the garden with me. I point to the seat and we sit together in silence. I can tell she's unsure of my behaviour. She looks at me curiously, and all the time I'm thinking of how to do this.

'Eleanor, do you trust me?'

'Of course, I do Freddie. What's all this about?'

'Would you close your eyes and hold out both your hands?'

She sits in darkness while I kneel on one knee. I take the ring from my pocket, hold Eleanor's left hand, the ring at her fingertip.

'Eleanor,' my voice shakes a little, 'will you marry me?'

'Yes Freddie. I will.' And with that she flings her arms round my neck and kisses me.

'Elly! No. Elly!'

'What Freddie?' she cries, and moves back as though she's made some awful mistake.

'The ring! It's flown out of my hand!'

She's horrified. 'Freddie, what have I done?' Tears roll down her beautiful cheeks as I hug her and say,

'It's alright. Come on, it can't be far.'

'What's happened?' William calls, and he's so near us I think he must have been listening.

'William, I can't explain now but we need some help. It's the ring. It's flown through the air and is somewhere here.'

We scrabble around in the soil, between the flowers and along the edges of the paths, but it's some twenty minutes before William raises his arm proudly.

'I've got it!' he shouts as he hands it back to me. I take Eleanor's hand and place it firmly on her finger. We have dirty knees and grubby hands but what does it matter. Once we stop laughing, William fetches fresh drinks while I take Eleanor in my arms and kiss her.

'It's my mothers. Violet gave it to you. And you called me 'Elly'. I like it.'

'I've always thought of you as my Elly and now you really are. Violet said that one day she hopes we'll have a baby girl to pass the ring down to.'

Eleanor goes home towards late afternoon. She's so excited, and wants to share the news with her family. William and me... well... it's been another tiring day, but a beautiful one, so we take our meal into the garden, where the smell of flowers, animals and our food mingle in the evening breeze. We lie on the grass after, as we often do, to take in the last of the sun, although we see clouds gather now, the air becoming muggy. Above us is a perfect circle of deep blue sky, edged with white, grey and some quite black clouds, but the sun still shines on us and lights up the feathery edges of the cloud circle. We do not speak. I'm at ease with William. I remember, as I lay here, thanking God a long time ago, for the gift of him, and think that He had William and Elly planned for me, that I've never been happier, that I'm the luckiest man alive.

A faint snoring comes from next to me. I almost laugh out loud, but put my hand to my mouth to stop it, for fear of waking him, so he doesn't see the first flashes. I leave him be, watch them become closer together, brighter, travel round the whole circle. Huge bolts of light leave themselves on my eyes. There's no thunder, just forks and enormous bright patches, which fly out from the clouds and into the darkening circle of sky. I wake him then.

'William. Look at this.'

'Uh… I drifted into sleep. Sorry old chap.'

'Yes. I left you for a while, but you should see this.' He rubs his eyes as the lightening continues.

'Where's the thunder?' he asks.

'Don't ask me. I've no idea. A storm like this… Well, I've never seen it before.' We go back to our silence, watch in amazement. I wonder how such things exist in this world, what causes them.

'Do you know what I think?' I say.

'No. But I think you're going to tell me.'

'I think the angels are playing ball with the stars, you know, throwing and catching. Every now and then, they crash into each other and explode.'

'Freddie… you have a wonderful imagination, old chap.'

43

Wedding preparations are well underway, with Eleanor's sister fussing round like an old mother hen. The dress has been made from Violet's wedding outfit, Eleanor delighted with the result and proud to be wearing both this and her mother's engagement ring. Freddie and William splash out on new suits, which hang ceremoniously in their bedrooms, both men looking quite unlike themselves in such grand attire. The church in the local town, has been booked for September 21st, with invitations sent to all the friends they have made since arriving. It will be a grand occasion, a topic of conversation among many of the locals. They decide if they save hard, they will be able to visit England at Easter the following year. The question as to where they will live gives rise to many different ideas.

'We could find ourselves a little house somewhere close and I'll be there to work with William on the farm,' says Freddie.

'But how will William manage?'

'I'm sure he's able to look after himself… He can always have some meals with us and we'd spend most of our time with him.'

'I think he'd miss you terribly. And… you know you'd miss him too.'

'Well yes… I would but we'd be married and isn't it only right for me to provide a home for you… for us?'

'I'd be only too happy to look after both of you. William is special to you and to me. I'm aware of how you feel about each other and I want to be part of that as well.'

After speaking to William, it is finally agreed, they would live in Freddie's home. Secretly Eleanor does not want to be the reason for the two men to be separated. She knows that what they had been through together had cemented their relationship. She was also a little scared of being far from her own family, which might be necessary, if they cannot find anything close. She is quite content with the arrangements, even though many will frown upon it.

Freddie and I wake on Friday to a beautiful still hot day, the wind having died completely and the cloudless sky a rich deep blue. Today should see the last of the harvest, but I've not been feeling good for the past week, being tired and listless.

'Are you alright to work today?' Freddie asks.

'Yes, old chap. Not much to do now, so we can look forward to a rest when it's done.' We walk to the far side, my scythe heavy even though I've not started work yet. We're both eager to complete the task before any rains come and ruin the crop, so we work through the morning and into the afternoon. By about three o'clock I'm feeling quite unwell, realising I've been slowing up and am now considerably behind Freddie. The day remains windless, so still the chaff and detritus isn't blowing away. It hangs about us as we move across the field. I can see it in the air, taste it on my tongue, feel it tickle the back of my throat. It must have reached my lungs because I start to cough. I can't catch my breath and I sweat profusely, until the weakness of my body stops me dead. I make an effort to catch up with Freddie, hear the wheeze of my voice as I say, 'I must have a drink and a short break,' and he acknowledges me without stopping. Back at the house I have no strength to make a drink, and fall into one of the chairs in the front room, lay my head back, try to slow the coughing and force relaxation on my body.

I don't know how long I keep harvesting after William goes back. The air is so full of corn bits, I can't see the end of the field, but carry on to try and finish. When I turn to make my way up the last run, I can't see through the haze, so walk along to find him, but he's nowhere. I make my way home, seeing how wonderful the house looks as the sun shines directly on it and feel a rush of satisfaction and even pride as I reach the door. It stands wide open. I go to the kitchen calling his name but he's not there and there's no sign of him having made a drink. I find him slumped in a chair, his head back, eyes closed and thinking him to be asleep begin to creep away so as not to disturb him but before I reach the door there's a cough.

'Freddie. Is that you?'

'Yes. Are you tired?'

'I am, but I think I'm not well too.' I move towards him, see that he's sweating.

'You have a temperature. I'll get some cold cloths and a drink for you.'

For the next few hours, I go from kitchen to living room, trying to cool him down, but there's no change, the coughing getting worse. I try to move him to the bedroom, but can't manage the weight, so leave him in the chair, fetch a blanket to cover him, watch him sleep fitfully, knowing I should go for help but all the while afraid to leave.

Elly is expecting me and it feels like hours later that she gives a gentle knock on the door before calling out.

'We're in here, Elly,' I shout. 'Come quickly. I've been trying to get his temperature down but I can't. I should have gone for help, but couldn't leave him like this. He's getting worse.'

'Stay there,' she says. 'I'm going for someone.' Help, when it comes, is the doctor from Altona. He takes one look at William and says we must make haste to get him into bed. He asks questions all the while he examines him and afterwards, we leave the bedroom, closing the door behind us.

'Mr. Tyler. It's not good news I have to impart. Mr. Trout is severely ill with what I believe to be pneumonia. It's highly likely he hasn't been well for a while and the harvesting has made a bad situation even worse. I'm afraid all you can do is nurse him and keep him comfortable.'

'What do you mean doctor? Elly!'

'Mr. Tyler, please sit down. There's nothing I can do for Mr. Trout. I'm afraid that he'll most likely die in a few days' time.'

'But… that can't be right… He was out with me today… we've been harvesting…. We've got lots of jobs to do.'

I can't take it in. How can someone be there one minute, laughing, walking about, working the field… and then… just die…? 'William's going to die?' I look at Eleanor and then the doctor hoping to find something in their faces that would tell me it wasn't true.

'Please make a good strong cup of tea,' the doctor says to Eleanor, 'you both need one for the shock, and make sure to put sugar in it.'

He returns to the bedroom while we sit in the kitchen, not speaking. Eleanor weeps quietly while keeping busy. I stare through the window into our garden, so full of colour and light; so full of life; so pretty and welcoming, but darkened by the moment. My head's full of troubled thoughts; the difficult times we've been through; the joys of what we've created; the love that's grown between us. *He can't die,* I think as I hear the door to the bedroom close.

'Is this real? Are you sure he won't get better?'

'Mr. Tyler... I'm sure. Your companion is dreadfully ill and there's nothing I can give him to reverse the damage to his lungs. You'll both need to be strong over the next few days. Keep him comfortable and give as much liquid as you can. You'll know when the end is coming... you must call me when it does.'

Eleanor holds me, her warmth comforting. She wants to help so we decide to watch over William between us, she during the day and me at night. He sleeps only fitfully, the dreadful coughing fits almost unbearable for us both, so that I lift his head and try to support him with extra pillows, all the while giving him sips of water. After three days he loses control of his bladder and bowels. Each morning I scrub at the linen we think can be saved, watch it hang on the line in our garden. The weather hasn't changed since last Friday. I see the sun wilting the plants, draining all their colour, browning their leaves and am thankful that William doesn't know how the garden dries and dies, like him. A week after he's taken ill, he opens his eyes and looks at me. It's early morning. His eyes are watery, pale, and deeper in his head, and while I smile my best smile, I know he's fading.

'How are you feeling?'

'Not good... old chap... My body... hurts more than... I've ever known it... I can't breathe.' I listen to the shallow breath coming between his words and the rattle in his chest is much louder.

'I'll get you a fresh drink. Make sure you stay here!' I say with a laugh, which makes his mouth turn up a little. I give him only small sips, and he says,

'You'll have the farm... old chap. Everything... that's mine is yours. There's been no ... greater friend... in my life than you Freddie... Look after Eleanor. Have a good... life together. Have courage.' As he speaks, I watch his face stream. 'I've never... had your... faith in God... but I always... admired you... for yours. Do you think I'll... see Annie again?'

'I believe so dear friend. And one day we'll be together again too.' He takes my hand, says, 'I don't want to leave you.'

Early on the Saturday morning, before the day has fully dawned, so that a hint of darkness remains over the house, William's chest and throat rattle loudly with each breath he takes. His eyes stay closed, his mouth open. I know it will not be long. I hold his hand, squeeze it every now and then to let him know he's not alone. As the sun breaks through, flooding the bedroom with its warmth and light, William takes one last deep breath, lets it out slowly and I see his body fall into the mattress. I take him in my arms, cradle his head, hold him to me. Still warm but now limp, he's no longer with me and I feel my own body shake as the sobs take over. I tell him,

'You will never leave me William. You will be in my heart for as long as I live.'

I don't know how many days pass, several sunrises and sunsets I think, but as to which day it is, I can't say. The house has been full of people, the doctor first, to tell me what I already knew. Then Violet, Henry and Elly of course, Ethel and Harry and others. John and David came, I remember that. I try every day to talk to whoever is here but it's so difficult. I can't think. I want to be on my own. When the house clears, I go in to be with William, curl up beside him, try to shut the world out. I hold his wedding suit to my body, draw in deep breaths to get the scent of him. I want to gather up all that is William, lock it inside me, carry it in my heart for the rest of my life. I dress him in the suit, before they come for him, his limbs soft now, giving to my touch, but he's so cold, so very cold and when it's done, I kiss his forehead. It's like an icy stone so that I wonder when his soul flew. I take his hand in mine, the cold of it entering me like a shock in my arm. As I hold it, his hand warms, my warmth flowing into him. I think if I stay like this his whole body will warm, that I can bring the life back, have my dearest friend here again, but it's useless. It travels no further than the part I hold. His head makes a hollow in the pillow, his hair, still dark against the whiteness of his face, lies in wisps. I comb it, straighten the bedding beneath him, kiss him again just before they take him.

Elly is wonderful. She makes me eat and drink, although it often sticks in my throat. She looks after the animals, sometimes makes me go with her, for the fresh air I suppose and I do feel better once I've stroked them. Then a memory comes, me and William laughing at something as we tend them, so vivid it might have been yesterday. I talk to them of him, tell them he'll never be here now. He's gone to be with the God he had no belief in, but one who would not turn such a good man away from the gates of Heaven.

We ride together, Elly's family and me, down to the little church in Altona. Other carts follow with many friends from the settlements, and as we near the town, more join us. Those we know from the shops, those who buy our goods, those who can't believe such a young healthy man can have been taken. It's Wednesday August 21st, one month before Elly and me are to be wed. Today I can only think of William, my friend, the man I love beyond all others, the man who saw something in me, gave me everything, asked for nothing, took my hand as it were, and led me to another world. Now I watch him inside his wooden box, slowly disappear into a hole in the ground. I feel my body bend forward, my feet still planted and for all the world I want to fall into it after him. Elly takes me under the arm, steadies me so my mind comes back to where I am. I take a handful of soil, sprinkle it over him, and my tears mix with it as it falls. 'I will see you again William.'

44

Henry and Violet are understanding when Elly tells them of her concern for Freddie, and the decision to postpone their wedding. They offer to organise everything and Elly is grateful not to have to worry, not have to feign happiness where only sadness dwells. One evening towards late autumn, Freddie takes Elly's hand and says,

'I don't think I can stay here… even though I don't want to leave him. It's too hard for me Elly. All the time… every day… every minute of the day… I feel him. I see him in the house, on the farm, with the animals, going to market together and it hurts so much. I want to go back to how it was. I hear all the laughter, like it's caught in the walls… his face is everywhere… on the chairs and the curtains. I even see it on the windows and doors. I want to go home Elly,' he says softly. 'I know it's a lot to ask, but will you come with me? It's a big decision for you, but I don't want to leave you here. I want us to be wed back at home. Please say you will dear Elly.'

'Of course, I will Freddie.'

Freddie writes home of William's death, the postponement of the wedding and their likely return. Violet and Henry see that Freddie is not the man he was, and agree they are probably making a wise decision, helping as much as they can, advising Freddie that the farm can be sold.

'You've done really well to develop your land as much as you have in the time you've had,' says Henry. 'I've taken the liberty of talking with Harry. We think that maybe we could take it on together… you know, adding to our land and working it between us just as you and William did. After all, the hard work's already done so we'd only have to keep it going… and the children are grown some, so they can all help. Of course, we'll buy it from you. What do you think Freddie?'

'Well… is it what you want? Please don't do this just for us. It's a huge number of acres you'd be left with and I don't want you or Harry to regret it.'

'We've talked about it. We know we won't get more land any other way and yours is right next to us! What could be better? If we struggle to cultivate it all, we can simply leave some as fallow land… our sons will be able to take it over when they're old enough… or maybe we'll increase your livestock. Who knows? It's a solution for you and us… it makes sense Freddie.'

'Well, if you're sure then I agree.'

'There's one more thing, Freddie,' says Violet. 'Where do you plan to go back to?'

'We haven't spoken of it. I thought we'd go back to Brighton and stay with my parents.'

'Henry and me… we think Eleanor would be better going to London to stay with our brother. It's just that she's never met your family… and I'm not saying that's a problem, but I think she'll be glad to have some of her own family around her.'

'Maybe you're right. I admit I hadn't thought about it much with everything that's happened.'

'Jobs would be easier to come by too, in London,' says Henry. 'Violet can write to Robert, as he's the brother most likely to have enough room for you.'

'I want to do everything I can to make this good for Elly, so if you think that's best, it's alright with me.'

Freddie, Henry and Harry meet early in January to seal the transaction. Tickets are purchased to Liverpool, which will have them back on English soil by the end of April 1890. There is much to be done; all their personal belongings need to be sorted and packed up once again; arrangements for their lodgings with Robert and his wife Eliza, in London, as well as farewell parties. The effort it takes to manage everything and continue the animal maintenance leaves little room for Freddie to become maudlin and so in contrast to the dragging of time after William's death, the months seem to fly.

Eventually the Red River Cart comes for the reverse journey. Freddie and Eleanor take a last look through the home he and William built together. They say goodbye to their much loved animals and lastly to those they might never see again; Eleanor's family; their friends. Everyone runs along the tracks as the cart squeaks its way through the ruts, waving and shouting, laughing, and crying.

'Write to us Eleanor,' shouts Violet. 'Write soon and often.'

'Safe journey,' yells Henry, his voice breaking just a little.

45

'The pain of parting is nothing to the joy of meeting again.' Charles Dickens: Nicholas Nickleby (1838)

London 1890

As the horses clip-clop their way from the station to Eleanor's brother's house, Freddie finds himself uneasily fiddling with the hem of his coat. He tries to stop but his fingers only go to other parts of his clothes, pulling at them, twisting them and scrunching them. He has not thought himself nervous of meeting Elly's family, nor has he considered what it would be like to be back in his home country, but he knows now, with a sudden awareness, that he is dreading the next few hours. A familiar voice in his head says, 'Courage old chap,' and he silently thanks William. His eyes grow wet. He feels Elly's presence beside him, her excitement not letting her settle. She points things out to him, most of which he either does not hear, or see, until she takes his hand and kisses it softly, bringing him back to the present.

Arriving at Winsor Terrace and alighting the carriage, they stand for a moment to look at the house they are to live in. It is part of a long row, there being no space at all between each house. They are used to open fields, with animals and crops, so they already feel claustrophobic. The front door opens and a tall man strides along the path, hand outstretched.

'Robert!' says Eleanor, as she flies towards him for a hug, and with his arm round her he takes Freddie's hand in a firm grip.

'Welcome to London,' he says, his face beaming. 'Come inside and meet the rest of the family.'

Eleanor holds Freddie's hand and almost drags him up the short path, into the long hall, which is gloomy, after the brightness of the day. They are led into the front parlour where a small table is laid with china and platters of little cakes.

'Freddie, it's so good to meet you at last. I've heard a lot about you from Violet… I think Eleanor's been too busy to write to me over the last couple of years! This's my wife Elizabeth and these two urchins are Penny and Alfie. Please say hello to your aunt Eleanor and her fiancé, Freddie.'

In unison they chant a hello before giggling and running away. They are still young, Penny at six and Alfie at four, and have not met their aunt before. Over tea and cakes, served by Clara, their maid, Freddie feels more comfortable and afterwards, they are shown to their rooms on the top floor. Their quarters, more than adequate, are a living room and another which can be used for visitors and two bedrooms. After unpacking, the family enjoy a wonderful meal together, before Eleanor and Elizabeth retire to the parlour. Robert and Freddie linger in the dining room. Freddie needs to fill the silence, so says,

'You have a lovely home Robert.'

'I've been lucky. This whole street was built by the owners of the gas works and as I've a good job with them, we were given this one.'

'What do you do for them?'

'I'm one of the managers for the plant. I've been asking if there are any jobs for you and Eleanor if you want one.'

'That's good of you. We have money from the sale of the settlement, but I need to keep busy, so I'd want to work and I think Elly would as well.'

'In that case, I'll see what can be done when I go tomorrow. When would you want to start?'

'As soon as I can. I must thank you Robert, for your kindness in giving us lodgings while we settle.'

'It's lovely to have Eleanor home with us again. You're most welcome.'

Neither Eleanor nor Freddie mind the work, though it is tiring and Freddie's legs do not like the constant climb of the ladders. They walk each day. The landscape, for as far as they can see, is desolate of everything but towering tanks and warehouses and even when the wind blows from the east, it bears no resemblance to the crisp cold they were used to, the beauty of Canada transposed, into a grey and forlorn wilderness, but as the weather warms and summer sun shines, they become used to it, even if only for short periods. Freddie takes Eleanor to Brighton for a weekend to meet his family, and seeing his home town as well as his loved ones, fills him with a sense of new belonging.

With summer on the wane however, Freddie's mood begins to fluctuate between happiness and deep sadness, sometimes bordering on depression. There are days when he cannot rid his mind of William, seeing him in all manner of situations and hearing his voice, always comforting. There are times when both of them miss Canada so much, they sometimes speak of returning, even while they know this can never be. One night, reaching home in great pain, Freddie inspects his legs as he changes from his work clothes, and sees veins, twisted lumps, rising like land masses from rivers of blood. He is shocked. They are tender, hard and it almost turns his stomach to feel them.

'Elly. I don't think I can keep doing this work. The pain in my legs is so great that I can hardly put one foot in front of the other,' he says.

'I realise how hard it is for you my dear. What do you think can be done?'

'Well... I thought I'd write to my doctor in Brighton to ask his advice.'

'A good idea. Maybe he can recommend something.'

Two weeks later, Freddie receives a lovely letter from his godfather, and news of an operation, which Elly, is much in favour of, although not pleased to hear that he wants it carried out in Brighton rather than London. Understanding of his wish, however, she says,

'You must make some arrangements and stop working so that the condition doesn't worsen. What will the cost be?'

'I don't know yet, but if you agree, I think it is needed so much that some of our savings can be used.'

'Of course, Freddie. We'll manage... I can stay here with Robert and earn as much as I can, and then when it's all over we'll plan for the future. What do you think?'

'I was hoping you'd say something like that! I'll give in my notice and hope the operation can be done very soon. Dr. Sayer says there'll be a lengthy convalescence.' He takes her hand in his, holding it tightly. 'I'll miss you so much Elly.'

'I'll miss you too. But it won't be for long and afterwards we have our whole lives to look forward to.'

Both legs are operated on in September at Brighton Hospital, and within ten days, Freddie is back in his old bedroom with his brothers, legs bandaged from thigh to ankle, and unable to get about. Nevertheless, with the aid of walking sticks and determination, the family soon have him taking short walks to the beach. His mood improves. His legs at last carry him without half the pain he is used to, and Elly's letters cheer him no end.

'You know Alice, we should have tried for this operation long before now. Freddie's so changed by it… his confidence is soaring,' says Alfred.

'I'm sure you're right…. I can't believe how quickly he's getting better… And I think maybe he'll be wanting to get back to London soon.'

'I wouldn't let him go back there Alfred,' says Lily in one of her increasingly intolerant tones.

'Why not mother?'

'After that expensive surgery? You want him to go back to work at that gas place… he'll just get them all back again.'

'Oh, I don't think so Mother. All the bad veins have been taken away. But I do agree with you that it's probably not the best type of work for him,' says Alice.

'Well… I should think about all the doctor's bills too. It can't have been cheap and what about all the checking up and things?'

'Mother. We're not paying Freddie's doctor's fees. He's seen to all that himself, so don't be so grumpy now,' says Alice.

'I was just looking out for you… there's no need for that.'

'Mother. You've been getting more and more grumpy lately. Is there anything wrong? Something on your mind you're not telling me?' Alfred asks.

'Of course, not… And I don't think I'm anything other than I used to be!'

Alfred and Alice look at each other with raised eyebrows. They have spoken of Lily's changing behaviour, her intolerance, petulance, and sometimes even hostility, and have discussed it with Dr. Sayer. He assures them it is not uncommon in aging people.

Freddie has been in his bedroom, writing to Eleanor while most of this conversation takes place, but is on his way to the parlour when he hears his grandmother speak of the fees. Without thinking, he stops outside and listens. It grieves him that his grandmother has changed in this way. She has been short tempered with him lately, making him feel uncomfortable and he does not understand why. He cannot remember doing anything to upset her unless, he thinks now, it is because she wishes he had not come home. But it also angers him somewhat that she thinks he is taking money from his parents to cover his bills. Entering the room now, he says,

'Grandmother. It hurts that you have such an opinion of me. I'm twenty eight and I make my own way in the world… and I pay rent for my lodgings here as well!'

'Oh, dear boy. Stop making such a fuss. I wasn't accusing you of anything… Just voicing my thoughts. Doesn't a mother have a right to state her feelings to her own son?'

'She does, but I believe we're perfectly able to manage the arrangements ourselves… though I thank you for caring about us,' says Alice.

'Now. That's enough. I'll have no more talk of this… I expect both of you to apologise for your outspokenness,' Alfred says, clearly upset at the tone his mother and son have taken with each other. 'Freddie, your grandmother means nothing by it… I should not have to remind you to respect your elders.'

Freddie softens because he loves his grandmother; because he does not wish to be rebuked by his father; because he knows he should not have spoken in such a way. The look on Lily's face is harsh though, as though whatever she has against him lies simmering somewhere, ready to flare up another time.

'Grandmother, I'm sorry for speaking to you like that. It won't happen again.'

'Hm. I suppose I am too, young Freddie. Just make sure that while you're here, you forget some of those ways you've learned in Canada. You're not the head of this household…'

'Mother! Stop right now,' says Alfred. 'I won't have you or anyone else upsetting the stability of this family. I think you need to apologise.'

With that Lily leaves without another word, an air of discomfort in her wake.

'She's not herself lately,' Alice says to Freddie. 'You mustn't mind her too much. She's become old while you've been away and can't manage change easily.'

'She takes things the wrong way, and argues, which isn't like her,' his father says. 'Freddie, please take no notice for the time being. We all know how it is for you being away from Eleanor and hope you understand that this will always be your home for as long as you want or need it to be.'

'I do Father and am grateful for everything you're doing for me, but I don't want to make things difficult... I'll try to stay out of her way for a while... let her calm down,' but Alfred interrupts him, 'No. You mustn't do that my boy. She is getting old, but we must not let her govern the way we live. We must be aware of her moods... that's all... and... not react to her in a negative way. I'll go and see how she is.

46

Freddie and Elly decide to be married in Brighton and in December, he obtains work as a porter with the railways at Brighton Station, having been recommended by a gentleman known to his father. The station is an imposing building and though Freddie has seen it for the purposes of travel, he has never really considered its beauty. As he approaches it on his first working day, he stops to admire its architecture, with its ornate decoration and central clock. The goods yard is east of the main station, so he makes his way to the right, eventually finding someone who can show him where to go.

The work is tiring with long hours of hauling goods from one platform to another. The loading of carts and vans is heavy too, but he does not mind. His legs no longer hurt, walking becomes pleasurable, and he does not want time to think, with Elly so far away, and William's presence still so raw he sometimes weeps for him. He wants to fill his hours, to be busy. His favourite task is that of delivering around the town for then he is able to sit behind the horses and watch the comings and goings of residents, but this is a rare pleasure.

Freddie becomes a familiar figure among the local townsfolk, often stopping to talk with PC Farncombe, who he has come to know well, interested as he is in Freddie's Canadian experiences. It is not the same with his colleagues at the station. The men he works alongside are long standing friends. He is the new man, and finds getting to know them difficult, although his improved self-confidence helps him try, but they are unforthcoming. They notice his 'nowhere times' which become more frequent in his anxiousness to be part of the group. They think him lazy, a daydreamer, and are not above speaking of it in his hearing. At lunch one day, the summer sun shining brilliantly, the air warmer than it had been, they sit outside at the back of the yard. One of them asks,

'What did you do before this Freddie?' He is taken by surprise that he has been spoken to.

'I've had an operation on my legs, but before that I worked a short time in London at a gas works.'

'And before that?' asks another, his voice harsh and cynical.

'I was eight years in Canada,' he says looking at them, a sense of pride as he speaks.

'You emigrated?'

'I did.' A third man looks up from his sandwich towards his mates and says, 'A Navvy I suppose!' Freddie cannot see the man's face properly, but knows he is meant to feel uncomfortable about his comment.

'No. I had a settlement, six hundred acres and made a good life. It's where I met my fiancé.'

'Why come back here then? Something go wrong did it? You get into trouble?'

He knows they taunt him, assume him to have failed and are enjoying what they are doing.

'It was a great sadness in my life. One I don't want to speak of.' He gets up, feels the tears swell his eyes, goes back to work thinking of William. After this, he does what is asked of him, but above being polite, keeps apart from them as much as he can. His twenty ninth birthday passes and he and Eleanor look forward to their wedding, just a few months away.

On Thursday December 10th 1891, the weather is wet and windy and Freddie listens to the drops hitting hedges and treetops, on his way to the bus, some large puddles already formed. His task that day is not as usual as he is required to work a delivery van, one of his colleagues having been laid up. He partners John Watts in delivering malt to Longhurst Brewery in Preston Road, a journey of about a mile. By the time they set out on the first of five trips, the rain has eased, John driving the horses for the first two deliveries, but as they begin the third journey, it has set in again and John hands Freddie the reigns so that he can sit comfortably huddled in his thick oilskin coat. Freddie completes the driving of the final three deliveries. When all is unloaded, John says,

'I'm going in for a drink. You going to join me?'

'No. You know I don't take alcohol.'

'Oh! Come on. You can still come inside.'

'I'll come inside out of this rain but I want none of your devil's drink.'

John raises his eyebrows at this, pushes his way through the door almost allowing it to fall back and slam into Freddie's face. Once inside and his beer ordered, John makes his way to a table where he joins friends, greets them heartily and sits down. Freddie follows.

'This's Freddie,' he says. 'Works with me at the good's yard. Doesn't drink though… Thinks he's better than us'… and he gives a short snort of derision before continuing. 'Calls it the devil's drink.'

He holds up his glass in a salute to the group and they join in with hoots and sarcastic remarks looking at Freddie with disdain. They want to know why he will not take the beer and when he tells them about the pledge, they stare in utter amazement, before breaking into loud raucous jeers.

'What are you a namby pamby?' says one of them and another asks,

'How'd you know it's the devils drink if you've never tried it? Tell me that then!'

As the intimidation continues, Freddie becomes agitated, the insults coming too fast for him to think of responses. Ready for another, John gets to his feet.

'Try it Freddie. It's a man's drink. Only men can take it. Prove you're a man Freddie. Have one with us men here,' and all the time he speaks he jabs Freddie with his index finger, in the arm, the shoulder, the back of his neck.

'I am a man John… soon to be wed.'

'Ha! Ha! Hear that. He thinks he's to be wed just like he thinks he's been to Canada,' John shouts to the entire room, arms outstretched. Freddie stands then, tall and straight, and looks his colleague directly in the eye.

'I'll prove it. I'll prove I'm as much of a man as any of you here.'

Almost instantly fresh beers are produced and one is handed to Freddie. He takes it, sniffs it, turns his nose up and almost places it back on the table, but their faces are turned to him expectantly and he halts. John stands, then leans into him and in a very low and depraved voice whispers,

'Where'd you pick up the lass then? In the Lanes eh.'

Freddie, instantly understands the slur against his beautiful Eleanor, drinks half the glass, places it on the table, makes a fist of his right hand and lifts it to punch John. Not quick enough though for such a street wise man. John side steps, sits down again and hands Freddie his glass, smirking all the while. To great cheers and applause, Freddie empties it straight down. More beer is called for and they ply him with another, and another, then another.

I drive the cart back to the station, but my brain's rolling about my head so I can't see the road clearly. The horses seem to take the way they know. I hold the reins loosely, my hands not doing what I want them to and we almost knock a lady down as she crosses the street. I feel sick. Something bangs the back of my head. I try to keep my eyes open but they close anyway. I want to lay down and sleep. John sits in the back, laughs at me and shouts out when the cart swerves behind the galloping horses. I can't say how we make it back to the yard without accident, but when we do, I get down, leave the horses where they are. I can't think about anything now. I walk about because I don't know what to do. Everything's a blur. I think it must be the end of my shift but can't see the clock properly.

'Drunk on duty Tyler! It's ten minutes before you can leave. Where've you been?' shouts Mr. Morley, my boss. I stumble on hearing him, but can't see him and don't answer. 'Where are the others?' he calls. I can't speak and he must leave then, because there's no more calling. I'm soaked from the day's rain, try to get my oilskin coat off, but it doesn't slip from my shoulder. My hand seems not to hold it tightly enough. I must be in the watchman's hut and see the clerk, ask him to help me. Free of it, it falls beside the hose reel.

47

Brighton Thursday December 10th 1891

Annie Thomson is five years old. She is a happy, bright young girl, the sixth child of eight, living with her parents in a poverty stricken district of Brighton, a district that is possibly one of the poorest of slums in the town. Bedford Buildings is a row of houses, built in the early part of the century, there being no more than four feet from their front doors to the back walls of the houses in the next street. The house they live in has just three rooms consisting of a kitchen, a living room, and a bedroom. At the back is a yard measuring six by six feet, hardly enough to hang out a line of washing. Many homes share one privy and cesspit.

On the corner, between Upper Bedford Street and Bedford Buildings, George Ward runs a pub, and in many of the streets, pigs and other animals are kept, neither of which helps the residents' in their fight for clean air and water. It is not just the dirty water and sour air they contend with. The buildings in front and behind, are so tightly packed together, they rarely have the sun on their backs when they go out, never mind it reaching through the small windows into living spaces.

Annie and her family are used to their lives here, having never had the opportunity to live elsewhere. Annie's father is a milkman, so at least they ha7e fresh milk every day. Her mother is a laundress which means the house is constantly full of wet or drying washing, causing year round moisture to run down the walls. At this time of year, even the fire struggles to keep the damp at bay and many layers of clothing are worn to compensate. Harold Thomson enters from the increasingly wet day, into an almost identical atmosphere. He kisses his wife and greets the children.

'Grace, this weather's got to end soon, surely. We might as well have no roof over our heads for all the water running down the walls!' he says, a smile playing across his lips. He knows all too well that Grace's laundry work makes the difference between eating and going without.

'There's so much Harold. I can't seem to get through it… and customers are expecting it to be finished.'

'Come on. Come and help your mother… There's something you can all do to make it go faster.'

With the children to help, Grace finally sees the end of her day's work but there is no let-up in the soapy, cloying air and two of her children have persistent coughs. She is afraid for them, her thoughts moving often to the threat of consumption, and she is constantly looking out for tell-tale signs of blood. Even though her chores are done, she is not able to rest. They need to eat. They rarely have more than two meals a day with just a crust of bread, or bowl of flour gruel for breakfast, but Grace always aims to provide something more nourishing in the evening.

'I need some more firewood and an egg, Harold. Would you get me some while I sort the children out?'

'I'm not warmed yet from being outside. Frank can go for them. Perhaps he can take Annie as well.'

'If you think so.'

'Frank. Annie. Put your coats and scarves on and do this bit of shopping for your mother. Here're some pennies. A bundle of firewood and one egg from Mr. Watson's grocery shop in Upper Bedford Street. You know where it is, so it shouldn't take you long. Here, have another penny to buy some chestnuts, as a special treat.'

'Thank you, father,' says Frank. He makes sure Annie is well wrapped up, stopping to adjust her hat to cover her head, before opening the front door. It is about eight o'clock on that Thursday evening, when Annie and her nine year old brother walk up the narrow passageway between houses, and under the arch at the top of Bedford Buildings, where the area meets Upper Bedford Street. They turn right onto a road lined with all manner of shops, and pass one which has bundles of wood cheaper than Mr. Watsons, and chestnuts too.

'Shall we get them here,' says Annie. 'The chestnuts look nice.'

The purchases are made, and they find themselves back on the street, where the rain is falling more heavily than ever. They hurry to the designated shop for their last buy.

'We can't take these things into the shop Annie.'

'Why not.'

'Well… Mr. Watson might think we're trying to steal them.'

'But we'll tell him where we got them from.'

'I don't think he'd believe us. You take my cap to keep the firewood and chestnuts in and I'll go for the egg. I promise I won't be a minute,' he says. 'Wait for me out here and keep as close to the window as you can to keep out of the rain.'

'See. I wasn't long, was I?' Frank says as he steps from the shop, and looking round for Annie finds that he is talking to himself. She is not there. The rain is still steady but even while he has been inside, the wind has increased, now driving the rain towards him as he looks up the road. He calls her name. He runs up and down. He feels angry with her for not staying outside, and worries that he might just break the egg, for he has no more money to replace it. When he cannot find her, he makes his way home, hoping she has gone back by herself.

Frank arrives about half past eight, drenched through, unhappy with his sister and needing to set down his egg while it is still in one piece. On entering the house, he asks his parents if his sister has come home.

'What do you mean?' asks his mother. 'Surely, she's with you.'

'No. I left her outside the shop with the bundle of wood we bought, while I went inside for the egg. I was only in there a minute mother, but when I came out, she was gone. I looked all up and down the street and called her name but she had disappeared, so I came home thinking she had gone ahead.'

He is suddenly afraid for both himself and his sister. Harold tries to reassure his anxious wife and children that Annie will be safe somewhere, puts on his coat, scarf and hat and goes to look for her. The night has become stormy even in that short time, the rain already dripping down his collar before he reaches the end of the buildings. His mind, full of how Annie will be, out in this wind and rain, he goes first on the route he knows they will have taken and then moves onto other adjoining streets.

'Have you seen Annie?' he calls to anyone he sees. Nobody has seen her. It is as if she has never existed. After about half an hour he is already feeling hopeless. Annie never strays far from home. Even when she goes to her friends to play, she is always home on time. He cannot imagine where she will be, and in hurrying through streets without knowing where he is going, finds himself covering the same ground twice. He needs help. He runs across Eastern Road, up Sutherland Road, past Kemptown Station in Coalbrook Road, all the paths already sloshing with water, great puddles collecting in the holes in the roadways. As he reaches the top of the hill, he can hear the rain washing down the street and it feels to him that part of his life is washing away with it. His clothing is saturated, his face wet with a mixture of rain and tears. Calling her name constantly he arrives at Freshfield Road, bursts through the door of the local police station, and leans his tired body against the counter to help his breathing.

'My good man. Whatever is it that brings you here in such a state?'

'My name's Harold Thomson and my little girl's gone missing. She's only five. I need some help to find her!'

The words come rushing from his body like the rivulets in the street. The policeman takes up pen and paper.

'Let's take down some detail, Mr. Thomson. What's she wearing?'

'A coat, hat and scarf.'

'Colour?'

Oh. Mm… well the coat's brown with some black fancy stuff on it. My wife was given it for her. It's a bit big for her though at the moment. She's wearing a black hat and the scarf is red… Gloves to match. Can't you hurry? I need to find her now… It's getting late.'

'Mr. Thomson. I realise this is exceedingly difficult for you, but we do need to know what we're looking for. Just be patient a while and my officers will have all they need to make a thorough search. Now. Does she have any friends she might have gone to?'

'Yes, but I've already been to those and she's not there.'

'Where was she last seen?'

'Frank… he's my son… left her outside Mr. Watson's grocers and when he came out, she'd gone.'

Desperate now, he persuades the police to accompany him in a search without any further questioning. Several men are hurriedly divided into groups, each to take a different area of the eastern side of Brighton. The main group, including Harold, begin once again at the shop where Annie had last been, only a few hundred yards from her home. As the search begins, Annie's mother, neighbours and friends join them. They search for most of the night despite the chilling cold and driving rain. They ask everyone they see. Shouts of 'Annie' ring out into the night, mingle in the wind and are lost to anyone who might just be about.

Not a fragment is found to suggest that Annie has been in any part of the town. Not a glimmer of hope is heard or seen. The search is abandoned in the early hours of the morning in the expectation that some news of her whereabouts will be heard of the next day. All the searchers silently pray that she has become lost and taken in, as a kindness, during the terrible night's weather.

Harold, leaves his distressed wife with their eldest girl, and begins looking for his missing child in the morning. The storm has passed, allowing a more thorough search of the area. His mind fills with any number of tragic outcomes which, while he attempts to keep them at bay, create lurid pictures before his eyes. His feet are heavy with weariness and many times he realises he is not really looking at all but simply wandering the streets in what is rapidly becoming vain hope. As the hours pass, people fill the roads, heading for work or shopping maybe. He stops to inquire of them, but nobody has seen her. As for the general public, growing rumours abound. People call on neighbours and friends to share the dreadful news, each one embellishing it with their own views. Had Harold stood still in the street, he would have heard the whispers, 'Have you heard?' 'There's a little girl gone missing.' 'Last night in that terrible storm.' 'Something horrible's happened to her, you mark my words.' Harold is not listening though, and if he had been, he would not have been able to take it in. Completely worn out, he returns home.

48

Brighton Friday December 11th 1891

My eyes open to the sky, grey and heavy. My head beats. The ground is wet beneath me but I can't think where I am. I sit up and everything goes hazy, lie down again as fear creeps up my spine. I think it's a field I'm in and when I manage to sit again, see it's the one close to home. How did I come to be here? Have I been here long? I think I must be late for work but don't know which day it is. I stand slowly, feel the aches in my body, see I wear my railway coat still. As I stagger towards the station, I try to think what might have brought me to this place, but the last I remember is driving the cart, being in the goods yard. I drank ale... Oh, dear Lord... please let it not be so... but I know I did... I broke the pledge... and everything it means to father. I can't walk on... the thought fills me with dread. What have I done? I bend with bile reaching my throat... see the marks on my clothes... damp, rust coloured... blood? Did I fight? Who? What over? I don't understand. Has the drink robbed me of my senses? How will I explain it?

When I reach the yard, I borrow threepence from two men and go to the baths. After that I feel better, cleaner at least, even if my mind still churns. The men look at me, whispering. Mr. Morley, and John talk for a long time together; turn their faces to me as they speak. I want to know what they say but can't move towards them for the fear that rages in me. My head is so heavy I can hardly lift it. I move away to part of the yard that's hidden from them all.

Mr. Morley finds me sitting down, not working and I wait for him to tell me off, but he puts a hand on my shoulder, sits next to me. I think I'm about to be fired.

'Freddie,' he says, 'you've been foolish… you're probably still under the influence of the ale today… I should fire you, but I'm not going to. I know what John and his friends did. It was inexcusable and I wish you'd been strong enough not to have been drawn in by their nastiness.'

'I'm sorry, Mr. Morley.'

'Well, it's done now, but I expect better of you in future. Stay here until your shift ends… it'll be nine o'clock now as you were late in. I'll make sure you're paid for the day.'

'Thank you, Mr. Morley.'

He leaves me. My heart beats so fast I think it might explode. I take deep breaths to calm myself, go back to my thinking, try desperately to remember what happened between leaving the goods yard last night and opening my eyes this morning. Nothing is there. No inkling of deeds, no colour, no light. Just a huge black hole. I wonder at the power of the devil's drink.

49

Two corporation gardeners, William Cooper and David Baker, begin work that morning, tending to the trees lining the road, in Rock Street.

'I'm glad we got this job today,' says David, 'I wouldn't have wanted to be out here in that weather we had yesterday. Proper storm was that.'

'Right,' replies William. 'We'd have been soaked to our under garments and no mistake.'

By about lunch time, much of the work is complete, when William comes across something for which he needs a different tool.

'I'm going to the shed for something,' he tells David.

The shed is in a corner of a field extending from the Eastern Road to the back of Rock Street and is enclosed by a wall with two gates, which are always locked. With no key to the gate on St Mark's Street, he has to climb the lowest part of the wall. William tramps across the field, sodden from the storm, his boots soaking up the water. He finds the shed door standing slightly open and this is unusual, even though it is not normally locked. He peers inside.

'Oh. dear Lord,' he utters, his hands immediately covering his face. 'Oh. dear Lord!' A small child lays on the floor just inside the shed, her clothes in disarray and bloodstained, her under garments removed, her face and hair matted with blood. William's legs shake as he runs back, climbs the wall into St Mark's Street and round the corner into Rock Street. Out of breath, more from shock than any distance he has run, he calls out,

'There's murder been done David. Come with me.'

While William goes to find a policeman, David waits back at the shed, unable to avert his eyes from the scene before him. *Who can have done such evil?* he thinks. Her clothes are dragged up to her waist, blood covers her lower body, and at her feet a cloth cap, trampled on, with firewood and chestnuts scattered close by. He takes a step back outside to breath and sees a doctor's carriage stopped by the road.

'I need a doctor to come over to the shed as soon as he can,' he tells the driver, his voice urgent. 'Will you get him please?'

The doctor pronounces the little girl dead, noting without touching the body further, that her hands are filthy as are her clothes. Her small pinafore once white, red with her blood. Her face is swollen and her throat distinctly marked. While the two men wait for what seems hours, they speak only in low whispers.

'How long do you think she's been here?' Asks David, thinking of his own children safe in the comfort of their home.

'I'm not able to say just yet. She may have been here most of the night, but there'll be an autopsy which will tell us more.'

David is now shaking, his mind no longer in charge, given way to shock.

'Are you alright?' the doctor asks him, seeing his disposition. 'Here sit down before you fall.'

William finds PC Farncombe in Sussex Square, not a great distance from the shed, and they arrive out of breath, and he is despatched immediately to the Freshfield Road police station for the ambulance. When loaded, its grim contents are sent to the morgue.

Annie Thomson's father, Harold, is sent for by the police at about one thirty.

'Mr. Thomson. I'm afraid the body of a child has been discovered. We need you to make an identification.'

Harold feels the groan rather than hears it, coming as it does involuntarily, his worst fears about to be confirmed. He is taken through dark corridors to a small windowless room right at the rear of the premises, where he is forced to look upon the body of his little Annie, once so joyous and full of spirit, now so still and cold, not twenty four hours previously so bright and beautiful; now so sullied and brutalised.

'Annie!' He cries out. 'Annie!' And he goes forward to touch her, to be close to her, a natural parent's desire to hold his child overtaking him, but is instantly held back.

'Please Mr. Thomson. You mustn't touch her before she's been fully examined. We'll get someone here for you.'

198

Harold walks out of the police station with his son and stands for a minute. Neither can believe what they witnessed. Harold does not want to go home because he will have to tell his wife, his family, what has befallen their little girl. It will become reality then. Now they can both suspend belief. It cannot be true. It never once occurred to Harold that his daughter would become the victim of some depraved animal, of what must surely be a deranged mind, for no sane human being could inflict such trauma on another.

He is in shock. Beyond tears himself, he holds his son allowing him to weep and finally, they begin the walk down Freshfield Road and into Upper Bedford Street. Turning left into Bedford Buildings, Harold notices, not for the first time, the darkness created by tall buildings and walls lining the all too narrow pathway. His home is without a front garden and therefore even closer to the opposing wall than some. Taking hold of his son's arm, he opens the front door, sees, the expectant faces of his children turned towards him, clearly full of hope, for why else would their father have been called to the station if not to collect Annie. Grace stands.

'Where is she Harold. Surely, they've found her.'

'Yes, my dear,' he says, trying to maintain his own strength to counteract the imminent vulnerability that will instantly fill the room. 'They found her body.'

'What d'you mean, her body? Has she met with an accident?'

'Grace,' he says, looking at his children, so much terror inside him he does not know how to form the words. He takes Grace's arms and leads her to a seat.

'Please… sit down Grace… Our… our Annie… she's dead,' and saying it, the fact finally registering, he buries his face in her lap and weeps. Grief sweeps the tiny claustrophobic room. Grace utters a sob, her heart suddenly beating too fast, her hands shaking uncontrollably. She wants to ask, how? She wants to be told, to know the details of her Annie's demise. She wants Harold to take her, there and then to see her child, but no words come. All she can do is stare into the room, to her children whose faces are creased and tear stained. She sees her eldest daughter cradling Frank in her arms, smoothing his hair, kissing his forehead. Her son who had left his sister outside a shop. When Harold finally looks up at her, she asks,

'Where is she? Where's Annie? Where's Annie Harold? Take me to see her. She needs her mother. She needs me to hold her; to keep her warm,' her voice rises in volume until she is shouting at him, drumming on his chest and then in a fit of screaming, she pushes him away. 'Take me to see my Annie.'

He holds her close to calm her and whispers that she cannot see her until after the autopsy.

'How did she die Harold?'

'It was no accident Grace. She's been… murdered.' Grace's hands fly to her open mouth. 'At the hands of a savage. It's a sight I'll never forget and won't let you see.'

'Oh no. Please dear God no,' and she is limp in his arms from fainting.

50

Rock Street, and the surrounding area, hum with activity for the rest of the afternoon. Police begin their search for the culprit as soon as Annie is found and identified. People come forward with sightings of a man talking to children and carrying a child in his arms. They name streets and provide information regarding the nature of him and the clothes he wore. Gradually a picture emerges of the route the man took on the night of December 10th, between seven and nine fifteen.

By five o'clock the Brighton Argus prints its afternoon edition, reporting the story, and going so far as to produce a plan of the field and a cross to mark the spot where Annie has lain. Horror occupies the town, its people shocked to the core from learning of these initial details. They gather together in small groups, gossiping, sharing their opinions of what they read or hear, opinions based largely on emotions rather than any factual basis. Some are telling of what they saw the night before, often grossly exaggerated for the purpose of their own importance. Edward buys a paper for his father, who is stunned at the events unfolding.

'I can't believe she lay there all night', he says to his brother David as they work. 'Let's finish for today. I don't think we'll be able to do any more... our minds won't be on it.'

Alice knows the child has been found but had not known until Alfred arrived, that Annie had been murdered.

'How dreadful. The poor child... her mother. I know what it is to lose a daughter, but at least our loss was through illness. To lose a child at the hands of another... I can't imagine what she must be going through.'

'What the little girl would have suffered,' adds Lily.

'They're saying she'd been outraged too,' Alfred says in a low voice.

'Dear God. Who can have done such a depraved thing?' asks Lily.

'Mr. Tyler. There's someone needs to see you,' says Rebecca at the parlour door.

'Bring him in please. It's too cold to be standing outside.'

'He asks for you to go out to see him.'

Alfred huffs and puffs but goes anyway, while mother and I share a smile. I hear murmured voices in the hall, then the door shuts, but Alfred does not come back. I find him leaning against the door, his face pale, his eyebrows knit at the top of his nose.

'What is it?' He takes my hand and leads me to the kitchen, asks the children and Rebecca to go and stay with Lily, then sits me down at the table. I feel his hands trembling in mine.

'Is it Freddie? What's happened? Is he hurt? Has he met with an accident? Tell me Alfred.'

'Freddie's been arrested my dear.'

'What could he have possibly done to be arrested for?'

'Murder,' he says.

I see tears roll down his cheeks, unchecked by any sense of manliness, and I feel the world stop, the only sound in the room the ticking of the clock, the only movement, its mechanism.

'I'm not sure I understand you Alfred. Our son couldn't do such a thing. I won't believe it. How can it be? What do you mean, murder?'

'Of that little girl, my dear. The one found in the shed.'

'Oh no. Our Freddie? Our loving son Freddie? It has to be a mistake Alfred.'

'The policeman says he's been identified, Alice. I know it has to be proved but all the same he's been arrested for it… I think it best we tell the family straight away.' We go together to the parlour, and I hear Alfred tell it all again.

'What shame he's brought to our door!' says mother, her face old and twisted as though she's swallowed something bitter. 'I knew he'd bring us down! This family's never seen the like.'

'Mother. He's not been found guilty. He'll just be a suspect at the moment. It doesn't mean it's true,' I say, 'How can you even think it?'

'It's fair made me weak. I should go home and let the others know. Perhaps I'll see you tomorrow,' and with that Lily leaves us all in a state of utter shock.

There is little sleep to be had in Rock Street, save for the sleep of total exhaustion which lasts but minutes rather than hours. Alice and Alfred spend most of it on their knees, praying to God for strength, for guidance, not knowing how they will cope in the days to come. When Alfred arrives in the kitchen, with daylight dawning, he finds Rebecca and his children at the table, hands cradling cups of tea as though the warmth alone might be a comfort. Not one face among them is without puffy eyes, tear tracts and drawn cheeks. They must have been there all night, stunned and afraid for their Freddie, but also for themselves. This room, which has known so much fun and laughter over the years, is now their hiding place, a safeness trapped within its walls.

Alice will not come downstairs. She lays in bed, too tired to sleep, though she keeps her eyes closed against the day. She is numb. She feels nothing, her head so crammed with thoughts of her son, of how she must have failed him somehow. Attempting to understand why such a gentle placid person should commit so terrible a deed, she thinks of his birth, remembers how ecstatic she was that God had been gracious and kind, had saved him. The memory breaks her. She rails against God,

'What sort of God are you? Did you save him just to murder a little girl? Was it part of your great plan for him, for her, for us? You are a cruel God. It was a cruel kindness!' She sobs uncontrollably, the shouts and cries reaching the kitchen. Nobody moves.

'Let her be,' says Alfred.

Across town, Grace is also in bed. Harold looks after the children and makes sure his wife is calm in between times. She succumbs to intense grief, a grief so all consuming, her body convulses. Like Alice's, her mind is full of thoughts and questions. Why? How could her little one come to such an untimely and tragic death. How could she have prevented it? Two families instantly fractured. So many lives. Parents, grandparents, children, brothers and sisters, aunts and uncles. Their worlds shatter like shards of glass raining down on them, destroying the very fabric of their beings. One event. Two families, broken by grief. Crushed by shame. Two mothers, who in different circumstances might have consoled each other, but who, under the bleakness of death, so cruelly caused, would never meet.

My eyes open to Alfred looking at me. He sits on the edge of our bed, his face grey, his mouth turned down.

203

'How do you feel now Alice?'

'I feel nothing...empty... an empty vessel... all its contents used up. What did you learn from the court, Alfred? Will Freddie be coming home soon?' He looks away and I see his fingers rub the palms of his hands as though scratching an itch. When he turns back to me, there are tears in his eyes... My Alfred who I've only seen cry once before, so I know instantly the news is bad. I raise myself up against the pillows, take his hands, kiss his fingers, ask him to tell me. He does. He says it was awful, the detail... the abhorrent act described so clearly. I know he leaves much out. He will protect me from the worst of it, but what he does say is enough. Freddie formally charged and detained. There's silence between us for a moment, so I try to make sense of it, but I still feel nothing, as though this's not about my child, but some unrelated event far beyond our lives.

When he next speaks the softness has gone and there is a hardening of his eyes.

'He broke the pledge. Thursday night he was drunk. I wonder how long ago he broke it. Has he come back to us used to the ale?'

'No Alfred. He's been here for months. When have you seen him drink? When have you smelt it on him? Never!'

'So why Alice? After all this time. Why?' He yells. 'Why now after all he's been through. After keeping the pledge so long. Did I not warn him of the outcome should he take the drink? Was I not clear enough? Did I not explain the evil things that taking alcohol would lead to? And this Alice... This most heinous of crimes against such a tiny child. How can I call him my son after this?'

He treads the floor, backwards and forwards, shakes his hands in the air as if to demonstrate the magnitude of his anger. I stare at him surprised at the speed with which the atmosphere has changed. I find strength in his weakness though.

'Alfred, my dear. We don't yet know the full circumstances. But he's our son. He came from us. He's made from you and me. Whatever he's done he'll only ever be our son, and though I won't forgive him if he's guilty of this act, I'll always love him. Alfred, my dear, you must find it in your heart to keep loving him too.'

51

'Pause you who read this, and think for a moment of the long chain of iron or gold, of thorns or flowers, that would never have bound you, but for the formation of the first link on one memorable day.' Charles Dickens: Great Expectations (1860)

My solicitor, Mr. Samuels, visits me the Sunday after I'm arrested. No other visitors have been allowed and I want to see father so much.

'Freddie. We need to discuss many aspects of this terrible situation so that on Tuesday, when we appear in court again, I'm able to support you as best I can.' Mr. Samuels sits beside me on the bench, but he keeps a distance from me. I wonder if I smell. I haven't washed since I've been here.

'I want you to tell me as much as you can about the night of Thursday December 10th. Don't worry about getting things in the right order for now, just say what happened.'

'I can only say what I remember, Mr. Samuels. The men goaded me. They said I lied about Canada and being engaged… they said I wasn't a man because I wouldn't take the drink… It made me mad Mr. Samuels and I wanted to defend myself… so I took what they bought me. And then they said I'd met Eleanor down the Lanes and that made me even madder, so I went to hit John… he moved though… I drank everything they bought me after that.'

'What happened then Freddie?'

'Well… he made me drive the horses back to the station… I managed it… remember it was difficult… I suppose I was so drunk…

I didn't know what I was doing you see. I remember getting back to the depot though because I couldn't get my leggings off and I think someone helped me in the end.'

'Who made you drive back?'

'John Watts. He tells me what to do mostly.'

'And when you left the station, what did you do?'

'Well… that's the thing Mr. Samuels. I don't remember anything else till I woke up in the field… I've tried to… I've had nothing to do here but think about it… I can't remember anything at all.'

'If you're unable to remember any of the events after that time, I can't put you on the stand… you have no personal defence to offer… do you understand what I'm saying?'

'I think so Mr. Samuels… I know I'll look guilty whatever I say.'

'Alright then. I'll next see you on Tuesday at the court. Is there anything else you want to tell me, or anything you wish to ask?'

'No.'

When he's gone, I walk round the walls of my cell, my mind full of terrible thoughts of what I am accused of, my fate and I pray it might not be true. Food is pushed through the cell door three times a day but I can't face it, not because I'm not hungry, but because it's tasteless gruel I'm not used. I've already lost weight. My trousers fall down and I have to keep pulling them up. I haven't shaved since I've been here. There's no point. There's nobody to see me. Nobody who matters anyway, and I think I must have the start of a beard.

On Tuesday December 15th, Freddie appears again before the judge, this time without the garments he wore on the night in question, for those have been sent to Dr. Clarke, an eminent Home Office Analyst in London. With news of this sitting, enormous crowds gather outside the Town Hall, attempt to gain access, though largely being denied, for all entrances are copiously guarded by police officers. It is a short session. Evidence is still being collated, and the case cannot move forward until Dr. Clarke's report is received. Freddie is remanded again, taken from the dock to await transport to Lewes Gaol.

The mass outside grows during the sitting, becoming increasingly hostile as they wait. They already find him guilty, wanting to lynch him for his unspeakable deed, but it is incumbent upon the force to protect their prisoner, and so his departure is postponed until late in the afternoon, amid hopes that the crowd will disperse. It does not. It gathers in strength and while they wait with a measure of patience on one side of the building, preparations are made to take

206

Freddie out on the opposite side. When it is believed safe to do so, the prison van is positioned at the correct exit, and Freddie is escorted out, accompanied by the Chief Constable, a Superintendent, and other officers. They are not to be unnoticed however. Before they make it to the steps of the van, a large group of people run down the narrow street, shouting, and jeering, encouraging others to follow them. Freddie is pushed up the steps from behind, quickly followed by his escorts. One officer only just manages to scramble inside before closing the door.

Inside, the van is close to darkness, only three small narrow slots on either side for ventilation. With it being high off the ground, suspended between two large rear wheels, what occurs next is frightening for all its occupants. Those outside, denied their entreaties, throw themselves at it, whereupon it sways initially and then, with more people joining in, its movement backwards and forwards becomes greatly exaggerated, so that inside they fear it might topple completely. The crowd consists of all manner of people, not just men and women but small children, even babes in arms. Not just the healthy but those with coughs and crutches, hobble along to take part in the frenzy. Not just the local population, but those who have travelled from other parts of Sussex to get a glimpse of the man who has killed a child.

All the while there are shouts of, 'murderer. Just let me have him. I'll make sure he never does such a thing again,' 'murderous villain'. The horses are frantic, held as they are by more of those rushing to the scene, before an officer manages to push his way through, mount the driving seat awkwardly, and force a passage out of the terrifying mob. It is nine miles to Lewes, the road not being particularly good and at times quite narrow. As soon as the main streets are left behind, the horses begin to gallop, but even so, many of the crowd run after them for some distance.

'What's it like inside the prison?' Freddie asks once he has recovered from the ordeal.

'We don't know,' says an officer laughing sarcastically, 'we've never been in it. We've had no cause to since we've never broken the law!'

The Chief Constable tells his men not to talk to the prisoner, but then says in a kindlier voice, 'You'll find out soon.'

Freddie tries to calm himself while becoming more and more afraid of how it will be. His thoughts turn to Eleanor. His beautiful girl.

207

He wonders how she is, how she has taken the news, and then to William, who he is sure would have stayed by him. But if William had lived, they would still be in Canada and this would not be happening. A picture of his mother, clear as day, appears before him, his mind struggling to comprehend what she now thinks of him. And there is Maud, his beloved sister, his rock all the while he was growing up. He has let them all down and he will suffer for it, even as he will suffer for the unimaginable thing he is supposed to have done. At several places along the route, groups of townsfolk gather to witness the passing prison van, their shouts of derision forced through the slots on the air. Freddie flinches with each onslaught until they reach the prison gates.

52

By contrast, on the following day, those who had been ready to kill Freddie themselves in fits of passion, are now out again, the anger dissipated to be replaced by sorrow. It is as though somebody has thrown a soft comforting blanket across the town, keeping out cold wind and rain. Keeping in a warmth generated by an understanding of grief. Never before has Brighton seen thousands come out to pay their respects. The funeral carriages wait and the entire distance from there to the sea is crammed with onlookers. Just after midday, the tiny elm coffin, so highly polished, the bearer's face is reflected from it, is placed in the open car, and surrounded by floral tributes from family and friends, Annie's school, her father's employer, market traders, and the local publican, who raised a sum of £30 to aid the cost of her funeral. Tributes from complete strangers and from places far outside Brighton, sit among them, the manner of her death touching so much of the county.

Grace weeps openly as she exits the archway, led by Harold, and takes her place in the first of the mourning coaches. Those nearby are visibly moved, as the cortege begins its solemn journey through the streets of Brighton. Travel is slow, befitting the occasion, and watched by groups numbering hundreds as it negotiates the narrow streets. The day is grey in every conceivable way, from the cloudy sky, through the misery openly displayed, down into black attire that lines almost every street, and onto the grimy roads through which they journey.

December Saturday 19th sees the resumption of the inquest into Annie's death. Freddie, now realising the gravity of the charge against him, sobs bitterly during witness evidence. A letter he wrote to his parents has not been sent to them, instead held as evidence against him and is now read to the court in full. In their next edition, the Brighton Gazette prints Freddie's letter for the world to know.

With Dr. Clarke's report still unavailable, a further remand is granted. Nevertheless, the jury finds that she has met her death by foul means at the hands of Alfred Maurice Tyler, returning a verdict of wilful murder. Freddie is led to the cells, to await transport back to Lewes Gaol, but before he can be taken, he has a seizure, followed by two others. Police surgeon, Dr Pugh, confirms that Freddie does indeed suffer from fits. Once completed, Dr. Clarke's report is put before another session, Freddie's clothes, worn on December 10th being produced. Evidence is given of where blood appears, and at the conclusion of the hearing, Freddie is committed for trial at the Lewes Assizes.

Freddie grows used to a strict regime over the weeks. His habit of waking early is not to be overcome, however hard he tries, so he has usually washed and made himself ready for the day well before breakfast. The food, though basic and unappetising, has to be eaten. He does not want to starve to death while there is still hope, as Mr. Samuels has told him there is. He trusts in God that it might come to pass. After breakfast and slopping out, he is put to work, never quite knowing what will be brought to him. His only respite is a daily exercise session and a weekly service in the prison chapel, so he is mostly isolated. The overseers are strict, ensuring every prisoner works as hard as possible throughout the day, but he does not object because it allows him to lose himself at least for daylight hours.

It is the evenings and nights that are most burdensome. However hard he tries, in the stillness and silence of his cell, his thoughts become uncontrollable. He worries about Elly, even though she says she loves him still, and can only conjure up the distress she must feel. He thinks of William, the only other person outside his family he has come to love, and he is thankful that his dear friend is not alive to witness this downfall. But wherever his train of thought begins each night, it always ends up in the same way. It always returns to the night of December tenth. *Why can't I remember? How could I have done such a thing? Where did it all begin?* It always comes down to the 'if onlys'. If only I had not lost control and taken the beer, I would have gone home that night. If only I had not needed that operation, I would still be in London. If only we had not returned to England, I would still be on my own land, in my own home, in Canada. If only William had not died. Was that it? Was that the first link in the chain of events that had finally led to this small, cold, dark prison cell? Round and round, they go, these merciless thoughts, until on most nights, sleep comes purely from mental exhaustion.

53

We make ourselves eat. The whole family comes to us, Rebecca and Emily cooking between them. We sit where we can. I have no appetite for the usual formality. Everything seems pointless now, but we do our best with shallow conversation. Alfred has forbidden newspapers in the house… they are full of every word spoken by everyone involved… apart from Freddie's of course. Lily sits quietly, tight lipped all the while but I see she eats well. She hasn't spoken to me in days, although I know Alfred has tried to persuade her not to shut me out. I think she blames me. I'm sad. I would love to have her to talk to, but maybe it's for the best at the moment. I need her support, not her anger. Even so I can't bear the silence between us, so say,

'You look splendid tonight mother.' After a short hesitation, she replies,

'It's about standards Alice. But I see you've not maintained yours.'

Each of Lily's sons turn to her with expressions between shock and horror. Alfred looks to me and his face says, do not respond Alice. He need not be worried. Everything smoulders beneath the surface of our façade without deliberately adding to it. When Lily leaves, Emily goes with her and I walk through the scullery and out into the night. It's bitterly cold and dark, but I need the chill air to remind me I'm alive. Enough light shines from the windows and street lamps to see the garden and I'm suddenly flooded with memories… laughing at starlings in the spring… a podgy little hand sowing seeds… pulling carrots in the warmth of summer sun… Maud and Freddie in the bath after a day on the beach. All so long ago, they melt in the past and take my life with them.

The children don't know what to do with themselves. Like us they are afraid to be seen, to be looked at, pointed at, afraid of the gossip that must be rife in Kemptown. Maud has already been told she's no longer required at Chesham Road. I think it premature, but suppose connections with even a suspected murderer are to be avoided. I go inside, feel the warmth of the fires on my face, see Rebecca and Maud clearing away after the meal. I look at them, try to smile, let them know their work is appreciated. They both cry silent tears and it breaks my heart all over again to know the pain they are in, these two women who mean so much to Freddie, who love him deeply, who do not understand what has happened to him.

Another Sunday dawns. My favourite day, normally full of sunshine even in the darkest days of winter, now takes on a metamorphosis. I want to wake to a different life. If I can only sleep long enough it might just happen. The children go to number eleven after breakfast, to read the newspapers with their uncles. They are unsure if they want to know. Knowing makes it real, but equally, I think the darkness of not knowing gnaws away at them, lets their minds invent the story, create lurid images that may be graver than the truth.

Reverend Williamson gazes across the congregation, his church packed to overflowing, and wonders if this is because those who do not normally attend church seek to indulge in gossip. He sees, unsurprisingly, none of the Tyler family. He knows them well, understands the effect Freddie's arrest is having on them, and thinks this is the first time, in all the years he has known them, they have not been here. His sadness is reflected in his sermon, his tone of voice leaving those who listen in no doubt that he is troubled by these events. He prays for little Annie Thomson, her family, prays for God to keep her safe through eternity. He prays for Freddie and his family, ignoring the murmur circulating about the congregation, asks God to look favourably on them through their crisis. He gives a sharp warning to all, reminds them not to exaggerate the story, to base their thinking on facts as they emerge, and not be swayed by emotion. But he sees many of them whisper and thinks his words fall on deaf ears.

The day passes slowly for Alfred, even though he goes often to see Alice and Lily, looking in on the workshop though he does not stay to be drawn into conversation. He sits in the kitchen with Rebecca as she makes work for herself, tries to read, but the words on the page do not stay in his head, and eventually he goes to the parlour, the fire warming and soothing his aching body. He does not realise he has slept until he wakes to find the time is five o'clock.

'Where are the children?'

'They're still at your mothers,' Rebecca says. He would have preferred them to be home by now, but does not dwell on it. Rebecca cooks dinner, although he cannot say who will to want to eat it. By eight, there's still no sign of the children.

Rebecca answers the door, and shows Freddie's godparents into the parlour. Alfred shakes their hands, thankful that they each clasp his firmly. No one speaks for a while after they have sat.

'Thank you for calling on us.'

'Alfred. I'm pleased to find you alone,' says Mr. Hargreaves. 'We've come specially to speak with you in the first instance.'

'It's wise. My family is devastated. I pray that your lives will not be adversely affected by Freddie's situation. I would apologise to all three of you right now... but he's not been found guilty yet... We're hoping that there's been some ghastly mistake.'

'Alfred.' says Dr Sayer. 'We've come tonight with the express intent of telling you something we realise now... I should have told you long ago'... He says no more, simply looks from Alfred to the others as though he can't continue.

'What can it be that matters more than Freddie's current demise?'

'Twenty six years ago Freddie had a convulsion... I was called to attend him... It wasn't a convulsion Alfred...'

'What then? Why would you say it was if it wasn't?'

'Freddie has epilepsy.' It hangs in the air between them.

'Why didn't you tell us the truth?'

'I'll explain later. Please let Dr Sayer finish telling you of the medical aspects,' says Mr. Hargreaves. Alfred looks towards the doctor, puzzled and shocked, and unable to believe there's yet more to contend with.

'Many children suffer from convulsions for one reason or another and they grow out of them. What I saw that day was in fact an epileptic fit, where the body jerks, the brain having lost its power temporarily, to order itself. Epileptics also suffer from absences without experiencing the full fit.'

'His 'nowhere times'? Is that what they are? Are you telling me that he's suffered this most of his life and we didn't know?' Alfred's face reflects his horror at this news and for a while nobody speaks.

'Yes. I am'

'Why tell of it now?'

All three of them are uncomfortable. Mrs. Hargreaves bows her head, unable to look at Alfred. Mr. Hargreaves squirms in his seat while Dr Sayer sits forward with his elbows on his knees and his face cupped in his hands. The doctor looks up, his face so contrite Alfred almost feels sorry for him. It's clear that Freddie's godparents are feeling desperately pressured.

'During fits and periods of absence, a patient is in a state much like a coma. Afterwards they have no memory of the event... There's medical evidence to prove that sometimes one period of absence can lead directly into others... sometimes lasting for many hours. The patient doesn't fall, as in a fit, but continues in some way automatically... Alfred... It's known that during such prolonged absences, both men and women have committed murder, and had no inkling of their deeds.'

Dr. Sayer sits back, exhausted, and Alfred looks at the ceiling, closes his eyes, against the ache. He does not know what to think. His head hurts and his body feels so heavy.

'Why did you not tell us the truth all those years ago?' He hears resentment he can't control, and sees Mrs. Hargreaves shed a tear. Her husband takes her hand as he says,

'I'll explain it to you as best I can.'

Alfred sits back against the comfort of the chair, listening to Mr. Hargreaves' voice retell the events of so long ago. Questions arise in his mind, which they answer as the story unfolds, and slowly he begins to understand more about his son, as well as why Freddie's godparents had made such a decision and kept the secret for nearly thirty years. They apologise for their action, assuring Alfred that they would provide every support necessary.

'I don't know what to say. I can't process this. I need time to gather my thoughts, to tell Alice and the family... For now... I thank you for your belated honesty, your heartfelt apology. I'm sure your decision was taken in the best interests of us all. I can't say how Alice will feel, but I'm sure she'll speak with you soon.'

When they have departed, Alfred collapses in the chair and weeps again... He thinks he will drown in his own tears... never before has he cried so much.

54

Waking early Alfred feels the warmth and softness of Alice, and for a moment it seems like any ordinary morning, until the images of his dreams say otherwise. Muffled voices float up from the kitchen. He goes down to find the boys eating breakfast or readying themselves for work. There is a less than a cheery chorus of good morning. He sees anxiety on each of them and Edward says,

'Will I go to the workshop today?'

'If you wish to keep yourself busy, and enjoy the company of your uncles, it may be best for you. There's plenty to be doing, but don't think you must.'

'Father. We read the papers,' says Edward.

'I know.' And David says, 'We need to understand what's happening Father… to be prepared for what's to come'… He looks at his brothers, 'and for what we might have to deal with at work.'

'I know… it's fine. You're all of an age to comprehend Freddie's situation… your mother and me…we appreciate how your lives will change now… and that includes you Rebecca. All I ask is that you don't bring papers into our home, or talk about in it in your mother's hearing.'

'Is there anything we can do to help, Father?' Walter asks. He feels for all his children but maybe more so for these boys who can't hide at home as their sisters do.

'There is. Lily and Isobel will need much looking after… Maud and Harriet will help Rebecca during the day, but I hope when you return from work, you'll also help.'

He eats breakfast before the girls rise then sits in the parlour to compose himself. He must talk to Alice of last evening, but before that persuade her to write to Eleanor. She must get up today. He is not aware of how long he sits, but eventually goes to the bedroom. Alice opens her eyes; asks what day it is.

'Monday my dear.'

'Is that all. I thought it might be the end of the week by now.'

'I'm afraid not Alice. Will you get up today?'

'I've a mind not to.'

'Please do. There are things we must talk about… I need you my dear… our children need you… it's hard for all of us.'

By the time Alice arrives in the kitchen, it's eleven thirty, the girls having gone back to their room to do whatever they do up there. It's possibly the most bedraggled Alfred has ever seen Alice… her normally beautiful hair, knotted about her expressionless face and down her back, testament to hours of sleepless tossing.

'There's plenty of hot water, Mrs. Tyler. Would you like me to fetch some clean clothes while you wash?' asks Rebecca, attempting normality.

'Yes please. I suppose it'll help me feel better.'

'It will my dear. When you're ready, I'll be in the parlour.'

Alfred is right to make me get up. I can't spend life hiding under blankets, however much I long for it, and putting myself before him and the children is selfish. I admit to feeling more alive once washed and wearing clean attire… I wish my head could be turned inside out and scrubbed clean of every vile picture it holds… of each thought of what my son is accused of, how he's incarcerated alone… of questions I ask… what I've done or not done… why God would allow it… how I will ever live with the knowledge of that little girl brutally killed by one of *my* children. I sit next to Alfred. When he turns to me, I see his eyes are red from crying… how could I not have noticed his heart breaking too… for all the strength we expect from men, they are, after all, human. I stroke the hair from his brow, hold his face in my hands, tell him I'm sorry for not thinking of him.

'We may not come through this,' he says, 'but if we do, it will only be because we travel together… us and all our family. You must write to Eleanor, my dear… straight away. I'll take it to the shop and it'll get the night mail.'

'Yes. You're right.' He prepares the table with writing paper, squeezes my shoulders as he helps with the chair… says to call him if I need help. Before he leaves, he tends to the fire, pokes it about so its warmth reaches out to me… I hear him do the same in the kitchen. For a while I do nothing, only look at the paper, wonder what to write… how to tell it kindly… how to tell it at all… and when words begin to tumble out, I see that it's grief they speak of, not ordered thoughts for my daughter-in-law to be. By the time it's completed, the floor is littered with screwed up paper. I feel exhausted, as though those words have cost me the day's energy.

I make fresh tea for him when he returns from the shop. We sit in the kitchen, the stove throwing heat into the room.

'Have the girls been down?' he asks.

'No.'

'I think we should have some lunch,' he says, as he gets up and calls them down to eat. I begin taking things from the pantry, soon hear the galloping thumps on the stairs as they come through.

'What have you been doing girls?' I ask.

'Reading mostly,' says Maud, always their combined voice. 'The days are so long, aren't they?' I kiss each one on their pale cheeks and think reading is not all they've been doing, stroke Lily's and Isobel's hair as I bend towards them and Isobel flings her arms round my neck, says nothing but holds on tight. When everything is cleared away, the girls use the parlour for a change of scene. Alfred asks me to sit by the stove, brings a chair to sit opposite me. I have an awful feeling he's about to give me bad news because his face takes on a frown.

'Last evening, I had visitors... Freddie's godparents came... they gave me news of something... but I'm still not sure how I feel about it.'

I listen as he tells me, think of what they did all those years ago, anger rising as he gets to the end.

'How could they have done such a thing? It's not for them to choose what we must know.' Heat flushes through me as I speak, only the secret deed at the forefront of my mind. I get up, walk about the kitchen, shout at Alfred, as though the secret is entirely his fault. He lets me be, his patience, as always, a testament to his character. 'How dare they. They're meant to look after him, to be his guide, to support him, not behave like God!' When I calm down enough, he collects me in his arms, takes me back to the seat, says,

'Alice, I felt the same last night. I thought they'd exceeded their role... but now I think their decision was made in Freddie's interests... there was no malice in what they did... I believe it's haunted them ever since and now they're devastated... We mustn't let this deed colour our thinking, because there is some good news in the knowledge.'

'What can be good about it, Alfred?'

'There's research which proves Freddie may have committed this crime without knowing it.' He goes on to explain as much as he can, hope in his eyes and finally in my heart.

55

Eleanor trudges home wearily after a difficult day, her boss taking his frustration out on the girls. It is cold, the wind blowing from the east and chilling her right through her winter coat. She longs for some word from Freddie, she longs to be back in the open fields of Canada, for life here without him is almost unbearable. Closing the front door behind her she looks, as she does every day, to see if there is a letter, and to her relief, there is. She grabs it, finds enough energy to run up the stairs. Throwing off her coat and shoes, her favourite armchair surrounding her, she tears open the letter, noting immediately that it is not from Freddie.

'Dear Eleanor,

I am writing to you because there is dreadful news that none of us here want you to know of from other sources. I am afraid, my dear, that there is no easy way to tell you of this, so I must simply come out with it. Freddie has been arrested and is being held in police custody. He is being accused of the demise of a little girl from Brighton and we understand that he broke his pledge to his father on the evening it happened.

He says he cannot remember anything of this event but the evidence seems to point to him having done it. We understand taking drink, being drunk, would most likely cause a series of seizures lasting maybe up to eight or ten hours, and that it is quite possible he does not remember anything at all. We have come to understand that Freddie has a condition, kept from us when he was a young boy. I cannot write of this now, but we will tell you all about it when we see you.

We are all in deep shock, as I know you will be reading this, but I believe Freddie will want to see you. We have little news of how he manages as we have not been able to see him, so a visit from you will be good for him, and I must say, for us as well. I am making up a bed for whenever you can manage the journey.

It is with deep sorrow that I write. I trust your family will be supportive of you and provide some comfort. Please let us know when we might expect you. Freddie loves you dearly so remember this as you come to terms with my news.

Alice Tyler.'

She reads it again, slowly, as though by doing so the words will carry different meanings and what she thinks she has read will not be so. Her face pales as she sits back in the chair, rests her now weary head against the softness of its filling. She wants to seep into it, let it cover her, and blot out the world. She cannot believe it… but then why would Freddie's mother say something like this? Without realising she is crying, she stands at the sound of footsteps on the staircase, and moves towards the door as her brother enters.

'Eleanor. You haven't been down for dinner,' and seeing her unusually wan features he says, 'Whatever is it?'

She is not sure she should tell him, but deep within, she cannot manage what is to come without him. Her whole body trembles as she says,

'I must go to Brighton first thing in the morning, Robert.'

'Why?'

'It's Freddie. Something's happened and I must go to him.'

'What's happened? What's so urgent that you must go tomorrow? What about your work Eleanor?'

'I can't even think about work now. It's not important. Freddie's important and I want to go.'

'For goodness sake! Explain yourself.'

The letter in her hand crumples as she wrestles with telling him. Robert snatches it from her.

'No Robert. Please No!'

She cannot look at him. She is afraid of his reaction. After all, she hardly knows her brother, both having been apart for so long. She knows him to be kind, but also short tempered and intolerant.

'What? This is outrageous. The man you're about to marry has killed a little girl?'

As he speaks, his voice rises and he throws the letter at her. His face loses its soft features, and is now hard, his lips drawn into a thin line, ruddiness born of anger colouring him.

'You can't go,' he says emphatically.

'I must, Robert. He's my fiancé and I must go immediately to be with him.'

'Eleanor... He's in prison. PRISON my dear. How can you be with him?'

'Please. I love him. I want to be near him. He can't possibly have done such a thing knowingly. I implore you to support me. I will go to him.'

'You will not. I forbid it.' He turns his back and leaves the room.

Eleanor packs as much as she can, while raised voices reach her from below. She wonders what Elizabeth thinks, hopes she might understand her need to be with Freddie. Unlocking the small drawer, she takes all their money and closes her purse with a snap. Not having eaten, her body feels weak. Her head aches. Her limbs are heavy as she walks the floor in a state of numbness. A gentle knock on the door rouses her.

'Come in,' she calls.

Elizabeth holds out her arms to embrace her, the friendly gesture causing her to burst into tears and fall into those open arms. She allows herself to be hugged and soothed.

'There now. You've had a terrible shock and Robert isn't helping at all is he? Come and sit with me.'

Worry, fear and longing pour from Eleanor as she gives way. Elizabeth holds her, lets it all dissipate, and when it has, she says,

'I want you to know I do understand, but Robert worries about you going there. He thinks you should break off the engagement straight away.'

'No. I won't do that,'

'Just listen for a moment. We think we know how you must be feeling, although I'm sure you'd say we didn't, but nobody can be blamed for breaking such an arrangement under these circumstances... After all, my dear, even if Freddie is found innocent of this crime, how can we all carry on knowing he's been suspected of it?'

Eleanor faces her sister-in-law. She clearly does not understand the power of loving someone, as she loves Freddie.

'Thank you for comforting me, but I think you'd better go and tell my brother that you haven't managed to change my mind as he'd hoped,' she says, the calmness of her words belying her inner feelings.

'Please give it some thought, as you must know how this will reflect on us all.'

Early the next morning, long before the household stirs, Eleanor makes her way quietly down the stairs and out into the street, leaving a short note on the hall table. Her bag is heavy as she makes her way to Beckton Station and boards a train for London's main lines.

Everyone is at home when Eleanor arrives at the front door in a state of great distress.

'Mr. Tyler,' she says at last, 'what has become of Freddie?'

'We're not too sure my dear. The only visitor he's been allowed is Mr. Samuels, his solicitor,' says Alice.

'Who has told us that Freddie is doing well and we mustn't worry over much. Both Dr Sayer and Mr. Hargreaves are helping him with his defence, but we won't know much until the next court date,' says Alfred.

'I want to see him… to be sure he's keeping as well as he can… you understand? Only I don't know how long I can stay. My brother doesn't know I've come… he forbad it… I couldn't stay there.'

'Of course, we do Eleanor. It's the same for us and I can try to get you a visit, but you must be prepared for disappointment,' says Alfred.

'You don't have to go back', Alice says, 'Please stay here with us.

In the event there is no persuading the authorities of a visit before the next court date. Eleanor stays.

56

Throughout the week between Christmas and New Year, there are never ending knocks at the front door of number 9 Rock Street, each one from a fashionably dressed lady, or sometimes a lady's maid, requesting the garments Alice has either completed or is making. None of them will cross the threshold, but wait while Rebecca brings them their gowns. Towards the end of the week, one of them turns back to the door as an afterthought, says in a low voice,

'Many of us have spoken together. We all appreciate the outstanding work of Mrs. Tyler, but none of us can possibly enter the premises once resided in by a murderer.'

Rebecca cannot help slamming the door before the lady has quite removed herself.

Before long, Alice has no business, her reputation in tatters. Alfred is faring a little better, the men being less disposed to searching for another good boot maker, though some customers simply fail to collect their orders. Local news reports contain every detail of what is occurring; even the London Times carries the story.

By the middle of January 1892, Alice has only left her bed for more than a few hours each day, and only then to see her children and husband. Rebecca knows what needs to be done and the work helps to ease her sorrow, so she does not complain about the lack of direction from her mistress. If money is needed, she goes to Alfred. Eleanor gets to know the family, her potential sisters, and brothers in law, helps Rebecca in her duties and gradually they become the hub of the home.

'Where's your mother girls?' Alfred says appearing at the kitchen door.

'Still in bed,' says Harriett.

'Would you like a hot drink, Mr. Tyler?' Rebecca asks.

'No. Thank you. I must see Mrs. Tyler and then get straight back to the workshop.'

He knocks gently on their bedroom door, not really wanting to disturb her, but hears a faint 'come in' from the other side. He sits on the bed and holds Alice's hand. Her face is so pale, wisps of knotted hair trailing over her pillow, and the sight brings a lump to his throat.

'How are you my dear?'

'I have no desire Alfred. My body feels so weighed down and my mind will not stop its constant dreadful thoughts. They go round like a carrousel and terrible pictures of murder and our son flash across my eyes. I don't know what to do Alfred.'

'Mother's not well my dear and has asked for you.'

'Why me? Can't Emily tend to her?'

'She only wants you my dear. Will you go and see her? It might help to talk with her.'

Reluctantly, Alice slides out of bed, finds something to put on, not bothered by her looks, and without hurrying, goes downstairs to the kitchen.

'Mother,' says Maud. 'Are you feeling any better?'

'I have to go and see Grandmother. She's unwell, but I would like something hot to drink before I go Rebecca, if you've time.'

'I've always time for you Mrs. Tyler,' she says with a warm smile.

'Good morning Mrs. Tyler. It's good to see you,' says Eleanor.

Alice finds the kitchen comforting and warm, not only from the stove, but from her daughters' presence and she kisses them for the first time in many a day. Rebecca asks,

'Would you like me to wash your hair for you when you come back? The boiler's on in the scullery so there's plenty of hot water and it may help you to feel more refreshed.'

'That's kind of you Rebecca, but I'll likely be going straight back to bed when I return.'

I slip a coat round my shoulders, venture out into the cold, step straight into a puddle left from last night's downpour, not realising I have my indoor shoes on. *Oh well. What does it matter in the great scheme of things?* I think. Up the road I see women returned from errands, their heavy bags almost dragging on the paths. I don't want to be seen, so bow my head for the short passage to number eleven, open the door and meet Emily in the hall.

'What's the matter with Mrs. Tyler?' I say.

'I don't know.'

'Why hasn't the doctor been called if she's ill?'

'She refuses to have him. She says it's only you she wants.'

My feet squelch as I make my way upstairs. I don't care about the wet marks left on the floor. In fact, I care little about anything these days. Without knocking on the door, I go straight into Lily's room and sit, uninvited, on the edge of her bed. She sits up, supported by many pillows, shawls wrapped around her shoulders, her face unnaturally drawn and blotchy.

'What's ailing you mother?'

She doesn't look at me or say anything for a few seconds, and then, almost exploding, says,

'Shame Alice. It's utter shame that keeps me here.'

Her voice is loud, raspy and cold, full of venom, and she looks at me as she says it, as though I'm entirely to blame. I understand Lily's distress. We're all distressed, but the implication cuts through me. I try for a consoling reply. 'Oh mother. We all feel it and I admit to spending most of my time alone.'

There's another long pause before she really does explode,

'Where's your pride now my girl? I told you long ago that pride's a sin. I warned you Alice... but oh no, you wouldn't heed me. You told everyone how proud you were of Freddie. Now we're all paying for your sin and I can't forgive you as I can't forgive him. He's ruined our lives Alice. Can't you see that? He's brought the whole family down with him.'

I'm mortified. I can't speak for the lump in my throat, and look away from her steely gaze, wanting to cry, but from somewhere deep inside, find the strength to stay calm.

'Is that what you called me here to say mother?'

'I did. And now it's done you may leave.'

I wonder where that woman is, I longed to know, how she can imagine I'm the cause of these events, why she believes that this is retribution for pride in my son. I will not allow her to intimidate me.

'No. Not yet.' I look directly at her, take time to gather my thoughts before responding. In the silence, Lily lays her head back as though too weak to hold it upright, closes her eyes to signal that the conversation will not be continued.

'Mother, you've been proud of Freddie... Do you not remember when he went to Canada? Do you not remember how much you enjoyed telling the congregation all about your wonderful grandson, who was making a good life for himself in the New World?... that was pride... Whatever Freddie's done now, I'll always be proud of his

226

achievements, and no matter what happens, I'll always love him… He's my son mother. Can you not find any compassion in your heart for us? Have you not understood the notion that Freddie may have had no idea what he was doing?… Are you so selfish Mother, that you can't comprehend how we're all feeling?' The more I say the stronger I become. I watch Lily's face grow crimson with either rage or embarrassment, I can't tell which.

'How dare you speak to me like that, Alice. I'm Alfred's mother and demand your respect.'

'You cannot demand respect, Lily'… I don't know where this comes from, how I am able to stand up to Lily, but I've already said more than I should, so continue. 'You have to earn it.'

'You're wicked Alice, like Freddie. You've both sinned against the Lord and we must all suffer for it.'

'Freddie is your grandson… Please don't forget that. I'll take my leave now mother.'

At the bottom of the stairs, I stop, heart racing with shallow breathing. My body shakes with anger and the energy it has taken to speak to Lily in such a way. A manner I never would have thought possible. I should go and see Alfred, tell him what has occurred, but decide against it. I feel suddenly, remarkably strong, as if the line between pride and shame is so thin, I have a foot on either side, both feelings coalescing into something I cannot quite understand. If I'm able to stand up to mother, I can be strong enough to support my family, love my imprisoned child and garner all our energy into fighting for him.

The girls, Rebecca and Eleanor are still in the kitchen when I arrive back, and it's warm and inviting, such a contrast to the cold unfeeling space I've just been in. I'm wrapped safely in its walls, loved and cosseted. The evening's meal is underway, the aromas actually making my mouth water, and I'm hungry for the first time in ages.

'How's Grandmother?' asks Maud.

'Oh. She's just fine.'

I hear a strength in my voice, like my old self, see them look at each other as though they suspect some strange force at work.

'Rebecca. I've changed my mind. Please will you wash my hair for me?'

'It'll be a pleasure, Mrs. Tyler.'

Alice's girls look at each other for the second time, raising their eyebrows now, wondering what on earth has occurred at number eleven, for whatever it was, it seems to have had an astonishing effect on their mother. They take over the cooking and other jobs while Alice and Rebecca disappear into the scullery.'

'What was all that about?' says Lily.

'I haven't a clue. But whatever's happened, it's brought her back to us,' says Harriett.

'And thank the Lord for it,' chimes in Maud. 'They'll be a while in there so why don't you two go up and whip the sheets off mother's bed and make it lovely and clean for them? We can put them in the copper once they've finished. I'll take care of things down here.'

Harriett and Lily complete the job in record time, come downstairs with bundles of linen which they stash away, so as not to be seen. Eventually the two women reappear from their hair washing and climb the stairs.

'What have those girls been up to?' I say looking at the freshly made bed and the tidy room.

'It looks as though they've been spoiling their mother a little.'

Rebecca begins brushing out the knots and tangles from my hair, apologising frequently for the pulling, but I don't mind. It's only then I consider how little I've cared for myself since Christmas. I wonder how I can have been so self-absorbed as to have neglected my family, every one of whom is suffering. Do my words to Lily apply to myself also?

'Rebecca, the girls can help with the meal tonight and I'd like you to eat with us.'

'But Mrs. Tyler. I'm just the domestic help. It wouldn't be seemly.'

'No Rebecca. You are, and have been for a long time now, more than just the domestic help. On this occasion, please join us in the parlour.'

'Thank you, Mrs. Tyler. It's truly kind of you.'

I wake up with renewed strength, knowledge of my own selfishness shaming me. I've no idea what my husband and children have been doing while I lay in bed. After breakfast Alfred and the boys go to work. Rebecca washes our sheets in the scullery with Eleanor's help, but I ask them to sit with the girls and me.

'I apologise to all of you,' I say. 'We've been hit hard by what's happened, but I've not done my duty as a mother, a mistress... nor to my son's fiancé.' I look at Eleanor when I say this, take her hand in mine. Guilt is a heavy burden. Nothing makes up for its cause and I feel especially distressed now for this poor girl, her life shattered, living in a strange home. 'What have you all been doing these past weeks?' Harriet looks at me with tears in her eyes and says,

'You don't need to apologise Mother… but we've missed you so much, and the boys too… we didn't know what was going on to begin with but now we read the papers… It's grim… but at least we understand what Freddie's going through in the courts and it does help.'

'I'm so sorry.'

'During the day,' Lily says, 'Harriet and Maud have been teaching us.'

'But you don't like learning Lily… you're the same as Freddie used to be… he hated school.'

'I know, but when Maud helps me, she makes it fun and it makes sense, that's right isn't it Isobel?'

'Yes. And Mother, we have tests to see how well we do. If we do really well, we get a farthing!'

'You're giving away our secrets now,' says Maud. There's laughter round this kitchen table. Is it the first time since before December, I wonder?

'I've decided,' I say, 'that we'll share everything from now on… the sorrow and the happiness… whatever comes to us, I'll not let you be on your own. Now, there's a particular job I want to do today and I'd like your help.'

'What is it first Mother?' asks Isobel. 'Can we say no if we want to?' I'm amazed to hear her so forthright, sure I have not noticed it before, and think how much like Alfred's mother she sounds.

'You may say yes!' I reply, 'for without your help I'll not be able to finish before your father and brothers come home. I shall not be making any more gowns, so today we're going to pack away everything in the front parlour, clean it and furnish it as it used to be. Who's going to help me?'

'We all will,' says Eleanor.

'I'll be there as soon as the washing is done, Mrs. Tyler.'

'Why don't I help you Rebecca. It'll go quicker,' says Eleanor.

We work hard with determination all through the house, seven women together, as though we are one body. Outside it's dark, grey clouds hang low, it rains constantly, but here there's light, warmth, cosiness, laughter as well as tears. We now have our front parlour back, extra room so the children don't have to hide away upstairs. I decide to purchase a larger table for the dining room, maybe we can all sit together. Whatever anyone else believes, whatever gossip flies down the street, whatever looks are directed our way, I will not be bowed by Freddie's actions. Actions I believe were not premeditated.

'I think your father and brothers will wonder what's happened to us,' I say. 'Eleanor, will you sit with me for a while?' We settle into the comfortable chairs round the fire.

'I'm so pleased to have you here, and only sorry that we can't visit Freddie.'

'I think it dreadfully unfair, Mrs. Tyler. Poor Freddie must be desperate to see us. I can't imagine how he's managing.' She begins to cry, so I hold her, let her weep.

57

Mr. Hargreaves and Dr. Sayer work tirelessly to search for any information regarding expert opinions about seizures. Nothing can restore little Annie Thomson to life. They can however, attempt to put the case for Freddie. They attend the local library, travel to London to search medical journals, and gradually build the evidence, providing the defence with their findings. They visit the family, all of them gathered to hear the news, including Lily, who has not been to their home since she and Alice confronted each other. Alice is pleased, feeling deep relief that Lily has not spurned her totally. A silence descends about the warm parlour, while they take in the information. Lily shifts in her chair, excuses herself and makes her way to the privy.

'Thank you for all your hard work and for being honest with us,' says Alice. 'It can't have been easy for either of you, and then there's all the time it's taken travelling up to London, coming to understand the information and of course we do so appreciate that you haven't denounced Freddie as your godson. It means a lot to us and to him.' Tears flow, but Alice is unsure if they are tears of fear, or relief from the hope been handed to them. Lily returns, hugs her daughter-in-law briefly.

'Mother,' Alfred says, when they are alone, 'will you stay and eat with us?'

'Yes, son. I'd like that.'

'How are you feeling, now we know all of this?'

'Well. To be honest Alfred, I feel rather conflicted. You see, Freddie has committed a terrible crime. He's broken one of the most important of the Ten Commandments, and my faith in God leads me to condemn him for that... but... well, you know Alice and I had an argument and we both said some horrible things, which I suppose we'll not find it easy to forget... I've had a long time to think about it in my solitude though, and I believe there was some truth in Alice's words. He is my grandson and what we've heard today does shed a different light on the matter… I'll do my best to support Alice and you through this.'

'Thank you, Mother. Alice hasn't spoken to me of the incident, but I know she's missed you and will be truly pleased to have you back.'

'Mind you Alfred, I still feel ashamed when I walk out.'

'Try not to. Freddie's crime was not committed wilfully. We know that, and must hold on to it for his sake.'

58

'Take nothing on its looks; take everything on evidence.
There's no better rule.' Charles Dickens: Great
Expectations (1860)

The courtroom at Lewes Assizes is full to bursting. Judge Justice Grant, raised high on his dais, surveys the faces before him, twelve jurors to his right, Mr. Wilkins the prosecutor and Mr. Robins for the defence, placed in the well of the room. There are faces he recognises from the press. Lewes and Brighton dignitaries also among the crowd. They all want to witness this momentous trial. He sees Harold Thomson with his eldest children, and Alfred Tyler with his sons and brothers, in the centre of the gallery. He is ready to begin.

'Bring up the prisoner,' he says authoritatively.

Handcuffed and escorted between two constables, Freddie is led into the court and placed in the dock, directly in front of the judge. He is much changed, a broken man, but has made serious efforts to appear well dressed in a black coat, a stand-up collar shirt with the points turned down and a black tie. He looks about him for anyone who might be other than hostile, sees his family and both godparents sitting together, and his eyes already full, overflow. They smile to let him know that they are there for him, but inside their guts are turning, their heads ache and their once happy worlds lie in pieces. Alice, advised by Dr. Sayer that she is too weak to attend, remains at home.

Mr. Wilkins opens the proceedings by addressing the jury. He states that he will produce very clearly the facts upon which the charge has been laid, and that they must pay close attention to the evidence brought before them. He also urges them to lay aside any preconceptions they might have, based on what they have heard or seen since December last, and in so doing to perform the duty required of them without prejudice to the man in the dock. He calls witnesses who have, from the start of the nightmare, given their accounts of the discovery of Annie Thomson's body and of Freddie's subsequent arrest. Their telling is so graphic, many in the gallery express their horror with sharp intakes of breath and whispered words of 'poor little girl', and all the while Freddie sobs, not understanding how he can have done such a thing.

Mr. Robins cross examines each witness, elicits from every one of them, that the prisoner has never before been seen to be drunk. Furthermore, they all state that he is a teetotaller and a very decent man, a good workman, a quiet, peaceful and sober man.

'I will now call witnesses who will shed light on the movements of the accused on the night in question,' Mr. Wilkins announces. 'Call Mrs. Mable Creswell.'

Mrs Creswell, in her mid-forties, takes the stand, dressed in her Sunday best for the occasion, her dark hair fashioned in contemporary style. She stands confidently, even defiantly, facing the prosecutor, who asks,

'Mrs. Creswell, where were you on the evening of December 10th last?'

'I was in Sidney Street, having come up from Gloucester Road where I'd been visiting.'

'Quite so. And at what time would this have been?'

'It was just after seven o'clock as that's when I left.'

'Now, will you tell us, in your own words, what occurred?'

'Well. I was walking up the road when I saw a man talking to a small child. I wouldn't have taken much notice but for the man picking her up. She screamed and he took a few steps away from me but then fell. The child being free of him, ran towards me and I took her home with me.'

'And where is home, Mrs. Creswell?'

'New England Street sir.'

'Did you see anything of this man's attire?'

'I did sir. He was wearing a railway coat.'

Mr. Robins for the defence, asked her if the man fell out of drunkenness, whereupon she replied that she did not know.

The next witness is a child of eleven, nervously fiddling with the ties of her dress as she is led in.

'There's no need to be afraid as long as you tell the truth. What's your full name?' asks the prosecutor.

'Rosina Early, sir.'

'And where do you live Rosina?'

'Number 47 Meeting House Lane'. Her voice is low and Mr. Wilkins asks her to speak up so all those in the room can hear her.

'Where were you on the evening of the 10th of December Rosina?'

'I was in Grosvenor Street sir.'

'Whereabouts in the street, were you?'

'At the bottom. There's a sweet shop at the bottom and I had a farthing to buy some sweets.'

'Now, you bought some sweets and came back onto the street. What happened then?'

'I saw a man. He whistled at me and then asked where I lived.'

'And did you tell him?'

'Yes sir.'

'Did anything else occur?'

'He asked me to go home with him.'

'And did you go with him Rosina?'

'No. I went into a house in Grosvenor Street because I was afraid.'

'Where was the man when you went away?'

'I left him in Edward Street.'

'No further questions.'

In cross examination, Mr. Robins asks,

'Hello Rosina. What can you tell us about the man you saw?'

'He had brown buttons on his coat and his face had little black hairs all over it.'

'Did you tell anyone about this man?'

'Yes. I told my mother when I got home.'

'What did your mother do?'

'She took me to the police station the next day.'

'And can you remember what happened at the police station?'

'A policeman asked me if the man was a railway man and then took me to see a lot of men in a line.'

'What did you do Rosina?'

'I pointed to a man.'

'Why did you point to that particular man?'

'Because he was wearing a railway coat.'

'Were any of the other men wearing railway coats?'

'No sir.'

'Now Rosina. This is a very important question, so I want you to think hard before you answer. What time was it you went for the sweets and came back out to the road?'

Rosina hardly takes breath before she says, 'It was about seven o'clock sir.'

'And you're sure that when the man whistled at you and spoke to you, it was about seven o'clock?'

'Yes sir.'

'No further questions for this witness, but may I approach the bench M'Lord?'

Given leave to do so, Mr. Robins and Mr. Wilkins walk towards the judge.

'M'Lord. We have witness statements that put my client at the goods yard just before seven and then in Sidney Street just after seven. From Sidney Street to Grosvenor Street is a fair walk for a sober man, so it is highly unlikely that he would be there at seven o'clock. Furthermore, the child was prompted by a constable to identify anyone wearing a railway coat and my client was the only man so dressed. I ask therefore that the witness testimony be struck as highly unreliable.'

Mr. Wilkins having nothing to add, the judge takes a moment to think before saying that her testimony will stand. The prosecutor smiles. Mr. Robins does not, knows the decision to be grossly unfair. Arriving back at their stations, Mr. Wilkins calls for the next witness, P.C. Shaw.

'P.C. Shaw, where were you on the night of December 10th last?'

'I was in Lavender Street.'

'Did you see the prisoner in Lavender Street?'

'Yes sir. It was about eight o'clock and I saw him coming down the street towards me.'

'Did you speak to the prisoner?'

'Yes sir. We said goodnight to each other. I noted that he was drunk.'

'In which direction did he go after you'd spoken?'

'There's a shop in St. David's Street and he turned there towards Bedford Street.'

'Did you notice what the prisoner was wearing?'

'Yes sir. He had on long mackintosh leggings, a railway coat and a cap.'

With no further questions from the prosecutor Mr. Robins rose to cross examine.

'How long have you known my client, P.C. Shaw?'

'About ten years sir.'

'Now. Mr. Tyler has spent some of that time in Canada, but since you've known him, have you ever seen him drunk?'

'No sir.'

'You've never known him to take the drink?'

'No sir.'

'How would you describe the prisoner?'

'As far as I know he has always been of good character. He is a religious man.'

'The constabulary have never had dealings with him in any criminal matters?'

'No sir.'

Mrs. Louisa Sharp is called, gives her address as seven Somerset Street, explaining that this is off Upper Bedford Street with Hereford Street opposite. In answer to the prosecutors questions, she tells the court that on December 10th, she left her house at the front and saw a man carrying a child on the opposite side of the road. The child was crying. Asked what she did, she says,

'I called to him not to hurt the poor little thing. He turned round and under the lamp light I saw his face.'

'Do you see that man in this court?'

'Yes sir. It is the prisoner in the dock.'

She tells the court it was just after quarter past eight and he went towards the east. She followed him to the corner of the street, because after she'd shouted out, the child had stopped crying and the man looked as if he was the worse for wear. He turned into Montague Place and then into Edwin Place which is close.

Under cross examination, Mr. Robins asks,

'Mrs. Sharp, I'm a little confused as to why you should follow the man you saw that night. Can you explain please?'

'Well… I thought they were father and daughter, but the child had little clothing on and it was pouring with rain.'

'Please tell the court, at which end of Somerset Street number seven is?'

'It's at the end of the street as it meets Upper Bedford Road.'

'And yet you say the man was going east, down the street and away from Upper Bedford Road. Is that correct?'

'Yes sir.'

'How heavily was it raining?'

'It was very heavy. We had storms that night.'

'It was very wet. Did you go back indoors to fetch a coat?'

'No sir. I just followed.'

'You have just testified, have you not, that you thought the man and child were father and daughter?'

'Yes sir.'

'How then did you think he was hurting her?'

'I don't know sir.'

Mrs. Louisa Sharman approaches the witness box with a straight back, wobbling in shoes that are clearly too large for her, but also perhaps, her best pair. Taking the stand, her face is free of expression, implying a manner of assurance that she will be a good witness. She confirms her address, says she had been out seeing her mother in Montague Street. On her way home, she saw a man dressed in railway uniform, looking at a little girl and stretching his hand to her. Mr. Wilkins asks,

'Whereabouts was this?'

'It was outside a shop in Upper Bedford Street.'

'Did you notice anything about the child?'

'She had a bundle of wood and followed the man into Somerset Street.'

'And what time would this have been?'

'It was nearly half past eight.'

Harry Robert Hutt is next called, and asked a series of questions by the prosecutor. In answer he states that he was on the Easton Road, close to Chesham Street, between eight thirty and eight forty-five. A man came towards him carrying a small child of about six or seven and he was drunk. Mr. Hutt says he could not see the man's face but noticed that his boots and trousers were very dirty. When asked if that man was in the courtroom, he replies that he is and points towards the dock.

When Mr. Robins stands for the defence, he looks puzzled, his left hand at his chin. He moves slowly across the floor, seemingly deep in thought. As he approaches the witness he says,

'Did you identify this man at the police station?'

'Yes sir.'

'And did you just testify that you were unable to see the man's face on the night of December 10th?'

'Yes sir.'

'Did you see any other garments apart from his boots and trousers?'

'No sir.'

'You were not aware of the coat he was wearing?'

'No sir.'

'If you were unable to see his face, or know what he was wearing above the waist, Mr. Hutt, how can you be certain that this man,' and he points towards Freddie, 'is in fact the man you saw on December 10th?'

'Well, I will not swear that the man I picked out at the police station is the same man I saw carrying the child.' At this there are gasps from the gallery, Freddie's family pleased to hear that not all witnesses are passing muster. As Mr. Hutt steps down from the box, he faints, to cries of concern, and when revived is led from the court.

Dr. Sayer, who performed the autopsy on Annie Thomson, is called to the stand, gives detailed evidence regarding his examination of the body and the result of the post-mortem. He states that in his professional opinion, the cause of death was asphyxia and that very great violence had been used against her. During his evidence, the courtroom is dulled into silence. Mr. Thomson weeps silently to hear yet again of such barbarism done to his daughter and his distress is the only sound to carry across the void. Freddie's brothers try desperately to stop their tears flowing, so affected are they by the descriptions given, and stunned to think that their own brother could have inflicted them. Mr. Robins stands to cross examine the witness.

'Dr. Sayer, please tell the court of your visit to Lewes Gaol on 30th December.'

'Yes. I was called to attend the accused who I found in the latter stages of an epileptic fit. When I arrived, he was being held by three men due to him thrashing about violently. I didn't witness the worst as he'd recovered considerably by the time I got there. I was informed that he'd had a seizure before and that the police surgeon was called to see him on that occasion.'

'I believe your brother practises also?'

'Yes. In Brighton. I know he attends the family of the prisoner, but I have no knowledge of them personally.'

'Now, if the prisoner had fits at a young age, would that affect his life growing up?'

'To an extent. He may be weaker in the brain. Before a seizure he'd probably be very violent. Once over he would most likely be confused but sane.'

'Is it not the case, Dr. Sayer, that violence follows fits rather than precedes them?'

'I'm not an expert in epilepsy, but in my experience, it precedes.'

'Are you aware of the term epileptic furore?'

'Yes.'

'Is it your understanding that many crimes ....?'

'No. No.' The judge calls out.

'Dr. Sayer has no understanding of this, M'Lord? Very well.' says Mr. Robins.

'Dr. Sayer have you had sight of Dr. Green's report, from the Brighton Sanitorium?'

'I have, yes. I agree with some of what he writes, but disagree in other aspects. I believe the epilepsy would be more violent after a long period of time without fits and that drink, if not having been taken for some time, or indeed ever, would most likely bring on an attack. During the mania, the person should be restrained, for fear of further attacks occurring. I do agree that there are a large number of dangerous epileptic lunatics who have also long periods of sanity, but they are likely to fit with violence. These are of course, confirmed epileptics. I also agree with Dr. Green, that it is a dangerous time for epileptic men, between the ages of twenty-five and thirty. I have no doubt that when not suffering, a patient might be seen as highly intelligent.'

With no further questions, Mr. Wilkins rose to re-examine his witness.

'Dr. Sayer. Would you say that the accused is suffering from epileptic insanity?'

'In my opinion, no. On the evidence I saw, he had an epileptic fit. He was unconscious and foaming at the mouth.'

'Would it be possible to fake an epileptic fit?'

'It would be possible, yes. On other occasions he was in possession of his senses and didn't have the appearance of a confirmed epileptic.'

With Dr. Sayer's evidence given, the prosecution rests its case

59

Mr. Robins rises, faces the jury, and begins his case for the defence.

'The prosecution case you've heard, asserts that my client did wilfully murder Annie Thomson on the night of Thursday December 10th last. Indeed, my learned council Mr. Wilkins has furnished you with a full account of this day, bringing forward witnesses who claim to have seen him. For my part, I've had considerable difficulty cross examining those witnesses... there is good reason for this... my client, the man who stands before you in the dock, has no recollection of the night in question, and therefore has not been able to take the stand in his own defence, to test the accuracy of prosecution evidence.'

'The key word in the accusation against Mr. Tyler, is 'wilful'... I ask you... all of you... to give great consideration to this small word in the charge against Mr. Tyler. Wilful. To perform something wilfully, consciousness is required. I will bring forward witnesses to prove that whatever happened that night in December, my client was totally without consciousness. Call Mr. Alfred Tyler.'

Alfred enters the courtroom, glances at his son as he passes, wishing with all his heart that he can say something reassuring to him. He sees Freddie's face stained with tears and has to turn away to prevent himself from breaking.

'Mr. Tyler, will you please state, for the record, where you currently live.'

'At number nine Rock Street, in Brighton.'

'And what is your relationship to the prisoner?'

'He's my son... I'm his father.'

'Now. Mr. Tyler, I understand that all was not quite as it should have been when your son was born. Please explain to this court what happened.'

'His birth was a difficult one and my wife didn't feel much movement as he was developing. When he was delivered, he didn't breath for many minutes.'

Mr. Wilkins stands to object, asking what this has to do with current criminal proceedings.

'What are you getting at Mr. Robins?' asks the judge.

'I aim to demonstrate, M'Lord, that my client has a long history of illness from epilepsy.'

'Overruled,' he says to Mr. Wilkins, but his tone betrays his attitude, and Mr. Robins is all too well aware that he needs to make his points succinctly.

'Please continue Mr. Tyler.'

'Alfred wasn't quick to progress and when he was two, he had a convulsion. We brought in the doctor who told us that many children have convulsions, but usually grew out of them. Alfred recovered at that time, but often awoke in the night screaming, taking a long time to settle again afterwards. He was a delicate child.'

'You say, he had a convulsion... was that true?'

'We know now that it wasn't, that in fact he'd had an epileptic fit.'

'M'Lord,' Mr. Robins says facing the judge, 'I'll come back to this at a later stage with further witnesses.'

'Did he attend school Mr. Tyler?'

'Yes, but he hated it, preferring to be outside in the garden or at the beach.' The memory somehow comforts Alfred as he speaks.

'What did he do after his schooling finished?'

'I had him with me in the business... you know... learning the trade. Then when he was fifteen, he went onto the navy training ship, the St. Vincent, but was discharged after three months.'

'What was the nature of the discharge?'

'It was said that he had a malformation of the chest, which we knew nothing of and weak legs.'

'So, his discharge was unconnected to any behaviour?'

'That's correct. His record said that his conduct had been good.'

'Quite so. What did he do after leaving this training?'

'He went labouring for about three years... then joined the Royal Surrey Regiment at eighteen.'

'How long did he serve?'

'Only a few months. He had varicose veins which had become quite severe since he was a child and he was passed unfit for duty.'

'And what did his army record tell you about his conduct?'

'This stated also that his conduct and character were particularly good.'

'Now, Mr. Tyler, please explain to the court how your son was after his return from the army.'

'Well… he tried to make good with his limited capacity for learning but had always believed he was a failure and by and large, that this was due to his physical difficulties. He became rather low and hit upon the idea of emigrating.'

'Where did he go?'

'He went to Canada.'

'And how was his time there?'

'He was there for eight years and made a great success of his life. His mother and I remain proud of his achievements.'

'He returned in 1890?'

'Yes. He went with his fiancé to London and took employment at the gasworks.'

'What caused him then, to return to Brighton?'

'He continued to suffer badly with his legs and came home to have an operation for his varicose veins.'

'Where did he next gain employment?'

'At the railway, as a porter. He started there in September 1890.'

'Now, Mr. Tyler… we've heard evidence from railway employees of his conduct up until the night of December 10th last. How did you find him during those months?'

'He always conducted himself well, his manner of a calm nature.'

'No further questions.'

Mr. Wilkins rose to cross examine.

'To your knowledge, Mr. Tyler, when was the last time you witnessed the accused having a fit?'

'Not since he was eight, have I seen what I believed to be the convulsions, but I understand that he had many while in Canada.'

Mr. Wilkins, having no further questions for Alfred, sits down and PC Cooper is called. He states he had been on duty at the Town Hall on December 22nd and was in charge of the prisoner. Asked if anything out of the ordinary occurred, he replies that the prisoner had a very violent fit, so that four policemen had to hold him down to avoid injury to himself.

'Was that the only occasion he fitted?'

'No sir. It happened again on the thirtieth and I was surprised to find the prisoner had such strength.'

With no cross examination of the witness, Mr. Robins calls two other constables who both testify to seeing the prisoner suffering fits, one of which was described as being extremely violent. Dr. Pugh, the police doctor, is called, who testifies to seeing the prisoner in an epileptic convulsion of some severity, adding under cross examination, that though confused after recovering, the prisoner was quite sane.

Arthur Smith, an attendant at Lewes Gaol had begun work there in February and had attended the prisoner for twelve hours every day. When asked by Mr. Robins, how Freddie had been, he states that he'd been admitted to the infirmary ward and had three seizures, testimony which was corroborated by the warder at the prison, who also stated when cross examined, that the prisoner did not foam at the mouth when in the fits.

The next witness is Dr Green, giving his occupation and position as a fully qualified doctor and superintendent of the Sussex County Asylum.

'Are you familiar with the condition of epilepsy?' asks Mr. Robins.

'I am. I've had several such patients under observation.'

'How was it you came to attend the prisoner?'

'I was instructed by the Treasury to see him. I saw him twice, on the twelfth and nineteenth of March.'

'How did you find him?'

'He was perfectly rational, which is not at all inconsistent with this affliction.'

'And in the light of your experience, have you formed an opinion regarding this particular case?'

'Yes. It is perfectly conceivable for an epileptic to become mentally unconscious without actually having a fit, after which he might become manic. It's also known that alcohol can affect the epileptic, giving rise to fits. Fits don't always come with the same severity, nor do they always make a man unable to move about. Statistics show that a man in such a condition might be liable to acts of a violent nature.'

'Did you report your findings?'

'Yes. I reported them to the Treasury.'

'Dr. Green, are you familiar with the works of physicians such as Jacobi, Jackson and Bourneville?'

'I've heard the names of Jacobi and Jackson, but not Bourneville.'

'Do you have any knowledge of research these two gentleman have worked on with regard to epilepsy?'

'I have to say that I haven't read into much of their work.'

'So, Dr. Green, you are not aware of a related condition known as 'Status Epilepticus?'

'No.'

'The eminent physician Bournville, has published his research, which can be found in medical journals in this country. His work has highlighted this condition which can lie somewhere between Grand Mal and Petit Mal and according to him patients sometimes move within an unconscious state for hours or even days at a time, with no memory of what occurs. But you are unaware of this?'

'I'm afraid so.'

'It has been documented many times, and over a period of some decades, that while in such a state, patients are capable of carrying out extreme violence quite outside their normal character. I'm surprised given your position, that you have not kept abreast of such research, Dr Green…'

Mr. Wilkins jumps to his feet. 'Objection. My learned friend is inappropriate in his comments of the witnesses behaviour.'

'Upheld.' Mr. Robins is nonplussed. He knew there would be an objection but has planted a small seed in the minds of the jurors regarding Dr Green's authority.

'Do you believe, Dr Green, that my client, Alfred Tyler could have suffered in this way?'

'Well. Given what you say, yes I suppose he could have done.'

'And do you think that if this was the case, the man in the dock was utterly without knowledge of his actions?'

'It may be possible.'

Mr. Wilkins stands to cross examine.

'You have worked with epileptic patients for how long, Dr. Green?'

'For many years both prior to my current position and of course since.'

'And you are renowned for your expertise in treating this condition?'

'I am.'

'What then, is your expert opinion regarding the prisoner's actions on the night in question?'

'Well… I am sure that the man is sane. Having witnessed him in fits it would appear that he falls into the known category of an epileptic, being of perfect sound mind between attacks. However, with the information…'

'Thank you, Dr. Green. That will be all.'

Mr. Robins calls Dr Sayer, Freddie's godfather and brother of the pathologist. He enters the courtroom, smiles at Freddie, and takes his place in the witness box.

'Dr Sayer. You have been doctor to the Tyler family for many years. Is that correct?'

'It is.'

'You attended at the accused's birth, and many times subsequent to that?'

'Yes.'

'You are one of his godfather's I understand?'

'Yes.'

'Dr Sayer, please tell this court, as succinctly as possible, the circumstances surrounding a secret you, and Mr. Tyler's other godparents, kept from the family.'

Without wavering, Freddie's doctor explains what occurred, why the decision to keep such a secret was made, and the necessity of enlightening the family at this juncture.

'So, Dr Sayer, my client grew up not knowing what was happening to him when he lost times of consciousness or why it should be.'

'That is correct.'

'Please tell us the effect alcoholic drink might have on someone suffering from the condition of epilepsy.'

'Epilepsy is a condition caused when the pathways of the brain become crossed, or stop working in the way they are meant to. Alcohol causes confusion in the brains of everyone if taken to excess. For an epileptic, it can trigger a seizure.'

'Thank you. What is the likely outcome of an epileptic aged twenty nine, who has never taken alcohol before, suddenly drinking to excess?'

'Catastrophic.'

'Thank you. No more questions.'

Mr. Wilkins asks,

'Dr Sayer. You have eloquently outlined the secret kept from Mr. Tyler and his family. Was it a mistake to do so?'

'... Life is always clearer with hindsight, but I will say that had the family known... had Freddie known... he may well not have emigrated... he may have been persuaded to remain here... live his life as a labourer... maybe end his life in our asylum. In Canada, my godson... our godson... flourished... achieved many wonderful things he could not have done here. So, no... I do not think it was a mistake.'

With this witness, the defence rests its case.

'All rise,' says the clerk to the court, as the judge leaves his dais for a short break, stating that summing up from both sides will take place within the hour.

Freddie's family and godparents meet briefly outside the courtroom. His father is in low mood, so Dr Sayer takes him outside for some fresh air and a kindly shoulder. Alfred asks,

'How do you think it went?'

'As well as we could have hoped for. Some of the witnesses were shown to be unreliable and Dr. Green profoundly demonstrated his lack of knowledge concerning the condition he supposedly excels in. We must trust in the summing up speeches and hope the jury keep an open mind.'

'I've been watching the jury. Some of them have hardened faces, even sour at times. I can understand this during the awful descriptions of the little girl's end, but only one or two seemed to soften on listening to the defence evidence, and I specifically looked at them when Freddie sobbed... None of them even turned towards him.'

'The jury have been told that they mustn't be biased or swayed by how things look, but that they must weigh all the evidence put before the court, in concluding their decision. I pray that will be the case Alfred.'

60

Within the hour court is resumed and a gradual silence falls about the place as the judge enters and seats himself.

'Both the prosecution and the defence have laid their evidence before this court. Each will now sum up their case.'

He turns, looks at the jury, takes his time, searching their faces for something nobody else is aware of. Backwards and forwards he goes along each row, and Mr. Hargreaves notes that throughout this time, some members look about them, at those in the gallery, at their neighbours, at Freddie, but not at the judge. There is such silence in the room that a pin might be heard, had it dropped on the stone floor, and after many minutes, those jurors, clearly unfocussed and distracted by their personal thoughts, begin to realise it is them the judge is waiting for.

'Ah. Good. All eyes are upon me,' he says with not a small amount of irritation. 'As I was saying, both parties to this trial will now give their final words and it is to you,' his head stretches out towards them, his finger points at each one in turn, 'that they will be directing them to. I sincerely hope that each one of you will take note of every scrap of evidence. Are you ready Mr. Wilkins?'

Mr. Wilkins stands. 'Members of the jury. I remind you of the strong witness testimonies given against the prisoner. There can be no doubt, whatsoever, that the accused… who stands in the dock… committed this outrageous crime… that he took a five year old child while she waited for her brother… carried her through the streets of Kemptown… broke into a shed… not just any shed… one close to his home… and there murdered her in cold blood. I remind you of those witnesses who saw the prisoner on the night of December 10th… with a child… and clearly intoxicated. I remind you of little Annie Thomson, so wilfully and cruelly killed… of her family… who will never see her grow to be a woman. The prosecution relies on you to do your duty today… I urge you to consider the drunken behaviour of the accused… remember how afraid this little girl would have been on a stormy night… taken by this man… brutalised… left for dead. The defence will try to persuade you otherwise… but I urge you to pass a judgement of guilty.'

Mr. Robins stands, walks calmly towards the jury, looks at each face.

'Members of the jury, you've listened to Mr. Wilkins's summing up, his assured conviction that my client is guilty of the crime… to the evidence of his witnesses which he maintains is proof of guilt. As the jury in this case, you are entitled, as suggested by the prosecution, to conclude that the man in the dock, is indeed the perpetrator of this child's demise… but I must remind you once again of the charge… one of *wilful* murder. *Wilful* murder.'

'As the jury, you must take all the evidence given. For what it's worth, it's circumstantial evidence… a type dangerous to act upon. Not a scrap of direct evidence has been put forward. Remember that Mr. Tyler has not been unable to offer any explanation beyond what you've already read in his letter… His mind is a perfect blank. My client has epilepsy. His epilepsy causes him to fit… to be unconscious… to have seizures that can last for hours.'

'It is incumbent upon me to remind you of some testaments that may have already slipped your minds… testaments that give rise to doubt. A young girl, for instance, who was asked by a constable if the man was a railway man… thereby implanting the idea in her head, before taking her in, to pick out a man wearing a railway uniform… perhaps you may be surprised to be reminded that my client had been the only man wearing a railway uniform in that line. Then there is the evidence of Mr. Hutt… the gentleman who testified that the man in the dock is the man he picked out at the town hall on December 11th… but who also said… in this court room… before you, the jury… that he did not see the man's face on the night of the murder… how then should his evidence stand?'

'You've heard considerable evidence given here today of Mr. Tyler's conduct over many years and in many settings… even from his recent employers… conduct which has been exemplary. You've heard him described as a calm natured man… a man of blameless conduct… a man known in Brighton as a kind, generous man who loves nature… and who has never committed a cruel act… a man who, with his family, believes fervently in God.'

'Members of the jury… You have heard evidence of the accused's epilepsy. A condition which can render a person bereft of

250

consciousness... for many hours... during which time he can have no inkling of his behaviour... his demeanour... where he is... and one in which after the event... there is no memory. You have heard testimony of research which proves that during such a time, gross crimes can be committed... murder has been committed... with no knowledge of it by the perpetrator.'

'I urge you, honest and upstanding members of the public, to consider, not only the dreadful death of this young child, a victim of beastly cruelty... but to consider also, the man in the dock, a victim of a medical condition, over which he has no control. Your task in this courtroom today, therefore, is not to determine whether my client committed this terrible crime... but to establish whether he was responsible for his actions on that fateful night.... You must be sure that *wilful* murder was done by him.'

Freddie's fate is now in the hands of twelve men. Those in the gallery listened intently to the content of the summaries, no doubt each making up their own minds as to which way they might vote, but whatever they had decided, the might of the judges' summing up to his jury would certainly have swayed the weakest. He uses strong language against the prisoner, leaves no one in any doubt as to where his views lay. He then tells them to rise, leave the court and return with a verdict. It is twelve minutes to six on the evening of April 6th.

Outside the courtroom, Freddie's family stand together in silence, none wanting to be the first to speak, their voices almost certain to betray them. After a few moments it is suggested they might return home to see mother, but Alfred does not want to leave his son alone in this building. Freddie has nobody with him, any further distancing seeming to Alfred to be disloyal. To their utter amazement, the call comes to return to the court room.

'It can't be,' says Alfred. 'We've only just come out!'

It is just eight minutes later, that twelve men return to the courtroom, with their preconceived ideas and hardened hearts, take their seats and are asked if they have come to a unanimous decision. The foreman rises and answers clearly,

'We have M'Lord.'

'How do you find the prisoner? Guilty or not guilty?'

'Guilty.'

61

I hear the word. Only one word. It rattles in my head, but as far off…
as though it isn't in the room at all. I cling to the railings of the dock
so tight the whites of my knuckles surprise me… I think the skin is fit
to burst. I look up… people are standing, jumping even, clapping
hands, shaking fists. The noise hits me then… like I've woken from
some dream. Every eye is on me… I look at Papa… at all my
brothers… my uncles… my godfathers. I see their crumpled faces…
tears drip onto their trouser legs. Papa's head bends low in his
hands… his shoulders shake… I swear I hear his sobs above the
shouts. He looks so small. What have I done to him?

The judge uses his hammer, a loud bang on the wooden desk.
It shocks me so much my bladder leaks. I try to take my hand down
there to stem the flow, but it refuses, its grip on the rails so tight I can't
move it. I shake with fear… with shame… with the knowledge of that
word. Did I hear right? Is this real?

I see the judge put the black cap on his head… my knees give
way… hands under my armpits force me up… force me to stand, face
the consequences. I am in the middle of the most awful dream. I want
to wake up… tell everyone at breakfast of my terrible nightmare. Dear
God… please no. I hear the judge speak.

'I will not add to the misery of the prisoner with words of
reproach' he says. 'I will say that you must make the best use of the
time you have left. You must seek mercy for your actions, wherever
that may be found. I now pass the sentence of the law.'

'You will be taken back to the place whence you came and
thence to the place of execution, there to be hanged by the neck until
you shall be dead, and your body to be buried in the precincts of the
prison, and may the Lord have mercy on your soul.'

62

The Thomson family give way to utter grief and a palpable sense of relief that the murderer of their beautiful little girl, will himself be killed. In Rock Street, Alice faints at hearing the news. Taken to bed, she cries herself to sleep. Everyone is stunned that the son and brother they all loved, the fiancé with a new life waiting, will end his life on the gallows. Their certainty of his condition having been the cause of his behaviour, cannot be rationalised against the decision taken by twelve men, who clearly made it without discussion of the evidence, provided by the defence. For how could eight minutes be long enough to move into a room, be seated, elect a foreman, discuss the case, and return to their seats in the court?

Freddie's godparents visit the following day, greeted by so many pale, tear stained and red eyed faces, to add to their own, they are not able straight away to speak, until Mr. Hargreaves says,

'We must continue to be strong and take some action to appeal the sentence. Dr. Sayer and I have spoken of drawing up a petition to send to the Home Office. We'd like to know what you think about this.'

'Yes,' blurts out Alice, looking to Alfred for confirmation.

'I think whatever we can do, we must do,' he says.

Time is now of the essence. The execution date is yet to be set, but is not likely to be far away. When complete, the petition asked people to sign in favour of commuting the punishment on the grounds of insanity and if this is not acceptable to the Home Office, that the sentence be reduced to detention as a criminal lunatic. The task galvanises them to work together and gives them all a clear purpose. It is circulated across Brighton as quickly as possible, but not without some distress for the Thomson family, and anger from many of the local inhabitants. However, it raises more than a thousand signatures, not only from those who know the family, but also from clergymen, local doctors, and even significant medical authorities. On the evening of Wednesday April 13th Freddie's solicitors send the petition to the Home Office. All they can do now is wait. Time seems to stand still and fly simultaneously.

The date for the execution is set as Tuesday April 26th, just a week away, and with no response from London, save a receipt of the petition, the Tylers fall into the darkest of places they have ever known. None of them can envisage a time without Freddie. How can it be? Maud will not face anyone but Rebecca, the two of them being the closest to him. What is a week? How quickly will seven days go by? Alfred wants to close the business for the week so that he can be with the family, but he also needs to be busy and if he works, he will at least be a little refreshed in the evenings when the family need him. The other boys continue to work as well. It takes their minds off these tragic events for a while. The women however, unwilling to be seen in the streets of Brighton, stay home, do their best to be strong for everyone, but mostly fail miserably.

Each day is a mountain to climb, a heavy burden to carry, like wading through knee deep mud and never reaching the opposite side. They watch the clock on the mantlepiece and when mealtimes eventually come round, they are not hungry. The minister calls on them, as he has done many times before. He knows that Alice has turned from her faith, but he is sure that in time she will return, understanding that not all events in this world are God's doing. For now, though, he simply speaks to her softly, as he does with them all, praying with those who want to and blessing the family in their time of stress. During his church services, he prays for both families equally and Alice is pleased to hear that, for she knows what the loss of a child means.

The night Freddie is told of the date for his execution, he writes a long letter to his parents, reiterates his inability to recall anything of that night, tells them he has tried hard to do so. The letter is full of sadness, apologies for having broken the pledge, love for his family, and sorrow for the little girl. He tells them he understands how they will be affected by his crime, and asks their forgiveness. He requests a visit from his parents, for he so dearly wishes to be able to say goodbye to them, even if he cannot say it to the rest of the family. He asks his father not to bring his mother to the prison though, if her health is poor and it will make her worse. He signs it, 'Your loving son, Freddie.'

63

'It was a long and gloomy night that gathered on me, haunted by the ghosts of many hopes, of many dear remembrances, many errors, many unavailing sorrows and regrets.' Charles Dickens: David Copperfield (1850)

Lewes Prison Sussex April 25th 1892

Freddie's father is escorted through the prison gates at about four o'clock on the afternoon of April 25th. With him are Maud and Harriet. The walk to meet Freddie is cloaked in the dimmest of light, metal gates and cell doors everywhere they look, the constable in front of them turning every now and then to ensure his visitors are still with him. He is a tall man, young, with a full head of dark brown hair, his uniform crisp and clean, but his shoulders sag forward, give him the beginnings of a round back and make him look much older from behind. Alfred does not envy him his job. Maud and Harriet hold hands as they walk, their shoes making a clacking noise on the hard stone floors.

Arriving at Freddie's cell, they are asked to stand back while the constable puts his eye to the spyhole, high up in the door, takes his large heavy set of keys and selects the right one. As he slowly opens the door, he says over his shoulder,

'You can never be sure how a prisoner's going to react to the cell being opened.'

They are allowed in, aware of the door being closed and locked behind them, and instantly understand something of what it is like to have this as a place to live, even for a short period. It is as dim inside as the corridors had been outside. A single narrow set of raised planks with a thin mattress and a cover, pass as a bed. A pail and bowl set into the corner, and then… Freddie. He comes forward hugs his father and sisters, offers his bed for them to sit. They speak for some time… of unimportant things, that do not have to be spoken of that day, but the tension is palpable and nobody wants to broach any matter to mar their visit. When they have been there a while, Alfred asks his son,

'Freddie, is there anything at all, however small, you've been able to remember about that night?'

'Father. If I could remember a single thing, you would know of it. I've had so much time to think but I cannot remember anything of it. Father, how is mother?'

'She's been strong for the last few weeks, but now, today, her mood has changed. She can't believe that she'll never see you again, dear boy.'

'It's the same for me Father. Can I ask what happened about the petition? There has been no news of it brought to me.'

'The response from the Home Office was that the police, in charge here, knew what they were doing and no interference of the case would be made. We're sorry, son. We did everything we could.'

'I know Father and I'm truly grateful.'

'You must try to be strong Freddie. There are many people of the town who understand what happened to you that night.'

When the time comes to leave, the pain they held at bay seems to flow from them, like a river in flood, coursing through their blood and gathering in their hearts. None of them wants this separation, the finality of it now becoming so real. Maud holds her baby brother, weeps on his shoulder, so that Alfred finds it necessary to pull her away, before he and Harriet can say their farewells.

'I love you son. I cannot ignore what has happened, but your mother and I, and all our family, will always love the man we know.'

Alfred takes an arm of each of his girls for the long walk back into daylight, and soon after their departure, Freddie has an epileptic fit, foaming at the mouth and has to be restrained. In the evening Rev. Williamson visits him, notices his previously calm demeanour has changed. His body shakes. He takes the minister's hand and begs,

'Please don't leave me, for I greatly fear being alone. Will you stay with me till the end?'

'I will,' says the minister, although he cannot bear to think of how he will accomplish such a dreadfully distressing duty.

'Freddie, do you have anything to say at this late hour, for if you have, I urge you not to delay?' Weeping and barely able to speak, his tone piteous, his heart broken, he replies,

'I'm sorry for what I did… wish that my sorrow, sincere as it is, be told to the parents of the child, for the great wrong I have done… But I have no recollection, Reverend Williamson, none at all.'

Freddie asks for messages to be sent to the press for print. He dictates them. The first is to Mr. and Mrs. Thomson. He prays for their forgiveness. He thanks his colleagues at the railway station for their kind letters. He thanks his solicitors, his godparents, friends and the church ministers for their kindness and the efforts they have made on his behalf. Soon after eight o'clock Freddie retires, the minister leaving him in the hands of warders, and he sleeps reasonably until about three in the morning. Afterwards his sleep is greatly disturbed. Rev. Williamson returns to his cell at eight o'clock, finding a considerably calmer man. They pray together and at Freddie's request, the minister reads two passages from the Bible.

'My time is short,' Freddie says, and he becomes agitated, his hands twitching nervously. He asks for pen and paper, writes again to his parents, a long letter, after which, and with the hour of his death approaching, he becomes more and more distressed. He kneels and prays, weeps bitterly, the pain of his fate all too clear to see. He pleads again for the minister to stay with him, prays for one last time, during which he says that God knows, he did not know anything about the crime he is about to die for.

64

Lewes Sussex April 26th 1892

The train leaves Brighton Station on its journey to Lewes, smoke issuing from its stack, steam powering pistons, which turn arms, which turn wheels, as it clatters its way through the countryside. Damp weather from the previous day has given way to a glorious spring morning, the sun clearing any mist lingering over the South Downs, in stark contrast to the night of December 10th. Passengers include those dignitaries who will preside over the events of the day, their conversation about only one thing. All agree that Mr. Tyler deserves nothing less than the gallows. However, expressions of sympathy are traded for the parents of little Annie Thomson and for Freddie's gentle old father who has spent his life in honourable work. For his mother, heartbroken at having borne a son who should commit such a deed.

Arriving at Lewes, passengers go their different ways. Those who walk over the bridge into Station Street and thence through the main street towards the gaol, note with surprise the peacefulness of the little town, even though it is gone eight o'clock. Very few people are about, seemingly uninterested in the imminent execution. Three members of the press have been selected to witness the hanging, and stand at the main entrance along with one or two others, gazing up at the flagstaff. Just before eight thirty the trio of press, having identified themselves to the warder, are ushered through the wicket gate into the prison grounds, there to wait for a further twenty minutes. From their vantage point they can see the chapel where Rev. Williamson has administered to the convicted man, the bell which would toll in a while. Two large men exit the chapel. They have been with Freddie throughout his last night on Earth. At exactly eight forty-five the bell begins its funeral knell, minute by minute,

259

whereupon the reporters are led to the Committee Room to clear a path for those who are required at the condemned man's cell.

As soon as officials disappear from view, the press representatives are taken to the place of execution, situated at the south east corner of the prison grounds, the gallows becoming visible as they approach. The structure is covered by a wooden shed, has no front and is therefore open to those who will witness the hanging. It is ghastly. A rope hangs from a black crossbeam, a noose at its end. It is a new rope, fastened to another scaffolding cord round the beam. Beneath the gallows, the pit is hidden by two stout oak doors, on which the warders will soon stand. At the opposite side of the yard and covered somewhat haphazardly by boards, is the grave into which Freddie's body will be placed.

Outside the prison meanwhile, people have begun to gather, their numbers increasing as the fateful hour approaches. It is an orderly crowd, policed against anything inappropriate given the gravity of the occasion. Some traps and other means of transport line the opposite side of the road, all quite full and some more than full, but there is little noise, only whispers and a few voices drifting on the gentle breeze. They hear the bell begin its mournful toll at eight forty-five and all noise abates.

65

At number eight Bedford Buildings, Grace and Harold Thomson have opened their home to family and friends, too many arriving to be held by the small property, so the narrow alleyway down to Upper Bedford Street and even into the street, is a mass of people from near and far, come to share this moment with them. Within the house, they sit on the floor, or on each other's laps, or on the sides of chairs. They stand in every tiny space. Many of those outside seat themselves on the cold concrete to wait. It is such a beautiful spring morning; it is as if God showers them and their little girl with righteous warmth and light. There are tears, but not many, for on this day the murderer of their child will meet his own death, allowing them to move on. Just before nine o'clock the house, that had been lively with movement and sound, falls silent. Hands are held, arms support and hug wives, husbands, and children.

In Rock Street, family and friends also gather to support each other, the ambience here of a totally different nature. Rebecca and Emily busy themselves providing whatever refreshment is required; it helps to dissipate those grave feelings going on inside them. In the back parlour Freddie's family do nothing but weep for him, their petition having come to nought. They hold each other, feel cold, although the day is quite sufficiently warm, but also to be as close as possible to those they love on this, the most tragic day of their lives. They watch the clock, fiddle with things. Great sobs sound every now and then from their broken hearts, as the hands of the clock move all to quickly towards nine.

66

Bradshaw, the executioner, who is short, clean shaven and about middle age, wears a black suit and skull cap, and arrives at Freddie's cell followed by the prison governor, the surgeon, and others. With no loss of time, he takes Freddie at the elbows, securing his arms. Freddie turns and shakes hands with those in his cell, and thanks them all for the kindness they have bestowed on him. Immediately a signal is given, whereupon the group establish a processional form, headed by Rev. Williamson, who begins his recitation of the burial service. It is one minute to nine. Freddie, escorted by two burley warders each holding an arm, is wearing the same clothes as at his trial, but his head and neck are bare, shaved of all hair. He walks steadily, holds his head up, until the awful moment when he is confronted by the appalling scene, his face then visibly paling. He turns towards the press with an expression of appeal. He does not falter though, but walks forward until he is positioned directly below the crossbeam, facing the back of the enclosure. All the time the minister continues to read the service as he turns to face the witnesses.

So many people are here to see me die. I pray silently as I walk between them. I think of mother and father, all my family, Maud who means so much to me, and Rebecca too. Poor Eleanor... she'll go back to her sister, I think. I'm so sorry. William. My legs shake as I walk, but I'll not flinch... William taught me to be strong... he knows, from where he is, I must face my death positively... he's looking down at me... will want to see I'm strong. I see the gallows as we turn a corner... know my death is only minutes away... my heart flutters like a butterfly...

I'm led to the platform. The executioner straps my legs... places the noose over my head and alters it round my neck. It's a thick rope. It scratches my head as it goes over and I want to reach up and smooth the scratch away, but my hands are tied. It feels so thick round my neck that I'm forced to lift my chin a little. It scrapes the bulge and comes to rest in the neat space at the bottom of my throat. It's almost as though the space is made for it. I look at the back of the shed, feel people behind me, hear Rev. Williamson as he keeps on with his chanting. I think time has stopped. I want it over now. The executioner takes the white hood, places it over my head and the light disappears. I call to William.

Mr. Bradshaw hesitates briefly. He hears the prisoner whisper something. It catches him unawares, so that he finds it necessary to complete the task quickly. He steps aside and the two warders supporting Freddie move away from the doors. The lever is pulled. The heavy oak doors fly inward. Freddie follows. There is no sway in the rope. Death is instantaneous. When the witnesses move forward to inspect the pit, as is their duty, they see the white cap has slipped to one side. Freddie's eyes are closed. It does not last long, the inspection, for who wants to linger? Signals pass from one warder to another until the black flag is hoisted, and Freddie's final words fly away on the breeze. 'Catch me William.'

ACKNOWLEDGEMENTS

There are many people I wish to thank for supporting the writing of this novel but I must begin with Kate Worsley of *The Writers' Company'* who read my third draft, encouraged me to move forward through her feedback, and gave me an insight into the craft of novel writing. Dr Richard Chin of the University of Edinburgh, provided generously of his time, through many emails, to help educate me about epilepsy, so that I could write with some confidence, and I am extremely grateful to him. Any medical errors in this work are mine, not his.

Keith Soanes is a retired Electrical Engineer in the Merchant Navy, and was always on the end of a phone to increase my knowledge of all things nautical. He kindly read the pertinent script to ensure as much accuracy as possible. David Grimwade, a Civil Servant at HMP Prison Service, Lewes, Sussex, shared his expertise, enabling me to understand the nineteenth century prison site and where Freddie was buried. Abraham Poorazizi, founder of Township Canada, to whom I owe thanks for helping me understand the complexities of the township grid system on line. To all those at the Sussex Archives, The Keep, Brighton, for their diligence in providing historical data, including maps, documents and plans from which to work. To 'Jericho Writers' for all the online material they provide for authors, and particularly for new authors like me. Their videos are informative and easy to follow. Their self-publishing information has been of immense help to this complete novice.

To my family, who have wholeheartedly given their support, encouragement, and sometimes critical feedback, kept me on track and suffered my often need just to talk things through. Finally, but by far the most important support I have had, is that of my friend Deborah Watts. She has been beside me through-out every draft, every plunge in confidence and every emotion I have experienced producing this debut novel, and I thank her from the bottom of my heart.

ABOUT THE AUTHOR

Sue Robertson Danells

Sue was born in Cambridge, England, and lived there until she was nine years old, moving then with her family to Staines. She attended Matthew Arnold secondary school, where she achieved reasonably well. Her career choice was always to become a children's nanny, and she secured a place to train, at the age of sixteen. However, during that summer, and for reasons unknown, even to herself, she decided to become a  teacher, eventually attending teacher training college. She has had a satisfying career in education, holding many posts from classroom teacher to education officer. Now retired, she lives with her husband and two cocker spaniels in a small Suffolk village.

email at: srobertsondanells@gmail.com
find me on: www.literarypleasures.co.uk

Printed in Great Britain
by Amazon